~~~ OO ~~~

Marcus tossed her onto the sumptuous coverings and she landed among the cushions and bolsters with a gasping laugh. Her skirts rucked up, showing long stockinged legs and rich petticoats. He began to strip off his jacket and then changed his mind—he couldn't wait—and flung himself down beside her.

They stared at each other, breathless, and it was as if he was on the verge of something he had never felt before.

"You know there is no future in this," she said, as if to convince herself as well as him. "Only this moment. Only now."

"I know," he replied, his voice deep and sensual. "I'm not a forever kind of man."

"Good," she whispered, tracing his mouth with her fingertip. He bit it, hard enough for her to feel his teeth, and then reached down, bunching up her skirts and petticoats, his palm gliding over her thigh.

SARA BENNETT

A SEDUCTION IN SCARLET

AVON
An Imprint of HarperCollinsPublishers

This is a work of fiction. Names, characters, places, and incidents are products of the author's imagination or are used fictitiously and are not to be construed as real. Any resemblance to actual events, locales, organizations, or persons, living or dead, is entirely coincidental.

AVON BOOKS
An Imprint of HarperCollins*Publishers*
10 East 53rd Street
New York, New York 10022-5299

Copyright © 2008 by Sara Bennett
ISBN: 978-0-06-133634-8
www.avonromance.com

First Avon Books paperback printing: January 2008

Avon Trademark Reg. U.S. Pat. Off. and in Other Countries, Marca Registrada, Hecho en U.S.A.
HarperCollins® is a registered trademark of HarperCollins Publishers.

Printed in the U.S.A.

10 9 8 7 6 5 4 3 2 1

For Joy

A Seduction in Scarlet

Prologue

Aphrodite's Club,
London
Late Spring 1850

Aphrodite, the famous courtesan, sat forward in her Egyptian style chair, her dark eyes bright with curiosity. "Lady Ellerslie. It isn't often that a woman of your position and social standing comes to see me at my club. Please, tell me what it is you wish from me, and I will make it come true."

"Madame, if only it were that simple."

"But perhaps it is. Tell me and we will see."

Portia, Lady Ellerslie, hesitated, and for a moment her well-bred calm wavered, giving the courtesan a glimpse of the seething emotion she was trying so hard to hide. "I am relying upon your discretion," she said with quiet dignity.

"We are all most discreet here, my lady."

It had seemed so straightforward in the hansom cab on her way here, but now she was face-to-face with the woman . . . No, it wasn't straightforward at all. But she had made up her mind to it, and once she decided on a thing, she went through with it. Besides, what was the alternative? Creep back home and do nothing? She could not bear it, not for another day, not for another moment.

Not for another night.

Portia drew a deep breath. "I am a widow, madame, as you know. My position is such that I must be extremely cautious, which is why I have come here today in a cab, wearing a veil and bearing a false name."

Aphrodite inclined her head, but her eyes said she had heard all this many times before. That gave Portia some comfort. She wasn't alone after all; there were others like her, who were desperate to escape the strictures society had imposed upon them.

Escape?

No, escape was impossible, but perhaps just for a brief time she might forget what was expected of her and pretend to be someone else.

"You would like some coffee or tea?" Aphrodite murmured when Portia did not go on. "A glass of something stronger, perhaps, to give you courage?"

"No, please, I don't want anything to drink," Portia said in frustration, her gloved hands clenching her reticule. Suddenly, the words spilled out of her, like a dam that had broken: "You are being polite, and I don't want politeness and good manners, I don't want to be hemmed in and suffocated with good intentions, I don't want to pretend to be happy when I am sad, and bite back my tears and my anger, to be so . . . so devoid of emotion because in the world I live in it is not the done thing to show how one truly feels . . ."

Aphrodite smiled and her dark eyes glittered. "Go on, Lady Ellerslie."

Her inner feelings, once set free, could not be stemmed, nor could her sense of desperation. "Madame, just for one night, for one hour, I want to be a living woman again and not a marble memorial to my dead husband."

Silence hung heavy in the small, chic room. Portia wished she could look away from the courtesan, but that would be cowardly —a denial of the words she had just spoken—so she kept her gaze still and steady. As if she were not quaking in her boots.

"I will let you in on a little secret," Aphrodite said, her voice conspiratorial. "You are not the only English lady of quality who has come here seeking my help, and you will not be the last."

"I am not? What is the world coming to!" She sounded just like the queen, Victoria, as she had meant to, but her smile took away the sting.

"The world is designed by men, my lady. I will say to you what I said to those others. There is absolutely nothing wrong in a woman wishing to satisfy her sensual needs; it is a natural thing. But in your situation you are taking a greater risk, and it might be safer, and more convenient, if you took a lover from among your own circle. A friend? A servant?"

Portia shook her head. "No. I must be beyond reproach, madame, and if the merest whisper reached the ears of my family or the palace . . . I cannot soil my husband's spotless memory. You understand that merely by being here today I put all in jeopardy?"

Aphrodite inclined her head. "You must be seen to uphold the pure perfection of Victorian womanhood," she mocked gently. "I understand very well, my lady, and I sympathize with your dilemma. You have been placed upon a pedestal and it is lonely up there. Especially if you are a sensual woman, and I think that you are. Forgive me, but can you not remarry? It has been two years since Lord Ellerslie died."

Portia wondered whether such a question was impertinent. Probably it was, but she did not care. This was the frankest conversation she'd had with a woman in many years, perhaps in the whole of her life. She hadn't realized until now that such conversations were even permitted to take place. Perhaps they weren't.

The thought that she might be breaking one of those interminable "rules" made her feel deliciously wicked.

"I do not think my remarrying would be looked upon favorably. I am the epitome of the faithful widow in mourning for her hero husband, and if I remarried, then the spell would be broken. Victoria—Her Majesty the Queen—prefers me to remain as I am. She is fond of telling me that I am a beacon that others may follow. Britannia in widow's weeds."

Unfortunately it was all too true. But it was what she had wanted, after all. Her mother's ambition and pride had brought her to this point, and her own sense of duty. Would she really want to change places with some happily married little cottage wife? If she was trapped, then it was a trap of her making and one she was content to inhabit—most of the time.

"So, you do not wish to take a lover and you cannot remarry. Instead you have come to me. Let me guess, you want an evening of passion, but without any ties or conventions. Just a stranger in one of my pretty boudoirs, with little or no conversation, and then good-bye forever."

If Portia was the sort to blush, she might have done so now, but hers was the cool, fair beauty of the English rose, and she had grown very clever at hiding her true feelings behind it.

"You have guessed right, Madame Aphrodite. That is exactly what I want."

"Connection with a man you do not know?" the courtesan asked, speaking forthrightly.

Portia tilted up her chin so there would be no mistake. "Yes."

Aphrodite smiled. "I am not trying to shock you, my lady. I like to be frank with my clients, and then there can be no misunderstandings."

"I am grateful for your plain speaking. It is not something I am used to. I find it refreshing, Madame."

"Then let me be plain again. You are not a virgin? I ask because your husband was a great deal older than you. He was still capable?"

Even her mother had not asked such a thing. Her mother would probably have fainted if she had discussed her husband's prowess in the bedroom. It delighted Portia to be able to say out loud secrets she had kept for ten years. "He was capable, but I was a virgin before I married. As a young girl I was kept so confined that there would have been no chance to be other than a virgin. But I wasn't interested in the young men about me. I was a serious girl, not inclined to flights of fancy or dreams of love, and my future had been drummed into me so thoroughly that I believed I had no other choice than to marry well. The family fortunes were riding on me, madame, and to hear such a thing day after day . . . well, I did not take it lightly."

It was true; well, mostly. There had been one man . . . a boy. Someone she had, briefly, fallen in love with and longed to give herself to, in the dreamy, innocent way of the inexperienced. Not that the boy knew that. They barely spoke, but she had fantasized about him all one summer. Come autumn, she was married. She hadn't thought of him for years, her life had changed so much, and then, one day, there he was. Inside her head. Her young and innocent love . . . only now her feelings were not so innocent.

Aphrodite didn't need to know that. Nor that he had taken a leading role in the fantasies she indulged in alone at night. Those dark wicked fantasies.

"After I married my husband I . . . I found I enjoyed the physical part of my marriage, but as you say, my husband was much older than me, and before long he became too ill to take the part of a husband. He was ill for many years before he died. That is not to say I begrudge my time as his nurse, but there was no physical intimacy between us."

"I see, my lady. You loved him, but now he is gone and for the sake of the public, the queen, your family, you must remain a perpetual widow."

"Yes."

"He was a national hero. They wish to preserve what is left of him."

"I do not mean to denigrate his name, I would never do that. But I am twenty-seven years of age, and I do not want to be old just yet. I want to feel what it is to be a woman again. I think if I could spend some time with a man who is young and virile, experience what other women take for granted, then I would be satisfied. Once would be enough."

Aphrodite's heavily ringed fingers tapped on the arm of her chair. "I hope you are right, but in my experience 'once' is sometimes the start of something rather than the finish of it." Her voice had taken on a warning note.

Portia smiled, confident she was in control. "I am willing to take that risk."

Chapter 1

It was far too early to go home, Marcus decided as he strolled though Covent Garden. Besides, Sebastian and Francesca would be there, glowing with connubial bliss. Since his brother had married, he didn't want to go anywhere unless Francesca was with him—in short he'd become a complete bore. Here he was, Marcus thought, freed from his stewardship of Worthorne Manor and a brief, disastrous stint in the Hussars, ready to experience all that London had to offer, and with no one to share it.

That evening, Sebastian had come to his room. "What are you doing with your life? You're drifting," he'd said.

Marcus had shrugged and grinned and told his brother he was jealous. "Not everyone has a purpose," he said, choosing his waistcoat. "What do you think? This one, or the new one from Bond Street?"

Sebastian sighed and shook his head and gave up, for the moment.

Afterward, he had been to the theater and enjoyed a

rowdy supper with some of his regimental friends, but they were called back to the barracks and now he was all alone. Although normally that wouldn't have bothered Marcus, tonight he was restless. Maybe he should visit one of the bawdy houses and while away an hour or two? Or attend one of the supper rooms in the Strand where girls in flesh-colored tights and short skirts kicked their legs up high? He considered his options.

A passing pretty woman in an expensive dress and bonnet smiled, glancing at him out of the corner of her eyes. Marcus recognized the look. She was plying her trade, looking for a wealthy gentleman for the evening. Just for a moment he considered being that gentleman, and then suddenly remembered that he did have an engagement, after all. He searched in his waistcoat pocket—ah, here it was! An invitation from the exclusive Aphrodite's Club.

"'An evening of pleasure, where you can sample the delights we have available just for you,'" he read under his breath.

Sample the delights . . .

Marcus grinned. That sounded exactly what he needed. Perhaps some of Aphrodite's delights would sooth the restlessness in his soul, and restore his usual carefree nature. His mind made up, he hailed a passing hansom cab and set off for Aphrodite's.

Portia felt as if everyone in the room was staring at her; not directly, but with curious darting glances. But they couldn't see her; the veil covering her face made certain of that. She might as well have been invisible.

The knowledge gave her power, and a sense of security. She was free to look and judge and make her choice, and no one would know. For someone who had spent much of her grown life with the eyes of others upon her, watching and judging her, it was incredibly liberating.

She almost hadn't come tonight.

Victoria—Her Majesty the Queen—was feeling poorly, and Portia had been expecting a summons to the palace to sit with her. Fortunately, it hadn't come. Portia felt equal parts of relief and guilt over that. Victoria was increasing again, and it frustrated her that she could not do all the things she wished to. She relied upon her friends and ladies-in-waiting to take her mind off her thickening body. But tonight Prince Albert had stayed at her side, and Portia was not required.

After supper she went early to bed, pleading a headache. Her mother, whose own headaches were infamous, did not need to be convinced and let her go without a quibble. Hettie, her faithful maid and only confidante, had been waiting. Her plain, good-natured face was creased with concern.

"Are you sure, *lieben*? You can change your mind."

"Hettie, you said you would help!"

Hettie took her hand, squeezing it. "And so I will. As long as you are not expecting to find love."

"Love?" Portia raised an eyebrow. "I am seeking

passion, Hettie. A warm body holding mine. I want to feel like a woman instead of a monument. Is that so wrong?"

"No, *lieben*, of course it isn't. Come and let me help you dress . . . "

When Portia was ready, Hettie wrapped her closely in a dark cloak, then Portia slipped out to the waiting hired coach.

Now here she was in Aphrodite's sparkling salon.

There were plenty of gentlemen present. Some were good looking but most were not. Portia did not expect a god. She was looking for that certain something, that moment of attraction, that spark that said this was the one. Behind the veil her gaze traveled from man to man. This one too short, this one too fat, this one whose voice was too loud, this one glancing at his pocket watch as if he had to be somewhere else . . .

Was she seeking fault? What if she did not find him?

Portia moved a little restlessly, and the scarlet silk rustled about her. The dress was tight and low-cut, giving her slim body a new voluptuousness and making her feel surprisingly sensual. Hettie had announced that it was a dress to wear to an assignation, as if she knew, and no man would be able to resist her. And the brilliance of the color . . . it had been so long since she'd worn anything other than mourning and half mourning.

She'd dreamed about the dress last night. One of her restless, feverish dreams in which a man held and caressed her in the darkness. And then, just before the end, he turned to the window and the moonlight fell upon his face and she saw that it was him. Marcus Worthorne. Her seventeen-year-old fantasy from that summer long ago.

Portia sighed now, and wondered if that was her trouble. She didn't want just any man; she wanted someone who didn't exist. Because of course the Marcus Worthorne who had grown and developed in her mind wasn't the boy she'd known at seventeen. He wasn't real. He couldn't possibly be.

When she had arrived that night, Aphrodite greeted her and spoke to her discreetly. "Do not worry if there is no one here who catches your eye. There is always next time."

But Portia knew it was quite possible there might not be another chance.

Ever.

She might not summon up the courage again, or circumstances might step in to prevent her. This was her moment, and she had to make the most of it. She had to take whatever Fate gave her.

So here she sat on her chair in her scarlet silk gown, with the ruffles of lace at the hem, and a scarlet veil covering her face and hair. The glass of champagne she held in her hand had been replaced three times. Or was it four? She no longer kept count. She was feeling light-headed, but it was not an unpleasant sensation. Rather like floating in a warm, comfortable cloud,

while all about her Aphrodite's guests moved and conversed, making their choices. Surely this was far more
honest than the dreadful debutante ball she remembered attending as a girl? If a woman was going to sell
herself to the highest bidder, then let it all be out in the
open . . .

She turned her head just as he moved into her field of
vision. Her spinning world came to an abrupt halt. The
sights and sounds around her merged in a meaningless
blur.

Dear God it cannot be . . .

Was Aphrodite a witch? For how else could she have
known? But of course Aphrodite didn't know. She had
placed herself in the hands of Fate, and Fate had given
her a strange and remarkable gift. Marcus Worthorne,
the man of her dreams, was standing in the salon here
at Aphrodite's Club.

Marcus hadn't visited Aphrodite's before. That was
not to say he hadn't visited houses of pleasure and
bawdy houses, just not this particular one. He had
made Aphrodite's acquaintance, of course—the courtesan was his sister-in-law's natural mother. But to visit
her club . . . no, he hadn't done that, hadn't felt it was
quite proper. Now, with the invitation in his pocket, the
situation had changed.

Aphrodite, an older version of Francesca, smiled at
him as he entered the salon, but she had not shown him
any particular favor. Good. He preferred it that way.

This was strictly private, nothing to do with family relationships.

For a time he prowled about the glittering and gaudy salon, enjoying the company of the beautiful women, sipping his champagne. It was as if he'd stepped into a fairy tale where the princesses wore very little and were prepared to make all his dreams come true—if his pockets were deep enough.

Well, and what was wrong with that? It wasn't as if he was looking for a respectable wife, for God's sake. Just a couple hours of pleasure with a companion seeking the same. They could enjoy each other and go their separate ways. But which woman? That was the difficult question. They were all lovely, all charming; it made it impossible to choose.

And then he saw her.

She was wearing scarlet, a dress that clung to her curves, the bodice so low her bosom was barely covered. It could have appeared tacky, but the woman's posture was so regal, so assured, Marcus thought she might well have worn sackcloth and still have the bearing of a queen. He wished he could see her face, but the veil she wore over her head reached to her shoulders, and he could not see through it. The mystery woman was seated beside a gilt statue of Cupid, and she was so still that she might have been a statue herself. Although he couldn't see her face or her eyes, Marcus had the oddest sensation that she was watching him.

He made another circuit of the room. The women

were still beautiful and so obviously wanting to please, but now they all looked the same. He didn't know what was wrong with him tonight, but his steps led him back to the lady in scarlet.

Marcus was intrigued by her. She was sitting so still, but wasn't like a thing of stone. Her skin looked too warm, too soft, too touchable. And he wanted to touch her.

She moved.

Just a slight shift of position, but enough to make him think that she was very aware of him. Perhaps she was as interested in him as he was in her? He thought it would be amusing to find out, to set her a little test . . .

Marcus began to prowl the room again, but this time he kept a surreptitious eye on her. Did the face beneath the veil turn a little to follow his progress? One of the beautiful demimonde wriggled up to him, smiling, stroking his arm as she spoke to him. He leaned down, giving her his full attention, and made a joke. She laughed and tapped him on the arm with her painted fan.

Marcus glanced over at the woman in scarlet. Oh yes, she was definitely watching him. Her head was turned toward him and she was leaning forward in her chair, to better observe him through the crowd. As if she did not want him to notice her interest, she turned quickly away, presenting him with the elegant curve of her shoulder, casually lifting her champagne glass to her lips.

Marcus strolled on, engaging another of the beautiful women in conversation, and then another, but the game palled when the lady in scarlet did not look again.

"Enough," he murmured, suddenly impatient with her and himself. He set off toward her, cutting his way through the small clusters of guests, his gaze fixed on her like a hunting jungle cat.

She heard his approach, or perhaps sensed it. She turned toward him just before he reached her. He saw her body stiffen, as if she was preparing herself. Was she shy? More probably she wasn't familiar with her surroundings. A first time visitor. An innocent.

Marcus smiled. This grew better and better.

The view from where he stood was truly delightful. Her breasts swelled over the bodice of her dress, plump and flawless, her skin like milk. A lady, then, and neither old nor wrinkled. He wondered whether she knew the effect she was having on the men in the room. Whether she realized how desperately he wanted to reach out and draw the scarlet neckline down that tiny bit, so that the peaks of her luscious breasts were disclosed to his gaze and his hands. And his mouth.

"Your glass is empty," he said, his voice deep and soft and intimate. "Will you allow me to bring you another?"

The veil appeared flimsy but was in fact surprisingly impenetrable; he could only just see the pale blur of her features. She was hidden from him, and he found it frustrating. He wanted to see into her eyes. He wanted to gaze at her mouth. He wanted to know her.

She said nothing.

"We seem to be unattached, you and I," he went on, as if her silence didn't matter to him. "We're watchers while the world goes by. Do you prefer to watch, is that why you're here? To watch?"

Still nothing.

"If you want to join me, I promise you I can be fascinating company." He took a step closer, and her head tilted to keep him in view. Her perfume reached him, something musky and sweet, teasing his senses. Her hand lifted, hovering over her cleavage, as if to preserve her modesty. "No, don't," he murmured huskily. "You are the stuff dreams are made of, lady. Don't spoil it by playing the prude."

He thought he saw the flash of her eyes. She hesitated, and then her hand returned to her lap.

"Thank you." He smiled as if they were lovers already, his eyes as hot as his need. "May I?" Before she could move again, he bent down and lifted her hand in his, raising it to his lips. She was wearing gloves, but her flesh was warm underneath the thin cloth. She didn't want him this close, he could tell, and when he released her, she folded her fingers tightly and dismissed him by turning her head away.

Marcus stepped back. "You wish to be alone?"

Nothing.

"A pity." He let his gaze run over her one last time, committing her to memory. "I think we would have enjoyed each other's company."

He bowed, sober now, but as he strolled away he struggled with a keen sense of disappointment. The veiled lady intrigued him. He wanted her. Marcus mocked himself: Why was he seeking the unattainable? The room was full of women. He was being ridiculous and childish wanting the only one he couldn't have. He drank a couple more glasses of champagne and watched as some of the women performed an elegant display behind a thin curtain, a naked rendition of the birth of Venus in a papier-mâché clamshell. He wasn't particularly interested and found it all rather silly.

It was time to go, before he became drunk and belligerent and sorry for himself.

Marcus was collecting his hat and coat when Aphrodite came gliding toward him in her black silk, her jewels glittering at her throat, her beautiful face timeless.

"Marcus," she said, "please do not leave yet."

"I think I must, madame," he said, polite but firm.

"Is my club not to your liking?"

"Your club is magnificent. Your girls are beautiful."

"But you are not in the mood to be pleased by mere beauty, *oui*? You want something more. Would it change your mind if you knew that there is a certain lady who very much wishes for your company?"

"I'm sure there are other gentlemen who would be more appreciative than I—"

"I speak of the lady in the veil, Marcus."

"The lady in scarlet?"

"You are surprised?" She smiled. "She was very taken with you, *mon ami*. This is a special commission. Her identity is a secret, and she will wear her veil while she is with you. One evening, Marcus, that is all she requires. Can you give her an evening to remember for the rest of her life?"

Marcus removed his hat and handed it to her with a droll look. "I think I can manage that, madame."

Chapter 2

Portia couldn't sit still. After she'd told Aphrodite which man she preferred, the courtesan led
her to this luxurious little room to wait. For the tenth
time her gaze flicked to the bed, placed discreetly in
a shadowy corner, the plump cushions slyly peeping
out from behind the lush draperies. The reason why
she was here. And for the tenth time she thought about
running away and forgetting the whole thing. But she
conquered her fear. Because this was what she wanted,
this was what she craved.

I want to feel like a woman again. I want to feel. *And
Marcus being here . . . it is as if it were meant to be.*

Marcus Worthorne was perfect. Oh yes. She thought
again of his eyes on her, burning her skin. She'd felt as
if he was touching her, and a hot ache had ignited low
in her belly. She had fantasized about him for so long,
but even in her wildest dreams—some of them very
wild indeed—she hadn't expected him to grow into
someone so perfect.

When she was seventeen, he'd seemed distant and unattainable. Perhaps that had been part of his attraction. He hadn't known she existed, and even now probably wouldn't recognize her as the shy girl he occasionally met in the lane while riding his horse, or the girl who embarrassed herself so dreadfully that day in church. But he'd certainly recognize her as Lady Ellerslie; all of England did.

Marcus the boy had shown promise of the handsome man he had become, the sort of man she'd always secretly admired. Tall and broad shouldered and slim hipped, with the arrogant good looks of someone who didn't worry about anything overmuch. Oh no, he wasn't concerned with what life might throw at him. In fact, Portia doubted that his life consisted of anything more than idleness and pleasure. Completely and totally her opposite, for she was very much a prisoner of her own conscience.

But what did that matter? It was the hot look in his eyes that was appealing to her senses, the sound of his voice that sent shivers skipping down her spine. Marcus was a man who knew how to please a woman, and he could give her the sort of pleasure she had been dreaming of. And then walk away without a second thought.

Perfect, Portia reminded herself. She didn't require any empty promises, or any pretense that there would be a next meeting—in fact such things would be an insult. It was simple mindless pleasure she wanted. There would be time enough to remember the world outside this room when she left the club. But for now she wanted to forget everything, just for an hour or two, and Marcus Worthorne could help her to do that admirably.

The door opened.

He stood a moment, silhouetted against the gaslight from the salon, and she wondered if he did it on purpose, because he knew how good he looked. But then she realized he was more intent on watching her, seated on the sofa by the fireplace, than striking a pose.

"May I join you?" His voice held the same amused tone she remembered from before, only now it was deeper, with a hint of seduction. She shivered, unconsciously responding to him. A jumble of memories filled her mind, but she shut them out, reminding herself of who she was and her position in the world. She had risen high from her origins, and although he would not know it, the reminder helped to restore her calm.

"Yes, please do," she murmured, her voice barely more than a whisper. Unrecognizable.

He closed the door behind him and strolled toward her with the graceful, loose-limbed walk she had noticed in the salon. Aphrodite's protégés had noticed it, too. He was the sort of man who would always be noticed. Women would look at him and want him. Perhaps they would even dream of him falling in love with them, but Portia was quite certain he would never love them. Instead he would break their hearts.

"We haven't been introduced," he said, smiling down at her.

The firelight was flattering, casting shadows over her skin, warming her flesh, and this time she didn't try to hide herself from his gaze. "We need no names," she murmured back.

"You're right." He sat down opposite her.

His eyes were hazel, with a hint of gold. Intelligent but with a cynical gleam that reinforced her belief that he didn't take life very seriously. But then, growing up in a wealthy and titled family, he'd never had to. In a way, she envied him his carefree manner—it must be restful to be so self-centered—but she knew she could never be like him.

"I'd very much like to see your face," he said quietly, in that voice that made her think of bed.

"No."

"You don't think you can trust me? I'm good at keeping secrets."

Was he? It didn't matter. She wasn't going to trust him with hers.

He must have read her answer in her silence, because he shrugged and smiled, as if it didn't concern him either way. Reaching out a hand, he touched her fingers, resting on the sofa arm. She could feel him through her thin glove. For a moment he simply smoothed the lace cloth with his thumb, gently caressing. He was watching her from beneath half-closed lids, trying to gauge her reaction.

"You're a very beautiful woman."

"How do you know?"

"You have an air."

"An air of what?" she mocked.

"Assurance. You expect to be looked at."

He was clever. She removed her hand, checking that her veil was firmly in place.

"Don't worry," he said, "I won't peek." For a moment his gaze caressed her idly, and then he spoke in a lazy voice. "May I do something I've been longing to do ever since I saw you?"

She was still fussing with her veil, but he didn't wait for her answer. In a sudden swift movement he was on his feet, reaching for her hands, tugging her smoothly to a standing position in front of him.

Portia gave a gasp, shocked despite herself. In her world, gentlemen did not manhandle ladies, and never so masterfully. She realized that beneath his well-made clothing he must be all hard muscle. She opened her mouth to reprimand him and then closed it again. Wasn't this what she wanted? Wasn't this why she was here? There was no going back now, she reminded herself with a shiver of excitement.

"What is it you want to do?" she whispered, taking a step away, giving herself room to breathe.

"This," he said, and before she could react, he slipped his finger beneath her low neckline and smoothly tugged it down a fraction.

She didn't struggle. She didn't reach up to cover herself, or shriek, or slap his face. She stood facing him, half naked now, and proud as a queen.

He remembered to breathe. "I apologize," he heard himself say. Apologizing wasn't something he did very often, but her bearing made him want to beg her pardon.

"Why?" she asked in that husky whisper that was playing havoc with his senses. "You said you wanted to do it."

"I should have shown more finesse," he answered. "I usually do."

"We could begin again, if you want?"

He laughed without humor. "I don't think so." It was difficult not being able to see her face, to look into her eyes, although he could see something of her against the firelight—the shape of her cheek, the curve of her chin.

He reached out and touched her breast, and then bent his head to taste her. She made a sound, a purr in her throat, and he drew her nipple into his mouth, rolling the hard bud with his tongue. Her hands closed on his head, fingers almost painful as she combed them through his hair.

That exotic scent rose from her skin, musky and alluring.

"Do you still want me to stop?" he said, sliding his hands over her shoulders, caressing her back.

"No, I don't want you to stop."

He knew then that she was his.

Portia trembled. He had found the fastenings of her dress and made quick work of them. He hadn't even begun to undress himself, so she did it. Hands at first uncertain, then growing in confidence, she removed his bow tie and unbuttoned his collar. His throat was strong and masculine, and she felt an urge to kiss him beneath his jaw and work her way down. Instead she reached her hands beneath the fine linen cloth of his shirt and touched his skin. He was very warm and there were hairs growing on his chest. She couldn't remember whether her husband had hairs on his chest; she did not think she had ever seen him entirely naked.

She raised his shirt for a better look. There was a line of dark hair running down his stomach and vanishing beneath the waistband of his trousers. She lifted the linen higher and found there was a wedge of dark hair on his chest. His skin was clean and warm, and the urge came again to press her mouth to him and taste him. To do all the things she'd dreamt of and longed to do.

But he had other ideas.

Her scarlet silk dress was pooled about her feet, and he dropped onto his knees in front of her. Good heavens, he was licking the inside of her thigh, his tongue hot and wet as it came closer and closer to . . .

Portia's head fell back and she gave a groan that came from deep within. All her pent-up desires and her secret cravings surfaced and she felt the beginnings of a pleasure so all-consuming her knees buckled.

He lifted her up.

She felt the back of the sofa sliding against her thighs,

and then he rested her hips upon the top of it, holding her firmly so she didn't fall. He began to kiss her, little butterfly kisses up the inside of her thighs. She tried to sit up, but the way he positioned her made her helpless. He was gripping her hips, keeping the lower half of her body anchored, but the top half was weak and unsupported. She fell back, arching, her legs splayed.

He closed his mouth over her.

Ecstasy erupted. She may have screamed.

Portia didn't remember much for several moments. She was still awash with that great maelstrom of pleasure, as if she had suddenly been lifted from London and spun around the stars, before being placed gently back down again.

Slowly she came to, blinking, and wondering why the room was patterned like lace. She realized then that she was still wearing her veil. Nothing else, just the veil. And she was lying in the bed that occupied the shadowy corner of the room.

Marcus Worthorne was beside her, and he was naked. She could feel his large, warm body pressed to hers, his fingers idly caressing her belly, her breasts, while he waited for her to regain her senses. "You were in great need," he said, and there was an unmistakable note of male smugness in his voice.

"Yes, I was." There was no point in denying it, and why should she?

"I'm glad I could be of service. Now it's my turn." And just like that he was on top of her, his body hot and heavy. He was a big man and she wondered if she should be afraid, but there was nothing frightening about him—she did not feel threatened. He reached down between them, fingers caressing, teasing the source of her pleasure. "Tell me when you're ready," he said as she gave a gasp.

Now. But she didn't say it. Her throat was tight as she fought the urge to beg and cry out for more, and her skin felt damp and feverish as those repressed desires rose to the surface again. She opened her thighs, instinctively pressing upward, to be closer to those wicked fingers.

"You like this?" he murmured, his breath warm on her cheek through the veil. He shifted slightly and she felt his male member seeking entry. "Let me kiss you," that devil's voice whispered. "I'll close my eyes. I swear it. Let me lift the veil just enough for me to kiss your mouth."

"No . . ."

He entered her a little, teasing her, withdrawing again. The tip of his member stroked her and she weakened.

"You must only kiss my mouth," she whispered.

He lifted the veil, just enough to uncover her chin and mouth. She felt his finger tracing her lips and then his breath warm on them. Then he kissed her. There was no easing into it, just the plundering of his mouth on hers, enjoying her fully and lustily.

A moment later his body drove deep into hers, and the shuddering pleasure rushed over her again, so intense that this time she couldn't even cry out. Wonderful. To think she might never have known this, that she might have gone to her grave with only her dreams for company. The reality was so much better.

Marcus gave a hoarse cry, enjoying her as she was enjoying him, totally lost in the moment. No emotion, no love or recriminations, no thought of the future. Just now.

Exactly as she wanted it.

She must have dozed, because when she woke he was lying beside her, his breathing deep and quiet.

She wanted to touch him, to stroke her fingertip down his cheek to his square and manly jaw. She wanted to explore the breadth of his chest with all those fascinating dark hairs, and the flat plain of his stomach, and all that lay below. But it was over now. Time to leave, before the evening that had so far been so marvelous became awkward and was spoiled. She would savor it, though. When she was seated, bored to death, at one of the endless functions she must attend, she would remember and smile a secret little smile.

It was just a pity that she could not see him again.

Why not?

The thought came from nowhere; sly, dangerous.

Abruptly, Portia slipped from the bed and stood up, her heart beating hard. That was not the plan, that had never been the plan. Once, yes, but more than once was far too risky.

Long, powerful fingers fastened about her slender wrist. Startled, Portia caught her breath, and when she turned to him, he was watching her through half-closed eyes in that lazy, teasing manner she was already growing to enjoy.

"Oh no, not yet, my lady. We are not done."

"I have to go." She meant to be firm but her voice treacherously wavered.

"Do you?" His mouth curved into a smile. He rolled onto his back and stretched, the powerful muscles in his arms and legs tightening, and she couldn't take her eyes off him. Portia didn't remember moving, she didn't remember making the choice, but the next thing she knew she was climbing on top of him, pressing herself to him, all that hard bare skin beneath her naked body.

He grinned, reaching up to stroke her back, following the curve of her hips down to her rounded bottom. She felt him hard against her thighs, and with a smile of her own she bent her head and lifted her veil, just enough so she could taste his skin.

"Well, perhaps not just yet," she murmured, feeling him tremble against her lips and tongue. "Perhaps I can wait a little longer."

"Marcus," he groaned. "That's my name."

I know, she thought, but didn't say it aloud. Instead she sat up, resting her hands upon his shoulders, and gazed down at him through the safety of her veil.

"You are mine for this evening," she said, her voice seductive and powerful. "I can fulfill all my fantasies, act out my wildest imaginings, and no one will ever know."

Except her . . . and Marcus.

"Please do," he said, and his smile was pure invitation.

Chapter 3

"**M**arcus? What time did you get in?"

Marcus opened one eye, hoping it wasn't his brother's voice, but unfortunately it was. Since Sebastian had married he'd become a first rate bore when it came to bedtime. But then again, he thought, if he had a wife as delicious as Francesca to retire with, he might be a little more prompt.

"Is that bacon I can smell?"

"Probably. Are you coming to breakfast or are you going to lie there on my library sofa all morning?"

The library had seemed as good a place as any to brood on last night's experiences. The mysterious lady with the body of a goddess. Oh yes, there was plenty to think about. Including why he had told her his name. It had been the perfect scenario. No names, no commitments, not even the need for polite pretenses. Just hot, exciting, bodily contact. And then he'd had to complicate matters by giving her his name.

Why the hell had he done that?

Moodily, he followed Sebastian into the breakfast room and threw himself down into a chair, still managing to appear graceful. His brother, after giving him a sideways glance, began to pour him a cup of coffee.

"I had a letter from my manager, Grieves, yesterday. There's a problem with some of the tenants at Worthorne Manor."

"Do they need their hands held?" Marcus retorted. "I know what you're doing, Seb. You're trying to find something for me to do, to keep me occupied. I don't need your help. I can run my own life."

Sebastian began to pile up a plate with a selection from the sideboard. "It seems to me you aren't running it very well. Months have gone by since you left the Hussars, and you still haven't decided on a new course of action, a new career."

"You spent eight years off playing, brother. I've only wasted a year so far. I think of a career as a new pair of boots . . . you have to find the one that fits without pinching."

Sebastian frowned and set the plate down in front of his brother.

Marcus gave him a charming smile of thanks and set to eating. His exertions last night had certainly given him an appetite. He wondered what she—the mystery woman, the lady in scarlet—was doing at that moment. Was she lying in her bed all warm and desirable, while her maids prepared her for the day ahead? Or was her husband lying next to her wondering why she didn't seem quite as vigorous as usual?

No! Now he'd gone and spoiled the image. No husband, then. She was alone, dreamily sipping her hot chocolate and thinking of him. She was remembering the pleasure they had experienced together at Aphrodite's Club. Now her hand had slipped beneath the bedclothes and was moving down over the soft curve of her belly, closer and closer to—

Sebastian cleared his throat meaningfully.

"What is it, brother?" Marcus said, stifling a yawn.

"You were sitting there with your mouth open. I thought in a moment you might start to drool. You were with a woman last night I take it?"

Marcus laughed. "Of course I was."

"And you're wanting to see her again? I know that glazed look in your eyes, Marcus. Lust doesn't become you. It's time you considered taking a serious view of women and finding the right one to settle down with."

Marcus's grin was smug. "I do take women seriously. You ask any one of my women if she has not been taken very seriously indeed, and she'll tell you she has. Thoroughly and rigorously. To both our satisfactions."

"And who is your newest lady love? Tell me it isn't another actress. Don't you remember the histrionics you had to put up with when you said good-bye to the last one? Not to mention the blunt it cost to keep her happy." Sebastian went on, listing his brother's amours, and his own objections to them, but Marcus wasn't listening.

He was thinking about the lady in scarlet.

He wished he could tell Sebastian all about it, if only so he could make a wager with him. Because he knew the odds were good that even though their arrangement was for one evening only, his goddess was going to ask to see him again. Women had a tendency to want to repeat the experience.

And he was going to accept.

Portia's feet tapped their way briskly along the gallery toward her bedchamber. This morning she'd been a domestic whirlwind, finishing her tasks in record time. She even replied to several letters she'd been avoiding for a week, and tallied up the household accounts, one of those challenges she particularly loathed but no one else seemed able, or inclined, to do. Now she was going upstairs to change her clothes before ordering the carriage around so she could pay a scheduled visit to Victoria.

Hettie was waiting for her with a smile. "The gray satin, *lieben*, or the lavender crepe?"

Portia had only recently left off her widow's black for half mourning in grays and lavenders and other subdued hues. She knew she should by rights have been returning to brighter colors after two years, but when she mentioned it to Victoria, the queen had looked so sorrowful and disapproving that she hadn't broached the subject again.

"Thank you, Hettie, the gray will do, and I will wear

the matching jacket. I doubt I will be staying for luncheon, but one never knows, so you will tell my mother where I am if I do not return?"

"Your mother is still in her rooms. She has the headache. It must be contagious," Hettie stated in a level voice, but her eyes were quizzical.

Portia had not spoken of last night.

"My mother is getting worse. Yesterday she forgot my father's name. Last week she couldn't remember where she was born. I wouldn't be surprised if one day she wakes up and doesn't know who she is. Or who I am."

"She is forgetful, that's all," Hettie soothed.

"I have mentioned her memory to Dr. Bryant but he is unconcerned, and I suppose I must listen to his advice," Portia replied in a voice that said she didn't entirely agree with the doctor. She knew her mother was not herself these days, that she had not been herself for some time. Her mind, once so sharp and acerbic, was now wreathed in clouds. The panic in her eyes was heartbreaking to see. When a word or a name eluded her, and she realized it was nowhere to be found, she would lose her temper rather than admit what had happened.

And what could be done? Dr. Bryant said it was a natural sign of aging and there was no cure. Portia, for all her wealth and position, was helpless to turn time around. They must just accept it, she'd decided.

"You are in fine looks today," Hettie said quietly, but didn't sound entirely happy about it.

Portia moved to the mirror and began to tidy her

hair. Her reflection gazed back at her, and for a moment she was startled by what she saw. Could one night of physical excess really effect such an alteration? She was glowing, her skin fresh and healthy, her eyes a spectacularly bright blue. She looked as if she had been on a visit to Victoria's beloved Scottish highlands.

"I am, aren't I?"

"What will you say if Her Majesty asks you what you have been doing to improve your complexion?"

Portia giggled, and then, shocked, bit her lip. She hadn't giggled since she was seventeen.

"My lady!" Hettie was horrified.

"I . . . I will be good now, Hettie, I promise you."

She had fulfilled her darkest desire and gotten away with it, but she must never, never risk such a thing again.

Marcus.

Why had he told her his name? She hadn't asked. She had preferred they remain strangers, in his eyes anyway. She didn't want to be tempted to search for him or to ask for a encore. A second meeting would surely be a disappointment; it stood to reason that it could not possibly live up to the first.

No, she had no plans to risk a second time.

"That is for the best," Hettie said, and Portia realized she had spoken aloud. "If you were to be discovered in such a place with such a man, *lieben*, the disgrace . . . "

Portia shuddered. "My mother would never forgive me." Although then again, she would probably have forgotten after a week.

"Her Majesty the Queen would never forgive you."

Portia considered Victoria her friend but was under no illusions as to what that meant. Powerful people, especially royalty, were motivated by greater issues than mere liking and friendship. If she were to be disgraced, Victoria would throw her to the wolves.

"You're right, Hettie. I cannot risk it. I have no plans to do so. It is over."

"Good." But there was a little crease between Hettie's brows, as if she didn't quite believe her.

Victoria insisted that Portia stay to lunch. The little princes and princesses were allowed to sit down with them at the table, and the royal family made a pretty picture of domestic bliss. Victoria and her Prince Consort led a life very different from that of former monarchs, who had scandalized the British people with their debaucheries and extravagances. Victoria and Albert were at pains to show they were obedient to the laws of God and man, and to set an example for their subjects. This new Victorian era was going to be very different from the royal eras that had come before.

Of course, there were many who scoffed. Some members of the aristocracy considered such ideas of respectability to be very middle-class, and others paid mere lip service to the royal insistence on proper and scandal-free behavior, while privately continuing on as they always had.

Portia could imagine what Marcus Worthorne

thought of it. He would wonder what all the fuss was about. Unlike her, the opinions of other people, and the demands of conscience, would cause him no lack of sleep. But she had always been "good" ; a proper little lady. Until last night . . .

"You are smiling, Lady Ellerslie. What are you smiling about? You must share your joke with us. I insist!"

Portia was momentarily speechless, but she had long ago learned to dissemble and did so now. "I was smiling because I wondered if we should continue with the little play we were rehearsing the last time I was here, Ma'am, that is all."

The children were delighted. The heavily pregnant Victoria clapped her hands. "What a splendid idea! My dear Albert might join us. It will do him good to take a moment from his work."

Albert was sent for and duly arrived. He was distracted from his lines, however, and when questioned admitted that he was concerned over a large meeting that was taking place in Soho. Some of the working-class poor were demanding that the land owned by the rich few be handed over to them, so they could share in the wealth and gain employment. Such radical ideas were not new in Europe, but they were worrying to the royal couple and the government.

"If these people wish to live in a republic, they should remove themselves across the channel to France," Victoria said unsympathetically. "I have not forgotten how they sang 'La Marseillaise' at Sadler's Wells rather than

'God Save the Queen,' and I have not forgiven them for it. Such rudeness and disrespect is intolerable to me."

"We cannot dismiss such matters just because they are unpleasant," Albert admonished her gently. "There are those in Britain who plot the destruction of us all. They wish for revolution and use the poor and disaffected as their tools. They would happily bring the guillotine to Trafalgar Square and set it to use."

"Please, I do not wish to talk about it in front of the children," Victoria said in a low voice, shuddering. "Let us enjoy the play. Lady Ellerslie does not wish to hear such things, I am sure."

Albert cast Portia a glance that said he understood it was his wife who did not wish to hear such things, but his smile was kind. Albert was in many ways a humanitarian and a forward thinker, but like Victoria, he was fearful of any ripple in the status quo. The rolling of aristocratic French heads into baskets was still very clear in the memory. The royal couple believed, as did most Englishmen, that a man should swear allegiance to his queen and his country and obey its laws, while a woman should be obedient to her husband.

Those were the rules, and woe betide anyone who stepped outside them.

"If your husband were still alive," Albert said, "he would have marched the army against these troublemakers and sent them fleeing like the cowards they are."

"Indeed he would," Portia murmured obediently.

"It is important we remember him," Victoria added, growing a little teary. "Your presence helps us to do that, Portia. Seeing you reminds us of Lord Ellerslie and all that is good in England."

"I am glad," Portia replied. She was Britannia in widow's weeds, just as she had said to Aphrodite. A perfect image of womanhood for others to admire and aspire to.

But she wasn't perfect. She had broken the rules. And now the memory of Marcus Worthorne was so wickedly delightful she had to lower her gaze in case the queen caught the echo of those licentious images reflected in her eyes. The things he had done to her, and she to him! Portia was quite certain she would remember them for the rest of her life.

Several days later Portia was no longer smiling. The memories and pleasures of her night with Marcus weren't fading; rather, they had turned on her. Instead of lightening her dull days, they were occupying her every waking thought. And the nights . . . he came to her in her bed, but now he wasn't some vague fantasy from her past. An incubus bringing dark and wicked pleasure. He was real, solid—the man he'd become.

In her dreams he promised to take her to heights she had never known, but though she begged him again and again, he always vanished, leaving her unsatisfied. She began to grow afraid that she might cry out his name in her sleep. What if someone heard her? In the mornings when she woke, her flesh aching with need, she automatically turned eagerly toward him.

But he wasn't there.

To her consternation, she was finding it more and more difficult to ignore that matter-of-fact voice in her head telling her that the only way to free herself was to do it again. That why shouldn't she enjoy herself like other women? That it wasn't fair to expect her to be a saint. This was Marcus Worthorne, after all, not just any man. If it was anyone else, Portia was certain she would not be having this crisis.

Hettie was eyeing her with increasing concern.

"She warned me."

"Who warned you about what?" said Hettie, with one of her worried sideways glances.

"'Sometimes once is the beginning of something rather than the end,'" she quoted.

Hettie's eyebrows rose very high. "You are not thinking of visiting that man again, *lieben*?"

"I think I must."

"But why? You said you would never see him again!"

"Because he is driving me to distraction," she said angrily. "It's as if he's awoken something inside me, and I can't banish it. I *must* see him. Just once more. This time it really will be the last, I promise you. Hettie, I am not asking for your permission. I will see him with or without your help." But Portia knew she wanted Hettie's support, if not her understanding.

For a long moment Hettie was silent and very serious, and then she nodded. "You are risking a great deal, but if it is your wish, then I will help you."

Portia grasped her hand. "Thank you. There is no one else I can trust."

"I know this, *lieben*. You are very much alone. Perhaps this is why you have fastened your thoughts on such a man as this; a man who sees you as nothing more than another conquest in a long line of conquests."

But Portia had stopped listening. She was already busy planning ahead. She would write a discreet note to Aphrodite, asking her to arrange a second meeting. Yes, that was what she would do . . .

Suddenly it occurred to her that Marcus might be otherwise engaged. The resulting disappointment made her feel physically ill, before she reasoned it away. No, in her heart she knew that couldn't happen. He would want to see her. He would come.

Marcus Worthorne was as fascinated by her as she was by him.

Marcus stared morosely into his brandy while the voices about him rose and fell. White's was full of his peers, men he knew well, but he hadn't returned any of their greetings, and after one glance at his face they left him alone. He'd been in a strange mood all week. Several times he'd set off to spend a night on the town, only to return home before midnight, having found the women boring and the conversation tedious.

"Good Lord, can you have turned over a new leaf?" his brother had drawled, eyeing him with cynical disbelief.

"I thought you wanted me home before dawn," Marcus retorted.

"Are all the pretty ladies staying in tonight?"

Marcus had grunted, but the truth was, there were plenty of pretty ladies interested in him, just not the one he wanted.

Now, he rubbed his brow and tried not to groan aloud. No woman had ever affected him like this before, and he was at a loss as to why it happened. He was obsessed by a woman whose face and name were a complete mystery to him.

He could almost hate her, because she had quite ruined his pleasure in the capital. Slyly, subtly, the lady in scarlet had crept into his mind, into his senses, and before he knew it, she was everywhere.

"Bloody annoying, that's what it is," he muttered to himself, swirling the brandy in his heavy crystal glass.

There wasn't anything he could do about it, either. He'd tried. Tonight, he'd been back to Aphrodite's Club, attempting to inveigle the name from Francesca's mother, but she'd only smiled her sphinxlike smile at him and said, "I cannot disclose that to you, Marcus. You knew the conditions before you agreed to the assignation. It was one night and one night only."

"But can't you bend the rules a little for family?" He'd given her his most engaging look.

Aphrodite shook her head at him. "Naughty boy. No, I cannot tell. Not even for you, Marcus."

He'd left, frustrated, and ended up here at White's.

The brandy was beginning to befuddle him, and he knew he should go home. "Home," where his brother and sister-in-law were so in love they made him feel lonelier than ever.

Surprised, he shook his head to try and clear it. Lonely? When had he ever been lonely? Life was an adventure, and he was a man who followed where it led him. He had friends, lovers, and the odd enemy or two. Marcus Worthorne was *never* lonely . . .

"Aphrodite said I'd find you here."

The voice was familiar. Blearily, Marcus looked up. Boxer's nose, hard gray eyes. He knew the face but couldn't place it.

"Jemmie Dobson," the man prompted him. "She sent me to find you, sir. To tell you that you are one lucky sod."

"Always have been," he slurred.

"Seems so. There was a note sent around to the club just an hour ago. Your lady love wants to see you again."

It took a moment for the words to sink in, and then Marcus grinned. "When?" he demanded, trying to stand up and failing.

Dobson caught his arm, steadying him. "When you're sober," he said dryly. "Come on, let's get you home."

"I knew she'd want to see me again," Marcus announced with certainty as Dobson helped him to the door. "Women always do."

How could he have doubted himself, even for a moment? With her veil and her mystery, he'd forgotten she was just a woman, and he had always had complete confidence when it came to his domination over the fair sex. With relief he put the strange feelings he'd been experiencing to the back of his mind.

And began to look forward to another assignation with his goddess.

Chapter 4

❦

Portia felt her hands trembling. She clasped them, tightly, until they stopped. There was no need to be anxious. This was her decision and she was in complete control of the situation. It was she who had requested another evening with Marcus . . . and he had agreed to her terms.

She stood up, the scarlet silk rustling. Marcus had asked, in his acceptance of her offer, that she wear the same dress. She had been flattered by his request. Besides, it made it all somehow pleasantly unreal, as if they were stepping outside real life and into their own private fantasy.

Now her body was trembling; little shivers. What was wrong with her? But she knew. Marcus Worthorne, he was what was wrong. He had made her his in a way she had neither expected nor wanted. She craved his touch as an opium addict craved the pipe. Her fresh looks had faded and she'd become pale and hollow-eyed. She wanted him with such an intensity she was afraid he would hear it in her voice, even if he could not see it in her face behind the veil.

You're being ridiculous.

He was a man, nothing but a man. She sat down to dinner with people from all over the Empire; princes and princesses, sultans and sultanas, archdukes and their duchesses. She had conversed with prime ministers and exchanged opinions with famous poets and writers and composers. What was Marcus Worthorne in comparison to them?

Portia closed her eyes and took a deep breath and then another. That was better. She felt calmer now. She felt like Lady Ellerslie. After a moment she found herself drifting, her thoughts slipping back into the past, and she allowed it to happen.

A long avenue of trees threw speckled shade onto the surface of the lane. She glanced along it, half afraid she'd missed him already. She had purposely awoken early to take her morning walk when she knew he would be out riding. But what if this morning he had ridden earlier still? Or what if he wasn't riding at all?

She breathed deeply, telling herself she was being ridiculous. Of course she hadn't missed him, and if she had . . . there was always tomorrow.

She heard the beat of hooves before she saw the animal approaching. A big bay horse, and atop it sat Marcus Worthorne, his dark hair tussled from the wind. The boy for whom she had been heartsore all summer. Her heartbeat quickened, her palms grew damp. What would she say when he spoke to her? Would he have that twinkle in his eyes, as if he found her infinitely fascinating—or a bit of a joke?

But to her consternation he was lost in his own thoughts, and didn't see her until he was almost upon her. He cursed and drew up his mount. "What are you about, girl?" he demanded, glowering down at her. His handsome face was tanned from the long summer, and she could see the vee of his throat because his shirt was unbuttoned and he wore no neckcloth.

If she had meant to dazzle him with her wit, this was the moment to do it, but her voice seemed to have dried up. She found herself staring at him like a child the sun.

His eyes narrowed. They were hazel, though more gold than green or brown. "Do I know you?" he asked, his arrogance tinged with amusement. His mouth twitched.

To her surprise, she could speak after all. "I am the Reverend Stroud's daughter, sir."

He gave her a slow grin, as if her identity was a matter of amusement to him. "The vicar's daughter," he said.

"Yes, sir." Did he know how avidly she watched him in church, her gaze caressing his profile while her father read his sermon? Her immortal soul was probably in jeopardy because of him, and he didn't even know who she was. It was a humbling realization.

"And what are you doing out here so early in the morning?" he asked. "I wouldn't have thought there were many needy families down this way."

"I am walking for my own benefit, sir."

"Ah, a healthy body means a healthy soul."

"Just so, sir."

He was laughing at her, she could see it in his eyes, but suddenly he sobered. "I've just recalled . . . there is something a mile or two down this lane. A Gypsy camp. Take care, Miss Stroud. Those fellows are rascals."

He was concerned for her. Portia glowed. "Th-Thank you, sir."

He paused a moment more, holding his restless horse, and she thought he was the handsomest boy she had ever seen. But he had already lost interest in her, she could see it in his face as his gaze shifted to the farther end of the lane. "Good morning, Miss Stroud."

"Good morning, sir. Perhaps I will see you in church?"

He nodded at her, briefly, noncommittally, and with a kick of his heels he and his big bay horse were off.

She stood, watching him go. Her heart ached. She was in love with Marcus Worthorne, and it was all so bittersweet and tragic because he did not reciprocate her feelings. Indeed, he hardly knew she was alive.

It hadn't been love she felt. Portia knew that now. It had been a young girl's fancy for a boy she never had a hope of attracting. It had been his very unattainableness that made him so alluring. If, in later years, he hadn't become her own personal night fantasy, she probably would have forgotten him as completely as he had forgotten her.

But now the fantasy was real. Marcus Worthorne the

incubus was threatening her peace of mind. He *must* be exorcised. Tonight she would rid herself of him once and for all.

Marcus met Aphrodite's gaze as she paused outside the door. "You remember the rules, Marcus?"

"Perfectly, madame."

She smiled and opened the door, and Marcus stepped in.

The room was lit by a candelabra, and the light was far more soft and romantic than the modern gaslights. His mystery lady was seated on the sofa, just as she had been last time, and she was wearing the same dress. It pleased him that she had agreed to his request. He had been dreaming of her in scarlet, and to see her in anything else would have ruined the fantasy.

She didn't turn as he closed the door softly behind him, but with the veil covering her face, he couldn't tell whether she was aware of his presence. He was certainly aware of her. He was focused on her with a single-mindedness that was new to him, every sense and fiber of his being standing to attention.

There was something else standing to attention, too.

Marcus smiled as he prowled closer. He wanted her and he didn't intend to waste time with idle chitchat. "My lady?"

She jumped. She hadn't known he was there after all. But in a moment she had regained her poise, her low-pitched voice unaffected.

"Marcus."

She surprised him. His name on her mouth was far more sensual than anything he had heard for years. He felt light-headed with lust.

"I'm glad you changed your mind," he said.

She bowed her head. "Aphrodite has left champagne," she said when he remained silent. "Would you pour me a glass?"

He glanced around, found the bottle, and did the honors. Her gloved fingers brushed his as she took the glass and she murmured a polite thank-you. She lifted her veil slightly with her other hand and sipped.

He watched her mouth.

"Why did you change your mind?" he asked her, unmoving.

She took another sip and stood up, exquisitely graceful, the scarlet silk rustling about her. She moved toward him, hips swaying gently, setting her glass down as she came. She reached out, lightly brushing his shoulder, then his jaw, her fingers making promises.

"I needed more," she said.

Marcus set down his own glass, watching her beneath his lashes.

He felt her catch her breath as he slid his arm around her waist and drew her hard against him. There was no mistaking the proof of his passion, if she needed proof. He could hear her little hitch of laughter, and then the soft warmth of her body as she leaned into him. Her arms twined around his neck and she pulled his head down to hers. He told himself he could see the gleam of her eyes through the veil.

"Let me see your face."

"No."

"Then let me have your mouth." He was frustrated and couldn't hide it.

She lifted the lacy cloth, and he saw that she was smiling a teasing smile. With a growl he ravished her soft pink lips.

She was no passive partner, his mysterious lady. She kissed him back, her tongue dueling with his, making little sounds of need in her throat. He slipped his hand beneath the veil, cupping the back of her head. Her hair was fastened up, but he could feel the silky strands, and longed to release it, tangle his hands in it, enjoy the color of it. Fair, he knew, remembering very well the curls between her thighs. The color of honey.

She had stopped kissing him and was gazing up at his face, as if sensing his abstraction. "What is it? Have you changed your mind?"

"Hardly." He caught her up in his arms, laughing when she made a purring sound in her throat, and strode toward the bed. "I was trying to decide which part of you I wanted to explore first."

He tossed her onto the sumptuous coverings, and she landed among the cushions and bolsters with a gasping laugh. Her skirts rucked up, showing long stockinged legs and rich petticoats. He began to strip off his jacket and then changed his mind—he couldn't wait—and flung himself down beside her.

They stared at each other, breathless, and it was as if he was on the verge of something he had never felt before.

"You know there is no future in this," she said, as if to convince herself as well as him. "Only this moment. Only now."

"I know," he replied, his voice deep and sensual. "I'm not a forever kind of man."

"Good," she whispered, tracing his mouth with her fingertip. He bit it, hard enough for her to feel his teeth, and then reached down, bunching up her skirts and petticoats, his palm gliding over her thigh.

"I'm not going to undress you," he murmured. "I can't wait."

"Neither can I," she gasped.

He climbed on top of her and she cradled him with her thighs. He took his weight from her, and when she looked up, he was watching her as if he could pierce the veil. It disconcerted her, and she pulled him down, nuzzling his jaw, his throat, tasting his skin.

I want to be free of him . . .

He moved against her, filling her, and the words spun out of her head as pleasure consumed her.

Portia had not believed this second meeting between them could possibly be as remarkable as the first. She expected it to be a disappointment—she *wanted* it to be so. Then it would be so much easier not to see him again. But now, as the feelings within her built, as she became lost in the giving and taking of rapture, she knew she had been wrong.

It was better than before.

Marcus was able to wring every last quivering sensation from her body. He trickled champagne over her skin and licked it off, his tongue rough and deliciously erotic. She did the same for him, reveling in the sensuality of it, exploring his body in a way she had never done with a man before.

Except in her dreams.

Portia gasped and groaned as he wrapped his arms about her, entering her once more, pounding against her. She strained to reach her peak despite being weary and sated. She was almost free of him, she knew it. Once more would do it. As he drove her toward ecstasy she arched against him, clinging and crying out his name as she climbed toward her goal. And then it came, and she was falling. Falling into nothingness. A place where Marcus Worthorne, and the need he engendered in her, no longer existed.

She had done it.

Her heart was pounding. She lay beside him in the wreckage of the bed, wrung out, beyond physical desire or any of the pitfalls that went with it, and knew that it was over. This time it really was.

"I want to see you again."

His voice was husky with weariness. She didn't

want to answer him. She didn't want to look at him. He brushed her shoulder with his fingers, and she struggled not to pull away. But he must have felt the change in her, because he propped himself up on his elbow and leaned over her.

His face was in shadow, but the candlelight from the room behind him shone gently upon his nakedness. He was so perfectly proportioned, his body fit and strong from a life of exercise. He might appear idle but he wasn't. In contrast to his taut, muscular body her own seemed fragile and soft and wonderfully feminine.

"We are not done with each other yet," he told her.

"We are. There is no more *us*, Marcus. When I leave here we will never meet again."

"Are you sure?" he mocked. There was a glint in his eyes.

"Yes! Yes, I am."

He smiled, and she didn't understand, not until he glanced down. Portia followed his gaze and, with a frisson of shock, realized that her fingers were entwined with his. They were holding hands.

He laughed but she was appalled. She jerked her hand away and slid out of the bed.

Her clothing was spread around the room and she was naked, but she collected it as if it was something she did every day. Let him watch her. Let him think of her when she was gone.

Maybe it was Marcus's turn to dream of her.

She adjusted her veil before the mirror over the fireplace. She could see the reflection of the bed behind her, in the shadows, and the lover she was leaving behind. When she was satisfied, Portia made herself turn casually toward him.

"I have enjoyed our time together very much."

He said nothing, but she sensed his attention.

"*Good-bye,* Marcus," she said, placing emphasis on the first word.

And then she walked out and closed the door.

Chapter 5

After she was gone, Marcus rose from the bed and began to dress. He took his time; he was in no hurry. He felt wonderfully sated but knew it wouldn't last. He'd be wanting her again by morning, and despite her pretending it was really good-bye this time, he was arrogant enough to believe that she'd be wanting him, too. But this time he wasn't leaving it up to her to arrange a rematch.

He would take control.

The salon was as busy as ever. Marcus recognized a visiting foreign prince being petted by several beautiful women. Aphrodite was keeping a close eye on him, but when she saw Marcus preparing to leave, she came over.

"Marcus? There is plenty of champagne still to be had, and pretty girls." She had a teasing expression and a sparkle in her eyes, as if she knew quite well her "pretty girls" had lost their appeal. He didn't know why she found that so amusing.

"Thank you for the offer, madame, but my brother

will be sitting up for me. Since he and your daughter married, he wants nothing more than to see me entrapped in similar domestic bliss."

"Ah, yes, they are very happy. The perfect match. And I take a small piece of the credit for making it happen, *mon ami*. I am formidable when it comes to the happiness of my family and their families."

Marcus wasn't sure he liked the look in her dark eyes, or the way they were fixed on him.

"I am happy with my life the way it is," he hastened to inform her.

"And what way is that?" she asked, head tilted to one side.

"Unattached."

"Oh, *mon ami*, you have much to learn."

Thankfully at that moment she was interrupted by one of her staff, and with a murmured farewell, she left him. Marcus strolled off into the chill night air with a sense of relief. London bustled about him, thriving even at this late hour. Omnibuses and cabs rattled by, and people strolled arm in arm, gentlefolk wearing the latest fashions and fresh from the West End theaters, and the poor, hurrying in their shabby best to the penny plays and sing-alongs to be found in the East End.

A juggler was giving an impromptu performance to the crowd he'd gathered about him. He was tossing oranges into the air, to the delight of the children, and when one fell, rolling and bumping over the uneven cobbles, they ran screaming after it.

Marcus passed by, deep in his own thoughts.

The lady in scarlet intrigued him. He admitted it. Whether their liaison continued or not, he wanted to know who she was, and why she was mysterious about her identity. She was going to extraordinary lengths to keep it secret. Why? He was not familiar with London high society—he found it a bore—and he probably would not have known her name if he did see her. So why this secrecy?

Well, tomorrow morning he hoped to have the truth in the palm of his hand, and then—he squeezed his fingers to make a fist—he'd have her! Marcus smiled to himself; it would be his turn to set the pace.

But it did not work out quite as he imagined. The following morning Martin O'Donnelly, his brother's former valet and now owner of the Thorne Detective Agency, was nowhere to be found. When Martin didn't call upon him as arranged, Marcus went looking for him, only to discover that he was out of town on another assignment.

Frustrated, Marcus went home to sulk.

As the days wore on and still no word from Martin, he grew increasingly frantic. What if Martin didn't know who the goddess was? What if he had lost his one and only chance to discover her identity?

"I'll have to go to every tedious affair in London to find her again!"

"What was that?" Sebastian was staring at him over his dinner. "Are you talking to yourself, brother?"

"Evidently." Marcus laughed, embarrassed.

"I believe it is the sign of an unquiet mind," Francesca said mildly.

"As a matter of interest, Fran, how many soirees and dinners and balls are there in London this week?"

"Every one, do you mean?"

"The ones that matter. The society affairs."

"Dozens, I should think. Why, is there any particular one you are interested in?"

"No." It was going to be tricky. And how did he know that he would recognize her when he did see her? After two intense meetings he could close his eyes and feel the shape of her against his palms and his mouth, smell her perfume and taste her skin, but that wasn't the same as coming face-to-face with someone in a crowded ballroom. He might not get the chance to get close enough to touch, and he couldn't go around sniffing every woman in London for a particular perfume. And as for tasting . . . he'd be arrested and hauled before the magistrates for lewd behavior, if he wasn't bundled off to an insane asylum.

"You are behaving very strangely lately, brother," Sebastian said, as if he'd read his thoughts. "Is there something you need to get off your chest?"

"Not at all. I have a puzzle I am trying to solve, but never fear, I will solve it. *I must*," he added, sotto voice.

"If you wish to attend any particular soiree or ball, Marcus, I'm certain there would be no difficulty. You are single and handsome and brother to the Earl of Worthorne," Francesca went on, her dark eyes twinkling.

"Thank you, my dear, but you forgot to mention feckless and penniless."

"Nonsense, that is neither here nor there. As long as you don't wish to marry into the royal circle, most girls could accommodate a little fecklessness, and there are quite a few heiresses looking for entry into the aristocracy—mill owners daughters and the like—so you don't need to worry about your financial state."

"I'll let you know."

He did attend a ball that evening, unwillingly partnering several attractive and eager ladies under the watchful eyes of their mamas and one jealous husband. He strolled through the saloon, a glass in his hand, certain he would recognize her.

He didn't.

There was no one there who reminded him even remotely of the seductress in scarlet, and he returned home even more frustrated than before. He could give up, he supposed, but knew that was impossible. The only course open to him was to continue the search.

But it turned out, after all, that it was unnecessary to begin a wild and desperate round of social engagements. The following morning Martin finally came to see him.

"A drink, Martin?" Marcus asked, strolling over

to the decanter and pouring himself some hair of the dog.

"Bit early for me, thank you, sir."

"Never too early."

"I apologize, sir, for taking so long to report to you. I hear that you'd been asking for me, eh, several times. If I'd known how urgently you wanted to see me, I would have written to you rather than waiting until I returned."

"Never mind, it's done now," Marcus said with a hint of impatience. "Now tell me, what did you find out?"

Martin gave him a curious look. "Is the lady in question a friend of yours, sir?"

"Of course." He cleared his throat. "Well, let's just say I want her to be. Come on, Martin, don't be coy, you've made me suffer long enough. Tell me her name."

Martin shuffled nervously. "I know that she lives in Grosvenor Square."

Marcus waited, but Martin said no more. "And?"

"It's the residence of the late Lord Ellerslie."

"Lord Ellerslie? The Nation's Hero?"

His goddess was a member of Lord Ellerslie's household? Immediatcly he dismissed the idea that she could be a servant or a maid. No, his lady was something more than that.

"But who is she, Martin?" he asked, frustrated. "I want to know her name, man!"

"She was wearing a veil and a cloak, sir. I followed

her to the house but I didn't have time to ask any questions because I had to go out of town. I'm sorry, but I've told you all I know."

Marcus took a turn around the room, searching his memory for information on the Ellerslie family. There wasn't much. He knew the old man had died two years ago, although the way he was still spoken about, you would not know it. He had been a hero of the Peninsula War and Waterloo, and then a dominant force at home. Queen Victoria adored him and gave him a state funeral, complete with muffled drums, a flag-draped coffin on a gun carriage, and plenty of somber mourners. Other than that, Marcus knew nothing. He certainly had never moved in such rarefied social circles himself, nor had any desire to.

"Very well, Martin. Thank you. I may need your services again, so for God's sake stay in town. And don't tell my brother about any of this. It's personal."

"Of course, sir."

Marcus considered his next step. Francesca was sure to have the information he needed. He'd seek her out and speak to her right now. But to his further irritation, she was out, and again he had to wait. The first chance he had to broach the subject was in the evening, as they gathered in the drawing room awaiting the call to dinner.

"Why do you want to know about the Ellerslies?" his sister-in-law demanded with a piercing look that reminded him uneasily of her mother.

Marcus shrugged and gave her a lazy smile. "The name cropped up. Come on, Fran, you know everything about everyone. Don't make me beg."

She smiled back, amused by him, as she always was. She'd told him often enough that she thought of him as her brother. With a family of two sisters, she had missed out on the male companionship a brother can give, and it pleased her to spend time with Marcus.

"Lord Ellerslie married twice. His first wife was a Gordon, minor Scottish aristocracy. They only managed to produce one child, a daughter, Lara. She married Arnold Gillingham. He comes from a good family, with money, but hasn't reached the heights that were predicted for him. I don't know why. Lord Ellerslie's second wife, now his widow, was much younger than he. Portia Stroud, a little mouse from the country who has blossomed into a . . . a . . . "

"A mouse can't blossom," Marcus said. "Now if you'd said she was a caterpillar, you could have spoken of butterflies."

"Stop it," she laughed. "Whatever she once was, she is a great lady now. Her Majesty the Queen considers her a friend, and she is loved far and wide."

"Is that all that's left? Just the daughter and the widow rattling round in that big house?"

"Well, the daughter lives elsewhere, so just the widow. But there are a couple of ancient sisters. One of them married an admiral, and the other a factory owner." She wrinkled her nose in pretended disgust. "Trade, my dear."

"Is that it?"

"In a household like the Ellerslies' there would be plenty of poverty-stricken relatives on extended visits. Cousins, second cousins. Hangers-on with nowhere else to go."

"How do you remember all this, Fran?"

"I'm interested, I suppose," she said. "Family means rather a lot to me, even when they're other people's."

He reached to take her hand, lifting it to his lips. "Seb and I are your family now."

She smiled and shook her head at him, but she was touched. He meant it, too. He was very fond of her and his brother, but he didn't know if he needed them in the way Fran needed her family. When it came down to it, he wasn't entirely certain he needed anyone, which was not something he was particularly proud of.

"Are you going to tell me why you wanted to know about the Ellerslie household?" Francesca asked, pinning him with her penetrating look again.

"Curiosity, that's all."

She didn't believe him but couldn't ask any more questions because just then Sebastian arrived. As they all went in to dinner, Marcus was busy wondering what his next step should be. He had an address and a name, even if it wasn't hers. Still, it was a start, and he was determined to find her.

It wasn't often that he set his mind upon something to

this extent, but there was a new resolve forming within him. He had taken control and he would have his way. His father, it was said, was a bossy and overbearing man. Marcus barely remembered him, and had never thought himself the slightest bit like him, but perhaps he had inherited the Worthorne strength of character after all.

"You're looking very pleased with yourself," Sebastian said, with a suspicious glance.

"Am I? I suppose I am pleased. I'm enjoying life in the capital, brother. I'm finding it all very interesting."

"Do you remember Duval Hall?"

Marcus looked at him as if he was insane. "Of course I remember it. Mother's brother owned it—Uncle Roger. The place is mine, isn't it?"

"Have you ever been there?"

"Let me see . . . no."

Sebastian sighed. "Our uncle Roger left Duval Hall to you over ten years ago and you haven't set foot in it. Doesn't that make you feel even the slightest bit ashamed?"

"But, brother, Duval Hall is in Norfolk."

Francesca giggled and shook her head at him. "Marcus, you are a terrible man," she said. "Aren't you in the least bit curious about it?"

"Not really. At the time, I had things to do and it just sort of slipped my mind."

"Perhaps now would be the time to remedy that neglect," Sebastian said, in what his brother privately thought a pompous tone of voice. Sebastian didn't used to be pompous.

"You're trying to find things for me to do again. I'm perfectly happy with my life."

And he was. Perfectly happy.

"There's a woman, you see." He heard the words falling from his mouth with a kind of horror.

Both Francesca and Sebastian turned to stare at him. "A woman?" his brother echoed uneasily, with a glance at his wife. "Not a . . . a . . . "

"A lady, I should have said," Marcus replied, sounding as pompous as Sebastian. "So, I don't want to leave London at this time."

They exchanged another glance.

"Is that why you were asking me all those questions about the Ellerslies?" Francesca asked.

"I'd like to drop the subject now, if you don't mind."

He took up his spoon and began on his soup. He could sense them exchanging more looks but carried on with his meal and ignored them. Let them think what they liked, as long as they didn't irritate him by trying to send him into far away Norfolk.

"I don't suppose it's Lady Ellerslie you're interested in," Francesca piped up, with a little laugh to show a woman like that was completely out of his reach.

Marcus raised his eyebrows.

"It is just that she and some of the family are sure to be attending the opera tomorrow night at Her Majesty's Theater in the Haymarket. They have a private box.

Lucia di Lammermoor is playing, Donizetti's opera, with Jenny Lind in the role of Lucia. Anyone who is anyone will be there."

"Opera." Marcus shuddered. "Thank you, Fran, but no. I can go to a cat fight and hear better singing."

"Philistine," Sebastian said. "Have you ever heard the Swedish Nightingale sing?"

"No."

"Well if you did, you might change your mind."

The conversation returned to more mundane matters and he was finally able to relax. His thoughts drifted. Perhaps he *would* slip into the opera, just to take a peek at the famous and perfect Lady Ellerslie, and her poor relations. His mysterious lady may well be one of the hangers-on Francesca had spoken about. That would explain her fear of being found out—the perfect Lady Ellerslie would be appalled and disgusted and demand she go back to where she came from.

Was there a chance here for him to play the hero? He could save his goddess from her uncomfortable circumstances and . . . Well, maybe not *marry* her, he wasn't the marrying kind, but he was a generous lover.

He lifted his head to tell Seb and Fran of his decision, and interrupted one of their long, sultry looks; the ones that meant they were planning an early night. With a sigh, Marcus returned to his soup. Even opera was preferable to playing gooseberry.

Chapter 6

Lucia di Lammermoor was renowned for testing the vocal cords of even the most accomplished sopranos. Mademoiselle Lind was singing her part perfectly. Portia, not a great lover of the opera, knew enough to know that. But who could not enjoy listening to Jenny Lind? The whole country was in love with her.

Portia was seated in the Ellerslies' private box with Lara and Arnold Gillingham, and her aunt Jane, one of her late husband's aged sisters. She was aware that she was under scrutiny; she always was. The other private boxes, the stalls, the pit . . . the constant curious gazes of those who came to the opera not to listen but to stare at the rich and famous. But Lord Ellerslie had taught her the art of polite indifference, something all public figures must learn, and she had been an apt pupil.

In the beginning she was a shy, young wife whom her elderly husband wanted to protect by keeping her out of the limelight. But in time Portia had come to realize that she could either rise above her own fears or remain a prisoner of them. Choosing to step out from her husband's shadow, she gradually grew as a person in her own right. It was ironic that now that Lord Ellerslie was dead, she found herself taking on his mantel again.

It was frustrating, too. The public might love and admire her, but Portia was under no illusions. Their feelings for her were in great part due to her position as the Widow of the Nation's Hero. Sometimes she herself could barely remember what she'd been like before she married. She was playing a role, just like Jenny Lind, but hers was not for an evening, it was for life.

Lara was whispering to Arnold. Portia ignored them, watching the stage with polite attention while her thoughts wandered where they willed. Lately, during her public appearances, she had found an immense satisfaction in replaying her feverish moments with Marcus Worthorne. It was amazing how the time seemed to fly when she was reliving the way he had carried her to the bed, or the expression in his eyes as he made love to her, or the exact timbre of his voice when he said, "I can't wait."

But remembering didn't mean she wanted to see him again. Having rid herself of the troublesome Marcus Worthorne, she didn't want him back. When she returned home from Aphrodite's she had barely been able to stay awake long enough for Hettie to undress her before falling into a deep and dreamless sleep. In the morning, she awoke refreshed and calm, and as yet there had not been a ripple upon those tranquil waters.

When Hettie had asked her, "So that is the last of him, *lieben*?" she was able to answer honestly, "It is."

By the time the curtain came down on the first act, Aunt Jane was growing restless. She was Lord Ellerslie's younger sister, and though nearing eighty, far from an invalid. But she was a stickler for her routine and was ready for refreshments. "Where are they?" she demanded in the loud voice of the hard-of-hearing. "I cannot do without my cake and Madeira."

"I'm sure they won't be long," Lara murmured, embarrassed. She glanced about to see if anyone had overheard and encountered a hard stare from a man in another box. "Do hush, Aunt Jane."

"No, I won't hush!" Aunt Jane was able to hear perfectly when she chose to. "When you are as old as me you'll understand the importance of keeping time. This might be the last opera I go to. The last time I partake of refreshments."

Below and around them opera goers were making their way through the vast interior, seeking their own refreshments, although some were content to remain in their seats, gazing up admiringly at the enormous chandelier and ogling the occupants of the private boxes for entertainment.

"My lady?"

One of the opera house staff had slipped in behind them and was bowing stiffly to Portia. He held out a folded piece of paper in his gloved hand. She murmured her thanks as she took it and unfolded it.

The writing was a menacing scrawl, and it seemed as if the words jumped up at her.

Meet me outside. Now. Marcus.

Her breath seemed to stop. She felt light-headed. Aunt Jane's complaints and Lara's impatient replies receded into a dull humming.

It couldn't be. It was impossible. How could he know? Even if he saw her, he would not have recognized her. She'd been wearing a veil. She'd been so careful, had taken every precaution.

No, no, no . . .

Portia stood up, the note crumpling in her hand. Lara and Aunt Jane stopped their mild bickering and looked up at her in surprise. Arnold raised an elegant eyebrow.

"I'll go and see what has happened to our refreshments," she said, which was the first thing that came into her head. She had not realized it was so easy to be untruthful.

Aunt Jane nodded. "Good girl. And tell them—"

But Portia didn't wait for Aunt Jane's instructions. She stepped outside the door of their box, into the corridor that led to the Grand Staircase. Just for a moment she was tempted to pick up her skirts and run. But where would she run to? There was nowhere. She was trapped by who and what she was. Her only hope was that it was some kind of mistake and she could bluff her way out of it.

There was a step behind her.

"Lady Ellerslie."

The deep lazy drawl was as familiar to her as her own face. She had been fantasizing about it only moments before, while the Swedish Nightingale sang. Portia took a sharp breath, her mind suddenly cold and clear. She must brazen it out, pretend he was mistaken, convince him that he had the wrong woman.

She straightened her back and turned to face him.

Marcus Worthorne was leaning his shoulder against the wall, watching her. His eyes, more gold than hazel, were gleaming with unholy glee. As if, she thought, he had just won a fortune at cards. He looked very pleased with himself indeed, and she knew with a sinking heart that it did not bode well for her.

She looked as if she didn't know whether to stay and fight or run for the Grand Staircase. God, she was beautiful. He would have been content with passing pretty, but this woman was an angel. Blazing blue eyes and golden hair and perfect features. He wanted to tear every stitch off her and have her naked in his arms.

He hadn't been able to see her properly from his box across the theater, but during the time it took for the first act to run its course, he'd seen enough to know it was her. The way she moved, the way she held herself, the set of her shoulders. The truth was, he'd known her the instant he lifted his gaze and saw her arrival—something clicked in his brain—and the rest of the time he'd just been enjoying the view.

It was Fran who'd arranged for him to borrow her sister Vivianna's opera box. He'd come along early, all togged out in evening dress, and sat in the corner, half shielded by the draperies, and waited. The Ellerslie party was late. As they took their seats, every eye was upon them. Then the murmurs began. "It's Lady Ellerslie."

"Portia."

"It's Portia."

There was a smattering of applause. She heard, smiling and bowing her head, as regal as a queen.

And that was when he knew who his mystery lady was. It was Portia, *the* Portia, Lady Ellerslie, Widow of the Nation's Hero.

It made perfect sense, far more than if she'd been some poor, put-upon relative. No wonder she was afraid of her identity being discovered. No bloody wonder! If it was known that such a pure and angelic model of widowhood was visiting a brothel to spend her time with a wastrel like him, she'd be finished. Destroyed utterly. Good Lord, he could hardly believe it himself. But yes, it was her. Distractedly, his mind had filled with images of her body clinging to his, the sound of her soft cries of pleasure and moans of passion. The scent of her; the taste of her.

Oh yes, his mystery goddess was definitely Portia, Lady Ellerslie!

And knowing who she was just made everything much more exciting. He felt wicked, as if he had done something bad, but he didn't want to stop. Thinking about it made him want to do it all over again.

"Do I know you?"

Her voice broke into his musings. She sounded imperious and irritated, as though he were an annoying insect. Marcus smiled. So that was going to be the way of it. She was going to fight. So much more interesting than running.

"Oh yes, you know me. Intimately."

"You're mistaken."

He straightened up, and she immediately tensed, becoming even more wary. Did she think he was going to grab hold of her and ravish her here? He smiled. Nice thought, but he prided himself on being more subtle than that.

"Trust me, I am very discreet."

"I don't even know you!"

Her cheeks were flushed, her eyes bright. In a moment she would be calling for assistance to have him thrown out. He wouldn't put it past her. She seemed determined to carry through with her fantasy that they were strangers. He supposed in her position she didn't have much of a choice.

"Why did you do it?" he asked her curiously. "Why risk everything? Not that I am complaining, mind. I'm glad you chose me."

"You are mad, obviously, and I don't know what you're talking about."

"I won't stop. I want you, Portia, and I'm going to have you again. And again."

"I think you are mistaking me for someone else," she whispered, but he could see she was beginning to lose her fire, as she realized her strategy wasn't working.

"We enjoy each other's company, Portia. We should keep on seeing each other. We can be as discreet as you like. I am the master of discretion."

"Leave me alone."

"No, I won't leave you alone. I can't. I'm going to persuade you to change your mind."

She shook her head. "You can't."

"I can."

He reached out his hand and brushed her cheek with the backs of his fingers.

She froze.

He was looking into her eyes and reading what was there, behind the mask she wore. Did he see a flicker of feeling? A hint of longing?

"I'm not giving up," he murmured. Her breath was warm and sweetly scented. He let his mouth hover over hers, promising the hot, deep kisses they had enjoyed at Aphrodite's Club. He had never wanted anything so much as he wanted to cover her lips with his and wrap his arms around her. He could take her against the wall. Just for a moment he allowed himself to imagine her thighs wrapped around him, his body deep inside hers, while the Swedish Nightingale sang.

She was thinking it, too. He was sure of it. Her blue eyes had darkened and her lashes fluttered. She arched toward him, just enough so that her breasts, enclosed in lavender silk, brushed against his stiffened shirtfront.

"I want you," he said.

Her fingers rested on his sleeve. Her wide skirts were pressed to his trouser legs, the many petticoats causing them to bell out behind her. Helpless invitation was in every line of her beautiful face and body.

Marcus smiled. If he wanted to, he could kiss her now. And he wanted to . . . but he also wanted to master her. Destroying her reputation would not endear him to her, or get him what he wanted.

He stepped back, and she opened her eyes wide. She looked endearingly confused, and cross.

"Good evening, Lady Ellerslie."

He bowed, then turned and sauntered away, leaving her standing there. He didn't look back. He wasn't going to ravish her just yet. She must agree to any ravishment wholeheartedly. She must agree to his terms.

The rules and strictures of high society meant nothing to him. It wasn't that he delighted in breaking them, just that he ignored them and went ahead and did what he wanted to anyway. He was a man who followed his desires, and couldn't understand why others denied themselves.

Just as Portia was denying herself now, and had to be shown the error of her ways.

* * *

Portia was shaking so much she wondered if she was going to fall down. She rested her hand against the wall, steadying herself, forcing her whirling thoughts to stillness. One moment she had been in control, and then . . . she would have let him touch her, kiss her, and more. She, who'd thought herself rid of him, was as entangled in desire as ever.

He will tell and you will be ruined! You should never have risked so much for a few hours of pleasure.

But as she began to think clearly once more, she realized that he had not threatened her with disclosure. He had sought her out because he wanted to see her again. It was an impossible madness. Yes, he must be mad!

But how had he found her? How had he known who she was? He had tricked her, followed her, broken their agreement.

There was no point in worrying about such details now, she told herself grimly. She had to deal with the facts, and they were plain and simple. He *had* found her and he *did* know who she was, and he wanted to continue meeting her. Somehow she must drive him away, make him understand he could not have what he demanded. Somehow she must untangle herself from the mess she'd created.

But her body gave the lie to her cool head.

There was an ache deep in her belly, a throbbing between her thighs, and a tingling on her lips. She was lying to herself when she said she didn't want him as much as ever, and he'd known it. He had shown her just how much of a lie it was, forced her to *see* . . . and then walked away.

"My lady?" It was the servant with their refreshments. Portia stretched her mouth into a smile and proceeded him into the box. Aunt Jane's sharp old eyes slid over her, but thankfully, she was more interested in the cream cakes and Madeira.

It was not until the curtain was set to rise for the next act that Arnold leaned across and pressed something into her hand. "You dropped this, Portia," he said smoothly.

She looked down and saw that it was the crumpled note. Had he read it? Did her expression give her away? She hoped not. Her smile was as calm as ever as she thanked him. He didn't seem to want an explanation, but then Arnold was so self-obsessed she would not expect him to ask for one. Lara hushed them as Jenny Lind began to sing once more.

But the evening was spoiled for Portia. Her life was in tatters, and although she would like to have blamed Marcus for it, she knew the fault was as much hers. He had hunted her down, and a treacherous, dangerous part of her was glad.

Chapter 7

Lara scowled. "I hate her, Arnold. I try to be charitable but I cannot help it. Why did my father marry her? He didn't need a wife, especially a parson's daughter with nothing to recommend her."

Arnold watched her, sipping his brandy, waiting for the anger and resentment to wind down. The wine at dinner hadn't helped. Lara tended to be louder and less cautious when she'd been drinking.

"I tried to persuade him not to. He wouldn't listen to me."

"Your father was a brave soldier and a clever general, but he was still a man, Lara."

"What does that mean?"

"He saw Portia and he was smitten."

"He felt sorry for her," Lara retorted. "He did not love her. My father was a compassionate man, not a fool."

She continued to rant, striding back and forth, more like her father than she knew. Arnold let her words wash over him. He had more important things to think about. When she was done, he would speak to her about the favor he wanted her to ask of Portia. And no matter how much Lara professed to hate her stepmother, she would do it.

She always did.

"So you want me to find out what exactly, sir?" Martin looked at him sideways.

"I want to know her engagements for the next fortnight. Which houses she is invited to, who she will be visiting, who will be visiting her, that sort of thing." Marcus waved a vague hand.

"And this is Lady Ellerslie?" Martin said, as if he couldn't believe Marcus was serious. "The Widow of the Nation's—"

"Hero. Yes, that's right."

Martin looked as if he wanted to ask more questions.

"This is a personal matter," Marcus assured him.

"Ah, I see." A twinkle came into his eye.

"And Sebastian certainly doesn't need to know."

"Of course not. This is between you and me then, is it?"

Marcus agreed.

"Then you'll be pleased to hear, sir, that after our last meeting I made a friend in the kitchen at Grosvenor Square. Just in case."

"Oh?"

"Amazing what a bit of bribery can do."

"Martin, just do what you have to."

He needed an invitation to one of the houses Portia would be visiting. He needed to be in the same room with her. He needed to look into her eyes and persuade her that continuing to enjoy each other's company was worth any risk. What was life without an element of danger, after all?

"You could always write to her, sir," Martin suggested.

"I did that. My letter was returned to me in the same envelope, torn to pieces." He smiled. The ferocity of her reaction had amused and pleased him rather than disheartening him. If he meant nothing to her, she would have tossed the letter aside, not ripped it up. Beneath that cool, calm mask she was passionate and bold, and although she was playing at respectability, Marcus was convinced that in truth she was far from respectable.

Besides, he ached to have her in his arms again and he could not believe she didn't feel the same. Denying them both was plainly ridiculous when they could be having so much fun together. She just didn't understand that there was no point to being miserable when he was here, available.

She needed him, and he was determined to prove it to her.

Victoria had kept her late at the palace rehashing memories of Lord Ellerslie. The queen had been brought to bed with the birth of her baby, another little prince, this one called Arthur. Both mother and child were well, but Victoria was bored and longing to get back to the things that stimulated and interested her. Despite the image portrayed of her, she was not a particularly maternal woman.

While she spoke, Portia had nodded and smiled and wiped away a tear or two. Sometimes she wondered whether Victoria was a little jealous, so many of her sentences seemed to begin with "If I had been Lady Ellerslie . . . " There had been speculation about the queen and her prime minister, Lord Melbourne, but Portia honestly believed that had more to do with Victoria's lack of a father than her need for a lover. Possibly, Lord Ellerslie had fulfilled a similar role in the young queen's life.

By the time she arrived home at Grosvenor Square, Portia felt exhausted. She hadn't been sleeping well again. Ever since she saw Marcus at the opera, she had been so tormented by regrets and wistful longings that she wondered if she was going insane.

"My lady."

Deed, her butler, glanced toward the drawing room. "Mrs. Gillingham is here to see you."

"Oh no," Portia wailed, and was immediately appalled at her lack of self-control. She never showed emotion in front of anyone but Hettie . . . and Marcus. "That is, it is so late," she went on, her voice calm again.

"I did mention the lateness of the hour, my lady," Deed said with a sympathetic note in his voice.

Slowly, Portia stripped off her gloves and reached up to remove her bonnet, at the same time paying more attention to Deed's expression. Her butler's face was always helpful in determining the mood in her household. "Mrs. Gillingham can be difficult, Deed, but she is Lord Ellerslie's only child."

"Indeed, my lady." He looked long-suffering now. "A very exacting lady, my lady, or so she was when she resided here with his lordship. Begging your pardon if I speak out of turn, but we here in Grosvenor Square are very happy with the current arrangement."

It was the nearest he could come to telling her he was her loyal and trusted servant.

"Thank you, Deed. I had better see her so that we can send her on her way."

Deed almost smiled.

As Portia walked across the marble floor toward the drawing room, she felt the weight of responsibility on her shoulders—a responsibility she did not want. Lara had never liked her, and although she had tried her best to build a friendship or at least some mutual respect with her stepdaughter, she had failed. Why couldn't Lara live her life, and let her live hers? Why did she have to criticize and judge and turn it into a contest about whom her father loved the best?

A great wave of weariness swept over her. She wanted nothing more than to turn around and hurry up the stairs to her bed. Pull the covers over her head. No more smiling, no more being polite, no more Lady Ellerslie. Just Portia, tired and worried and confused.

But she knew she couldn't do that. All the people in this house were dependent upon her. She had a duty to them. Usually she did not mind. In fact she prided herself upon carrying out such duties to the best of her ability. But tonight the souls in her keeping weighed heavy upon her.

"Portia?"

Lara's voice was strident, breaking the spell. She had come out of the drawing room and was watching her.

"Why are you standing there in the dark? Didn't Deed tell you I was waiting?"

Portia hoped Lara hadn't read the chaotic thoughts in her face. Her stepmother's moment of crisis would be another thing to save up and throw back at her the next time she was feeling spiteful.

"Yes, he did tell me," she replied levelly. "It is late, Lara, that is all, and I am tired," she added, following her into the drawing room.

"Is it so very late?" Lara replied artlessly. "I was at the Fenshaws' ball and decided to see you on my way home." She had her father's nose, the poor girl, but she was still a handsome woman, or could have been if discontent and resentment had not begun to draw lines around her mouth and creases beside her eyes.

"Where is Arnold?" Portia sat down, forcing a polite smile.

"He had someone or other to visit at his club. You

know men." Lara plunked herself down onto the opposite chair with a throaty laugh.

No, thought Portia, surprised, *I don't.*

Her father was a stern man who had little time for his daughter's flights of fancy, and her husband, though kind, was of a different generation. In her life, she had only known two men intimately, her husband and Marcus . . . And did she truly know him? She doubted it. Apart from being dangerous and careless, more interested in his own pleasure than anything else, he was as much a mystery to her as the rest of mankind.

"You are looking very grand," Lara said.

Her rise in tone seemed to imply that she thought her young stepmother was overdressed. Portia, long used to such barbed comments, no longer felt the need to justify herself. Tonight she didn't even bother to answer.

"How is Her Majesty the Queen?"

"Victoria is well. The baby is well. They are both healthy."

Lara clicked her tongue. "You should not call her that. It shows a lack of respect."

"I don't do it to her face, Lara. And I respect her a great deal. We are friends, I think. As much as a queen and a commoner can ever be."

"You are friends only because of my father." Lara's voice was sharp, all pretense at manners suddenly gone.

The two women were of a similar age and could have been close. But Lara did not want to share her father with anyone, especially a new wife. Portia assumed that was why Lara resented and disliked her so much. Yet it was not as if his marriage had made him treat his daughter any differently, for he had always loved her. Unfortunately, it was the guilty love of a father who was disappointed in his only child and had never been at home long enough to discover her finer points. And instinctively Lara had always known it.

"It is my father Her Majesty thinks of when she looks at you," Lara went on with a curl to her lip. "It is my father the people loved. You are just a reminder."

Portia was tired, her head ached, and she was fed up. She had troubles enough of her own without listening to Lara's. For the first time in their rocky relationship her patience deserted her.

"What do you want, Lara? Tell me so that we can stop pretending we enjoy each other's company." Her own words shocked her and she almost wished them back, but it had been so good to say the truth out loud for once and not pretend.

Lara's eyes widened. She didn't appear to be insulted. In fact there was almost a hint of admiration in them for such plain speaking. "Very well," she said slowly, "I will tell you. I came here to ask you a favor, Portia."

"What sort of favor?"

"You needn't sound so suspicious. If you can house and feed all those Ellerslie relatives, as well as your own, you can surely grant your stepdaughter one request."

"I only have one relative and that is my mother, as you well know, Lara. And your father would not want me to turn out his family when we have more than enough room to keep them. Can you see Aunt Jane in the workhouse?"

Lara gave a mocking laugh. "I had forgot you were a parson's daughter."

"I am not ashamed of that." Portia lifted her chin.

Lara probably was, though. She was a snob, whereas her father had been a humanitarian, boasting that he judged a man by his actions rather than his birth. All very well, Portia often thought, and easy enough to say when your own breeding was impeccable. But this time she kept such disloyalty to herself.

"What is the favor you want to ask of me?" she said again, curiosity getting the better of her.

Lara glanced away as if embarrassed, but more likely hating having to ask Portia for a favor at all. "Arnold will not ask so I must. He has heard that there is a vacant position in the royal household . . . secretary to Prince Albert. Arnold would be perfect for the post. Perhaps a word from you in Her Majesty's ear . . . ?"

Portia sighed inwardly.

Lara's eyes narrowed. "And don't tell me you don't have any influence, because I know you do!"

"Lara, Victoria has her own mind. She does not listen to me. Why should she? As you say, I am nothing but a parson's daughter."

Lara ignored her gentle mockery. "She does not like

Arnold. Last year, when he was referred by a number of very important men for a position in the Home Office, she appointed someone else. A man far less clever and not nearly so handsome."

"She says she does not like his eyes."

Lara stared at her.

This time Portia did wish she could take the words back. But perhaps it was best if Lara knew the truth, then she would not ask her for impossible favors.

"I did not mean to hurt you, Lara," she went on cautiously. "It is nothing Arnold has done, I promise you, but sometimes Victoria takes a . . . a dislike to certain people, and she has taken one to him."

Lara's face went red. "Oh, don't spare me! Why does she dislike him, pray? He is handsome and intelligent and well-bred. Which is more than can be said for her husband! Tell me, Portia, what has she said?"

"Only that she finds his eyes cold. As if . . . "

"As if?"

"He has no heart."

Lara was furious. "And she's wed to gloomy Albert!"

"Lara, hush!"

"Well, it's true, everybody says so."

"Albert cares a great deal for this country."

"I wish Papa were here," she whispered, wiping at her cheeks, but her tears were of anger rather than sorrow. "He would have helped Arnold. He always said Arnold would have made a fine general."

His actual words had been: *Because he doesn't give*

a damn about anyone but himself, so he'd send his men to their deaths with impunity. But Portia didn't say anything.

"You've always resented me," Lara said in a low, angry voice.

"Lara, you know that isn't true."

"It is true! Papa loved me best and you hated that."

"Lara, please . . . "

"Well, you'll give me your help whether you want to or not. You owe it to me. You will come on Thursday night and no one will say we are not the best of friends."

"Thursday . . . ?"

"My soiree. You promised to be there. People are expecting you. Don't you dare let me down."

"I don't know if—"

"You promised! And wear black. I want you in mourning."

She marched out, slamming the door.

Portia stood in the ensuing silence.

Dear God, in *mourning*, like some freak at a fair. It was a wonder Lara did not post bills around London, advertising the fact that the Widow of the Nation's Hero would be appearing at Curzon Street.

She would do it. Of course she would. But in her heart she knew that what she said or did would make no difference. She could never make Lara happy.

Suddenly, she longed to walk out of the house and not come back. Just keep walking, until she was free of the squabbles and the need to constantly think of others. Free to do as she wished.

And what is it you wish?

She knew the answer. To lie in the arms of Marcus Worthorne. Because in those brief moments she felt freedom—more freedom than she'd known since she was a child.

But that was impossible. And it was no use thinking and wishing for things that could never happen. She had chosen her life—or it had chosen her and she had made her decision to accept—and there could be no turning around now. The assignations with Marcus would remain with her, delicious memories, but any liaison between them was over. She could not risk it again.

Then why did she feel this sense of loss? Of grief? Or longing for something she could never have?

Why was it that she had to please everyone but herself?

"I did try!" Lara cried, wringing her hands.

Arnold remained unimpressed. "It wasn't much to ask," he said, petulant. "I don't ask much of you, Lara, and when I do ask something, you do not even try."

"She refused," Lara insisted, her voice rising. "If you must blame someone, then blame her."

Arnold said nothing.

Lara hated his silence more than his hurtful words. She could never bear it. She loved him, didn't he know that? She would do anything for him.

As usual, it didn't take her long to cave in. "Please, forgive me," she said breathlessly.

"Forgive you?"

"Arnold, please, what do you want?"

"I want you to show me you care, Lara. Is that too much to ask?"

"I do care!"

"Then you should prove it, shouldn't you?"

Lara's lips trembled but she didn't cry. Arnold hated it when she cried. He said it made her ugly.

"Tell me what to do," she begged, "and I will do it."

Arnold gave her his beatific smile. "I may have something for you to do, Lara. I have a plan, and I will need your help with it."

"Anything, my love," she said feverishly. She touched his cheek and felt him freeze. He didn't like to be touched, not even by his wife. Arnold, beautiful as he was, was a cold man. Lara told herself such things were unimportant if one loved, but some nights she lay awake and wished he were a little more interested in the physical side of marriage. Even a kiss and a cuddle would be enough, he did not have to do more.

But she would never ask him. Not after that one time when he had flown into a rage, accusing her of being as base as the women who plied their wares in Covent Garden after dark.

Their love had to be a spiritual union. A meeting of the minds.

"Is Portia attending the soiree?" Arnold asked, breaking into her thoughts.

"Yes. In black."

He smiled. "Very good, Lara. I am pleased with you. Everyone will be there to see her. It will be a hit. The angelic widow, so untouchable, so pure. Or is she?"

"What do you mean, Arnold?"

"There is something very erotic about Portia. Her untouchableness, the very thought that she is so unattainable, makes her desirable."

"But Arnold, you—"

"Not to me, you ninny," he said impatiently. He shook his head. "Never mind. Go to bed, Lara. You have much to do for Thursday's soiree. Good night, my dear."

He leaned down and kissed her temple, before he turned away toward the library. Alone, Lara floated up the stairs to bed, tears of joy in her eyes.

Chapter 8

Marcus strolled toward the house in Curzon Street. It was spectacularly lit up, and there was a small army of servants in livery directing carriages as they arrived. Ladies in beautiful evening dresses and gentlemen in sober jackets made their way past the footmen standing rigidly on either side of the doorway and into the Gillingham residence.

Marcus followed them inside. It had been no easy matter to get hold of an invitation. For the past three days and nights he had been on the hunt for someone who knew the Gillinghams well enough to get him inside. In the end he had been reduced to begging Lady Annear, Sebastian's godmother. She surprised him by managing to secure the invitation within an hour.

"I don't know why you want to go to Lara Gillingham's gathering," she'd said, waving aside his thanks. "Dreadful snob of a woman, and as for the husband . . . looks like a poet. All that flopping hair and soulful eyes. I never trust men who look like poets."

Marcus smoothed his cuffs and felt no such qualms. He knew he was looking his most elegant; the perfect gentleman. No one would dare question his credentials. Just because he chose not to mingle with the blue bloods did not mean he could not, if he wished to. He had the breeding, the education, the contacts to charm a duchess at twenty paces. It was true he found situations like this a dead bore and avoided them like the plague, but this time was different.

Portia Ellerslie made it different.

What would she say when they came face-to-face? She would not be expecting him to seek her out on her home ground. He could catch her off guard, get under her skin. He smiled. Oh yes, he'd very much like to get under her skin.

Anticipation buoyed him up as he handed the invitation to the bewigged servant waiting at the salon door. Inside, a sea of guests seemed to wash back and forth beneath the brilliance of the gaslit chandelier.

He saw her at once, mainly because she was wearing black. Her deep mourning stood out starkly against the other women's whites and pinks and bolder colors, making them seem frivolous and somehow shocking. For a moment he wondered whether she had worn her widow's weeds as penitence for her meetings with him, but he doubted it. She did not seem like a woman who punished herself for her pleasures. There had been nothing furtive in the way she took her fill of him at Aphrodite's Club; she had impressed him as being confident and certain of herself and her place in the world, and what she wanted from it.

The bewigged footman had been squinting at his invitation, but now he cleared his throat and read aloud: "Mr. Marcus Worthorne!"

Marcus watched to see Portia's reaction. She was standing in line with her stepdaughter and husband, greeting newly arrived guests. She was with an elderly gentleman, clasping his hand and smiling gravely as he leaned toward her, but at the sound of his name, her head came up. Her face seemed to pale as she looked straight into his eyes.

He allowed himself a moment to drink in the sight of her—the perfect O of her mouth and the wild glitter in her eyes. All that pent-up anger couldn't be good for her . . . she needed to be tumbled into bed, and often. But her true feelings only registered on her face very briefly, and then the mask was back in place— polite, cold, her vapid smile focused on the elderly gentleman.

Marcus sauntered down the steps and joined the line. He was looking forward to seeing what she did next.

"Mister, eh, Worthorne. Good evening." The sharp-eyed woman with the large nose was inspecting him curiously. "I do not think we have met."

"Mrs. Gillingham, you look magnificent." She did, or would have, if she was not outshone by Portia.

"Thank you. I don't remember exactly where we've met . . . ?" She gave him a questioning smile.

"Ex-Hussars," he murmured in explanation.

"Oh. Yes, of course. You must have known Papa."

"Your father was a great inspiration to us all."

She beamed at him.

Well, that was easy. Marcus moved on to the husband. Arnold Gillingham was an indolent-looking gentleman with rather long fair hair, pale blue eyes, and a handsome if horselike face. With his faintly otherworldly air, he did give the impression that he was composing poetry.

"Ex-Hussars?" he repeated with a cool glance. "You knew my father-in-law, Mr. Worthorne?"

"His fame encompassed us all."

"Just so." But there was a flicker in his eyes, as if he was fully aware that Marcus had not answered his question. "Enjoy your evening, Mr. Worthorne."

Finally Marcus took the step that brought him face-to-face with *her*. The hem of her skirt brushed his shoes. The black mourning accentuated her pale beauty and the bright glory of her hair. He could smell her scent, warm and sweet but with an exotic overtone. She seemed to be trying to decide whether she could withhold her hand from him without anyone noticing her lack of good manners.

"Lady Ellerslie," he murmured, and held out his own. He was prepared to stand here for an hour, but it didn't take that long for her to give in to a lifetime of training and conditioning.

Slowly, unwillingly, she reached for him. He did not

allow her to rush their clasp, sliding his fingers down to grasp hers firmly before squeezing them through her glove.

Her eyes flashed up at him in angry frustration as she realized she was trapped by her inability to forgo the social conventions. She was her own prisoner as much as his.

"Mr. Worthorne," she said through stiff lips, and pointedly looked beyond him.

"I don't imagine any of these people know you have a small beauty spot, just to the left of your spine, where the swell of your—"

She gasped, the color rushing into her cheeks. She opened her fan—an elaborate affair of painted feathers—and used it to good effect, hiding her emotion and cooling herself at the same time. Over the top, her beautiful blue eyes narrowed in fury.

"Not quite the angelic widow now," he murmured, pleased he'd flushed her out of her cover.

"How did you get an invitation?"

"I used to be a brave Hussar. Your husband's old company."

She stared at him, trying to evaluate his words for truth or lies. "Are you saying you served with my husband?"

"I met him once," he said.

"I don't believe you," she replied in a low, angry voice. "I don't believe anything you say. You were never a Hussar, Mr. Worthorne . . . "

"But I was, Lady Ellerslie, and dashing in my uniform, too . . . "

" . . . you do not have the staying power. I cannot imagine you exerting yourself to be anything worthy."

That stung. He was surprised he cared enough to let it. Was he beginning to want Portia to think well of him? Surely not; he had never cared for others' opinions.

"You wrong me, my lady," he said in a lazy drawl. "I'll have you know I come from a long line of England's best."

Her fair brows lifted skeptically. "England's best soldiers?"

"England's best lovers."

Her mouth twitched.

"We Worthornes pride ourselves, I'll have you know, on our swordsmanship."

She giggled, and then looked chagrined, as if it was he who had forced the sound from her.

"Portia?" The voice was heavy with disapproval.

She stilled and then glanced toward Lara Gillingham with all the appearance of a child caught out. Marcus decided she was utterly adorable, and he was more than ever determined to enjoy her until they had exhausted whatever was sizzling between them.

"You are holding up our guests, Portia."

"I apologize, Lara." When she turned back to Marcus, the vapid smile was once more plastered on her mouth. "Good evening, sir."

There would be time later, Marcus reminded himself as he strolled away. She was the reason he was here, and she could not hide beside the Gillinghams all night. He would corner her, and then . . . He smiled in anticipation and reached for a glass of champagne.

Portia realized with despair that she hardly knew what she was saying. Her head was spinning, her hands felt damp inside her French kid gloves—dyed black—and her thoughts were all over the place.

She shivered. He had sought her out and confronted her, and trapped her again. But that wasn't the worst of it.

He'd made her laugh. Not just laugh, but laugh as she used to laugh when she was seventeen. He'd stripped the years from her just as he intended to strip her clothes. She might think about the lingering effects of his smile, the timbre of his voice, the promises in his gaze. She might consider the warmth of his fingers as they clasped hers, all the more potent because they were both wearing gloves. But it was when he made her laugh that he had won her, because he made her forget that he could so easily bring about her destruction. Despite everything, he made her enjoy herself.

She still didn't understand why he was pursuing her. Was it really because he wanted her body? Or was it sheer devilment, because he wanted to ruin her for his own amusement? Such an act of random cruelty did not seem in character, but then she reminded herself that she knew only the sketchiest details about him.

Apart from having tasted most of him.

Portia moved restlessly. The elderly duke at her side was talking about her late husband, and she, who prided herself on never allowing her inner concerns to interfere with her duties as the Widow of the Nation's Hero, felt the urge to turn and walk away. She could even picture the duke staring after her, his mouth hanging open.

Unforgivable!

How could she contemplate such a thing? Somehow she managed to remain at the duke's side, the smile fixed to her face, until it was possible at last for her to politely excuse herself.

She accepted a glass of champagne from a passing servant. The room was so stuffy, and the noise of the crowd made her head ache. She looked around, frantically searching.

Where was he?

Feeling like a hunted creature, she edged her way around the room. A smile here, a polite comment there, now and again pausing to listen to those who wished to speak to her, to touch her . . . She had noticed before that some people liked to touch her, as if she were a holy relic or a good luck charm.

But her black dress felt hot and uncomfortable, and the weight of the cloth, as well as the expectations of those present, began to tell on her. No matter how hard she tried to remain calm, her sense of being under siege grew. Eventually, no longer able to bear it, she looked about for somewhere to escape. A few hasty steps took her to a closed door, and a moment later Portia slipped inside the unoccupied room.

Blessed peace and quiet. The room was cool and dimly lit, and she gave a ragged sigh of relief.

If she had to smile once more or listen to one more tale of Lord Ellerslie's cleverness and bravery, she thought she might scream. Lara would have her taken to Bedlam in a closed carriage, to be locked up with the other lunatics. And then Marcus Worthorne would have to rescue her. It might be worth it if he would wear his dashing Hussar's uniform.

The nonsensical thought made her smile as she began to prowl the room. That was when she noticed where she was; in the Campaign Room. Lara had gathered together her father's military memorabilia—tattered maps and diaries and military honors, as well as the boots he wore at Waterloo—and now they were all here on display. Portia had not been to worship at this shrine for ages.

Her stiffened petticoats and black silk skirts rustled loudly as she moved from glass case to glass case, peering at the contents. Here was a specially struck medal from the Prince Regent, and an urn presented to him by the Prussians. She bent to read a page from one of his diaries, struggling to make out the smudged writing by the single gaslight.

Lara had hung a portrait of her mother, the first Lady Ellerslie, above the fireplace. Dark-haired and gently pretty, she wore what Portia always thought of as a long suffering smile. Not surprisingly, perhaps. In his younger days, Lord Ellerslie had a reputation as a ladies' man, and that, and army commitments, meant he was never home. Just as well that Lara's mother was the sort of woman who suffered in silence. Portia didn't think she would be so forbearing, but by the time he married her, Lord Ellerslie was too old to stray and his soldiering days were behind him, so she never had to worry about losing him to other pursuits.

He had met and married her within weeks. Her mother, Mrs. Stroud, discovering that he was staying with the brother of an old school friend of hers, had taken her on an impromptu visit. Years of telling her daughter that it was up to her to raise the family profile, and the family fortunes, had paid off. Portia had done her duty, received the elderly Lord Ellerslie's attentions, and his subsequent proposal, with serenity.

They were married in the autumn.

She was carried off to London like a trophy of war, she remembered now. Another of the great soldier's conquests.

Portia realized, with a little frisson of shock, that she was jealous of her hero husband. Not because he was loved by all and sundry, but because he had lived such a full and interesting life. He had done so much and achieved so much, and when he died, he had famously stated he held no regrets. She knew she couldn't say that.

What had she done with her life thus far? What had she achieved? It seemed to her that she had lived her life entirely for the sake of other people; her mother and father, her husband, Lara and Aunt Jane, and the British people . . . Even Victoria expected her to behave in a certain way, *be* a certain person. Where was Portia Stroud in all of this, the vicar's daughter who once wandered the country lanes? Had she completely vanished behind the mask of the woman she'd become?

Behind her the door opened, and she knew even before he spoke that once more he had found her.

"Portia . . . "

She spun around, her voice uncharacteristically shrill. "What do you think you're doing? This was never part of our arrangement!"

He moved toward her in that smooth, catlike way, as if stalking her, hunting her. "Let's make a new arrangement then," he was saying. "I never did like the old one."

"You know very well I cannot—" she began, stepping around him on her way toward the door.

He blocked her. "That word isn't one I like either. You can do whatever you wish to, and so can I. Who is there to stop us?"

"We move in different worlds. If I did what I wanted to, I would soon lose everything. I have people who rely on me. I have people who depend on me."

"How tiresome." He sounded bored.

Perhaps it was because she knew it to be the truth, or

because a moment ago she had seen her life with such depressing clarity, but she lost her temper. It went from tepid to boiling point in the blink of an eye. All the years of restraint and good manners—"Do not show the servants how you feel, Portia, it is not befitting a lady!"—of holding herself back—"My dear, it is most unladylike to laugh in front of others, even your husband. Now, now, do not weep. Be a strong little general!" It was suddenly too much, and a red mist formed in front of her eyes.

She went for him, whether to hit him or push him, she didn't know, only that she was so furious she needed some physical outlet. He caught her wrists and pulled her, struggling, against his body. She could feel him laughing and it only made her more furious.

"Let me go, you scoundrel!"

"Is that the best you can do?"

"You shouldn't be here . . . "

"I wanted to see you again," he said in a low voice, "and I didn't intend waiting for your permission, not when it was clear to me that you wanted to see me, too."

She gave an angry laugh. Good God, were those her fingers, crooked like claws? The emotions surging through her frightened her, but at the same time she was elated. She was showing her feelings and the relief was wonderful.

"You will destroy me," she reminded him, and herself. "I will lose everything."

He smiled, damn him. "How so? I won't tell anyone. Will you?"

"Of course not!"

"Then where lies the problem, Portia?"

He let her go, but only so he could wrap his arms around her and drag her in closer to his body. She wanted to scream. He bent his head and kissed her, hard, taking away her breath. Angrily, she tried to bite him. He laughed, avoiding her teeth.

"Bitch," he said mildly, and kissed her again.

His mouth was warm and tasted of the same champagne as she had sipped earlier. He was good at kissing—he'd probably had plenty of practice—and it didn't take him long to gain a response from her. Or maybe she wanted to respond. Maybe this was what she'd wanted all along.

Just like that, the anger inside her switched to desire. Bold, shuddering need that could not be denied. She clung to his neck, her fingers now caressing his hair, his skin. She melded herself to his body despite the restrictions of her stiffened petticoats and wide skirts.

His palm slid over her breast and squeezed her flesh through the lined bodice and tight stays. She barely felt him but her body knew his touch and craved more.

That was when, dizzy and breathless, she lifted her head and remembered where they were. "No, don't," she gasped, trying to evade his grasp.

"Why not? It's what we both want."

"Not here," she said, her voice regaining some of its strength.

He looked around him and seemed to realize for the first time what sort of room it was. His handsome brow wrinkled with distaste. "Good Lord," he muttered. "A tomb. Was this your idea?"

"Lara's. She was always trying to please her father while he was alive, and she's still doing it now that he's dead."

"Please, when I die, give me a Viking burial."

"What is that?"

"Put me in a boat, set it afire, and push me out to sea. I'd rather be food for the fishes than end up in some bloody great mausoleum."

"Lord Ellerslie is buried in St. Paul's."

"Exactly. I want my soul to be free, not locked up in a stone box."

Dazed, she let him take her hand in his, holding onto her as if he expected her to escape, while he glanced about the room. Apparently he was considering their options. He spied the second door by the bookcase, and pulled her across the room with him to open it. Inside, she saw an anteroom containing a table and chair and a daybed without mattress or bedding.

Hardly welcoming, but at least there was nothing in here she recognized. This was neutral ground.

"Well?" He was watching her, waiting for her decision.

Portia nodded.

He drew her into the cramped space and closed the door, just as the outer door opened and Lara Gillingham called out, "Portia? Are you here?"

It wasn't completely dark; there was a high window and light enough to see his face. She stared up at him with wide eyes. Smiling, he put his finger against her lips and then traced the shape of her mouth. He bent again and kissed her, slowly this time, drawing her back into the sensual world he had so recently opened for her.

"Where has she gone?" Lara's voice, closer now, her muffled footsteps crossing the rug before the fireplace. "There are people asking for her. What am I to tell them?"

"I was sure she came in here. I must have been mistaken." It was Arnold Gillingham, sounding as if he couldn't care less. "Forget her. Come and have some supper, Lara, before those swine eat it all."

The footsteps retreated. "I should have asked Portia to invite Her Majesty."

"Come now, Lara! Even Portia couldn't ensure an appearance at your soirée by the queen."

"Why not? I'm sure she has the queen under her thumb, just as she had my father. Do you know, I don't think she has been in this room more than once or twice since he died?"

The outside door closed with a snap.

Marcus lifted his mouth, and Portia heard her own ragged breath. "Remind me not to allow a shrine to be built to me when I die," he said, his leisurely gaze scanning her face.

"There would be nothing to put into it," she managed, dredging up an echo of her former rage.

"Isn't that an ill-mannered thing to say?"

"Yes!"

He laughed at her. "Good. You're learning."

"You're a good teacher."

He cupped her face, tracing her beauty with his eyes. "I'm a *very* good teacher, my lady."

He meant the sensual arts. Portia supposed he was right to be smug. He was every bit as good in the flesh as her fantasy Marcus. Better. This real Marcus did things to her that the dream man hadn't even thought of, things her imagination had not been able to conceive of.

"Now," he said, serious again, "I'm about to do what I've been wanting to do since I first walked in the door and saw you dazzling that elderly gentleman with your smile. Are you going to try and stop me?"

Portia shook her head decisively. "No," she said, "I'm not going to stop you, Marcus. Stopping you is *not* what I want to do."

Chapter 9

He could see the desire in her face, and it increased his own even more, if that were possible. Her blue eyes were dark and dreamy, her mouth swollen from his kisses, and her cheeks were hectic. All signs that the woman in his arms was ready and eager for him to take her.

And yet he waited, relishing the moment, enjoying his victory.

It was Portia who broke the stalemate. Standing on tiptoe, she reached up and kissed him, her mouth open to his in long, hot kisses that made him groan. She slid her fingers over his shirtfront, down to where it was tucked inside his trousers, and tugged it out. Her palms were warm against his stomach, smoothing the skin of his chest, caressing him as though she couldn't get enough of him.

She was on fire.

He hadn't been mistaken. Whatever was between them sizzled, and it needed to run its course. They would burn with it until it burnt itself out. And experience told him that it would go out, eventually. It always did.

Her hand had wormed its way inside his trousers and he gasped as she ran her nails lightly over the hard length of him. Her eyes gleamed in the pale light from the narrow strip of window high above. And there was just enough light to see her smile, too. A wicked, wanton smile that he'd wager very few people had ever seen curling Portia Ellerslie's adorable mouth.

"What are we going to do about your bloody petticoats?" he said hoarsely, as she continued to stroke him into raging desire.

She laughed and stepped away, drawing up her skirts, which seemed to consist of miles and miles of black silk and crepe and ribbons. Her petticoats were numerous. The first was very beautiful and made to be seen—satin, with flowers embroidered on it and layers of lace trimming the hem. The second was plain white cambric, the third another plain garment, and then another, and finally a knee-length petticoat of horsehair and wool weft, to hold out her voluminous skirts so they assumed the fashionable dome shape. Some of the petticoats were tied at her waist, while others were buttoned to the tied ones.

He watched, fascinated, as she untied the ribbons, working swiftly, and then she gave a cry of triumph as the whole lot came away and collapsed onto the floor about her feet. Taking his outstretched hand, Portia simply stepped out of them. She was still wearing her drawers, but these were quickly removed.

With a growl, he swung her around, his hands planted about her waist. Now, without her petticoats to hold them out, her skirts hung far below her feet. He lifted her, resting her with her back against the wall, and began to bundle them up, carelessly, while she tried to help. And then at last she was free to wrap her thighs around his hips, gripping him while clinging to his neck, fingers tangling in his hair, kissing his face and making little sounds of need.

Marcus pushed into her, smoothly and easily. She was so ready she almost peaked at once, but he held her hips so she could not move, forcing her to wait.

"Please, please," she gasped.

"How much do you want to see me again?" he whispered.

Her body trembled around his. She jerked her hips, forcing him to release his iron control. With a groan he began to thrust into her, listening to her soft cries, feeling her pleasure as the ripples passed through her and into him, until he couldn't hold off any longer.

Her climax became his, as he died in her arms.

He came to with his heart slamming in his chest. Leaning his forehead against the wall, he attempted to slow his breathing and regain his mind. She was lying limp in his arms, her head heavy on his shoulder, her arms loosely linked about his neck, her thighs still hooked about his hips.

He hoisted her up, gaining a firmer grip on her, and carried her to the wooden base of the daybed. He sat down with her still in his arms, and she sighed and nuzzled against him.

"I want to see you again," he said, the words so familiar to him now, but no less true.

She shook off her languor and looked up at him. "That doesn't mean you *should* see me again."

"Oh, come, Portia. You can't pretend any longer. I've seen into your heart and soul, and I know what you want."

She smiled. That wicked, teasing smile he knew was for him and him alone. She reached up and with her fingertip traced his left eyebrow and then the right. Then she ran it down the center of his nose, over his top lip, and finally pressing it to his mouth.

"You're a dangerous man, Marcus," she murmured.

His expression turned fierce. "I love the sound of my name in your mouth." He felt his body stirring, wanting her again, but she stood up, shaking her head and reaching for her wretched petticoats. She began to wriggle back into them, a crease between her brows.

"This is madness. Marcus, you know it as well as I. We can't see each other again. We must end it now."

"Not if we're not found out, and we won't be."

She stared at him in silence, and it was as if he could read her thoughts in her face. She wanted him, and she felt as if drawn into something she knew was dangerous, and yet she couldn't seem to resist. But she was trying.

"Marcus, we can't continue to do this. We will be found out."

Exactly, and the chance of discovery only increased the sexual tension between them. But he didn't tell her that.

"Meet me again, Portia. Do I have to beg?"

She was straightening her skirts, bending to smooth the creases, and she turned and looked up at him, her face pale and beautiful, glowing from their lovemaking. Marcus was filled with a burning determination to have her. *He had to have her.* Whatever the cost.

"We can go outside London, if you wish," he went on levelly, convincingly. "Somewhere no one knows you."

Portia gave a shaky laugh. "Marcus, I doubt there is such a place."

"We can stroll along the seaside. Take off our shoes and stockings and run in the sand or splash in the waves. We'll pretend to be there for a holiday. I'll be a . . . a clerk . . . "

"I've never seen a clerk who looks like you."

" . . . and you'll be a draper's assistant. No, wait, an expert petticoat seller!"

She laughed, even as she shook her head.

"We can pretend that this is our first time away together, and that normally we live in a little house in Deptford, with your parents, but they hate me because they don't consider me good enough for their only daughter . . . "

The story grew, becoming more and more preposterous—he even knew how many dogs and cats they
owned—but as he spoke, embellishing and elaborat-
ing, he could see the longing in her eyes. Even so, she
continued to fight him—and herself.

"Marcus, I don't—"

"You do, Portia. We both do. Let's enjoy ourselves.
Why not?"

"Why not?" she mocked, and walked past him to
the door.

Outside, in the Campaign Room, Portia tidied her
hair before the mirror, checking her appearance from
all angles while Marcus watched her in silence. He
had said all he could. Now, the decision was hers.
Was that one of the reasons why she attracted him?
Because she was not easily seduced by his justly
famous tongue?

"You promise me that no one will recognize me in
this seaside paradise?" Her shoulders were unnaturally
tense, her gaze fixed on his in the mirror. "I cannot
afford a scandal."

"I promise."

She took a breath, then nodded brusquely, almost as
if agreeing against her will. Perhaps she was. Perhaps
it was a case of her desires overruling her brain—he
knew all about that phenomenon.

But he didn't let her see his sense of victory. He
might have triumphed over her scruples, but he had yet
to win the war. Still, it was quite something to have

corrupted the Widow of the Nation's Hero, the angel in widow's weeds.

Except his Portia was far from being an angel.

"I'll make the arrangements," he said lazily. "Don't worry."

Portia glanced at him over her shoulder as she reached the door. "Of course I will worry. I cannot help it." She pinned him with a look. "I'm trusting you, Marcus. Do you understand just how much I am relying on you?"

He gave her a deep bow, and spoiled it by grinning. "Until we meet again, Lady Ellerslie."

She opened the door and slipped through, closing it softly behind her.

Marcus barely gave her scruples another thought. He was already considering the arrangements he had to make for their next meeting. It had to be soon. He was too impatient to wait, and there seemed no reason to do so.

When he thought enough time had elapsed since Portia departed, he followed, quickly losing himself in the crowd.

Arnold watched as Marcus Worthorne weaved his way through the thronging guests in the direction of the door. The arrogance of the man! It was only luck that had caused Arnold to pick up the note Portia had dropped at the opera and read it. Then, tonight, he'd noted her odd behavior when she'd greeted Mr. *Marcus*

Worthorne. Arnold knew that if he hadn't put those two facts together he would have been as ignorant as the rest of the onlookers here tonight, although he prided himself on his sharp wits. He had learned over the years to keep a close watch on those who might be of help to him when it came to his secret ambitions. And his pretty stepmama-in-law was currently at the top of his list.

It was amusing that Portia had always seemed beyond reproach when it came to matters of propriety, something that Lara found difficult to swallow. If Portia had been a foul-mouthed slut, then Lara might have found her more palatable. How did one fight perfection? And Lara, as he well knew, was far from perfect herself.

He had taken his wife to the Campaign Room on purpose, to see if he could catch Portia and her beau, but they had slipped into the anteroom. He'd thought about flinging open the door and exposing them *in flagrante delicto*, but on reflection decided it was probably best to leave them be. Lara would only make a terrible fuss, and Portia would be tarnished, possibly beyond repair.

Such a scene was better saved for another time, when it could be used to his advantage.

Arnold stood in the shadows and observed Portia playing the grand dame as if she was born to it. For someone of such lowly breeding—a parson's daughter, egad!—she certainly had a way with her. One smile and the crustiest old soldier fell instantly in love with her. And she had captured the crustiest and oldest soldier of all and married him. Arnold had to admire her, even as he despised her.

His own family came from a long line of Englishmen whose blood was far bluer than that of the minor German aristocracy who now ruled Britain. The Gillinghams went back to the Normans and beyond—they were true Britons. They belonged. It was time the people of Britain were brought to understand just how wrong it was that their country was being destroyed by a never ending influx of foreigners. One had only to walk through the East End to see the seething mass of people who had no right to be here, no right at all.

It was not that he disliked other races. Not at all. They were perfectly fine as long as they stayed in their own countries. But England was for the English, and had to be kept that way.

The English race must remain pure. It was something his father had often said and written about, and when his father died, Arnold had taken up the challenge to make his dream a reality.

And his time was coming, he could feel it. Not long now until he had his chance to show the monarchy, the Parliament, and the people the error of their ways.

Chapter 10

Portia hurried along the platform at Waterloo Station, while Hettie came grumbling up the rear. Waterloo had only been open for a year or two and still wore the gloss of the new. Steam was rising from the stationary train, and passengers burdened with luggage, some with children in tow, hurried to find their seats, while uniformed porters wheeled baggage trolleys and looked officious. Their own porter, striding a few paces ahead, was leading them to the private first class carriage that Marcus had reserved.

She had read his letter of instructions until she knew every word by heart. *Board the 9:09 train at Waterloo Station. Disembark at Little Tunley at 10:17. The train will stop for you only, and I will be waiting.*

"Why didn't you wear your veil?" Hettie tightened her grip on the picnic hamper as she tried to keep up. She had refused to allow the porter to take it from her, clutching it as if it were treasure. The contents of the hamper had been collected earlier from Fortnum and

Mason's, one of London's famous food specialists, because Portia didn't want questions being asked in her own kitchen as to why she was taking a picnic hamper on a visit to an old school friend.

"Everyone knows I am going on a train journey, Hettie. There is nothing wrong with that. I do not need to wear a disguise."

"A place like this . . . the whole world and his dog are here . . . you never know who you might run into . . . " Hettie panted.

"That's the whole point. If I act like I have something to hide, then everyone will assume I do," Portia said. "But if I am going on a train journey for the whole world and his dog to see, then how can I be guilty of anything morally unacceptable?" She smiled as a group of elderly ladies turned to stare and whisper her name. "And nobody knows *where* I am going. I've told my mother and Deed that I am going to visit my friend, but our ticket says Southampton, and it will be assumed by anyone who sees us that I am traveling from there to the Isle of Wight, to Victoria's residence, Osborne House, when actually we are disembarking before that at—"

"He has rehearsed you well! But I still do not like this, *lieben*," Hettie said darkly. "You are risking so much for so little. What is he, after all? A nobody, a nothing."

"Surely one day, even with a nobody and a nothing, is not too much to ask? A single day, when I give up so much of my life for the sake of others?" She sounded as if she was pleading with Hettie for understanding, but Portia knew it was really her own conscience she was attempting to pacify.

"This man . . . " Hettie puffed, not to be sidetracked. "You do not even know him. He could be anybody."

"I thought he was 'nobody.'"

Hettie humphed, or perhaps she had just run out of breath.

Portia was glad. She did not want to think negative thoughts. Now that she had her heart set on this special outing, she did not want anything to spoil it. No doubts, no what-ifs, no dire predictions. This was *her* day, and she meant to make the most of every minute of it.

The porter had reached their carriage and Portia climbed the three steps, holding her skirts up and negotiating the narrow doorway. Daringly, she had left off two of her petticoats today, and the dress itself was new; gray and white striped, with gathered flounces on the skirt and full, bell-shaped sleeves. She had also lately purchased a round wide-brimmed hat made of straw, and this seemed the perfect occasion to wear it. Besides, her tiny and elaborate parasol of black silk with red trim was far too small to keep the sun from her pale skin.

Or at least that was the excuse she used when Hettie cast her a look that seemed to Portia's raw conscience to scream "frivolous."

Their carriage was luxuriously upholstered, with polished brass fittings and looped velvet curtains over the windows, but Portia found she was too wound up to admire the appointments properly.

I will meet you there.

His words echoed in her head. After their wild and deliciously dangerous mating at Lara's house, Portia hardly dared think what he planned for her next. And yet she *did* think about it. She thought about it all the time. She was addicted to the touch and taste of him. He was becoming as essential to her as breathing air.

Hettie was fussing with her own bulky woolen skirts and muttering to herself in German. Her faithful maid was not usually so grumpy, and Portia suspected it was because she was worried. She had been willing to support her mistress when she thought it was just one assignation—Hettie was always more than happy to ensure that she was happy—but now the situation had assumed greater proportions, like a child's lie that grew and grew, and neither of them knew how it would end.

On impulse, Portia reached out and took her maid's plump hand in her own, squeezing it comfortingly. "You don't have to approve of what I am doing, Hettie, I wouldn't expect it of you, but I need to know you are on my side."

The steam train blew its whistle.

Hettie sighed and returned the pressure of her fingers. "Of course I am on your side, *lieben*. I worry, that is all. I am no prude, it is not that. I think if it were simply the urges of the flesh you were feeling, then I would be happy. But this . . . this *man*." She rolled her eyes. "He wants more from you than he has any right to want, and he is careless of your reputation. He takes risks. Perhaps that is because he has nothing to lose, or perhaps he is one of these revolutionaries who does not believe that rules and laws apply to him. He worries me. Such men are dangerous."

The train shuddered, jerked, and then slowly began to move forward. The whistle blew again, loudly, and there was a loud puff of steam outside the tightly closed windows as the locomotive chugged out of the station.

Portia laughed. "A dangerous revolutionary! You are imagining Marcus at the heart of some terrible plot, Hettie?"

"Could be," Hettie said stubbornly.

Waterloo Station was receding, and with it London, and all of the noise and dirt and sprawl that was an increasing part of that great city. With it, too, went her life, and the minutia that it was made up of. She felt lighter with each turn of the wheels, the pressures of family and public life lifted from her shoulders.

Suddenly, Portia turned and grinned at Hettie, feeling like a naughty schoolgirl skipping her lessons. "I am having my very own adventure today. Please don't tell me I mustn't."

Hettie smiled back with an effort. "I promise I will not say a word to spoil it, then, *lieben*. At least . . . not until we get to Little Tunley."

Portia settled into her soft leather seat as the outskirts of London gave way to countryside. Marcus Worthorne would be there at the other end of her journey, and despite her outer poise and calm appearance, inside, her emotions were very different. She felt young and carefree and alive. She had to grip her hands together to stop herself from fidgeting with impatience. She had to bite her lips to stop herself from smiling.

She and Hettie disembarked a little over an hour later, when the train made the unscheduled stop at Little Tunley. The noisy, smoky locomotive left them standing on the empty platform and puffed off into the distance.

As the sound of the train faded and the silence grew, Portia felt a sense of peace begin to settle over her. Unlike London, this sky was blue, with hardly a cloud to be seen. Red geraniums spilled over wooden tubs in front of the station house, birds were singing, and the air was tangy with salt. Portia knew the sea must not be too far away; this was meant to be a journey to the seaside, after all.

I'll be a clerk and you can be a draper's assistant. No, a petticoat seller!

She smiled at the memory of his nonsense, just as clattering footsteps heralded the arrival of the astonished station master, who was hastily buttoning his uniform.

"M-My lady!" the poor man stammered, recognizing her at once. "No one told me *you* would be paying us a visit. Not that you're not welcome and we're not grateful . . . I mean . . . "

"It is a private visit. Please do not concern yourself."

Portia took pity on him. "You have a very pretty little station," she added with a smile. "I envy you living here; London fogs grow worse every year."

The man opened and closed his mouth, flushed with pleasure.

"Someone is meeting me. Is this the way to the vehicle yard?"

"Yes, my lady. Through the arched doorway."

Portia snapped open her parasol of glistening black silk with the daring red fringe, and strolled in the direction he indicated, Hettie trotting along behind her with the Fortnum and Mason's hamper. To her disappointment, the vehicle yard was empty. Beyond the open gateway a narrow lane ran at a right angle, bordered by flowering thorny hedges. The lane was empty, too.

"He's not here," Hettie said unnecessarily.

"He will be." She supposed she should have felt worried or apprehensive, but she didn't. The air was warm and scented from the honeysuckle growing up the wall behind them. It was a beautiful day.

"You are very trusting, *lieben*." Hettie, the voice of doom.

Just then Portia heard the sound of an approaching horse and the rattle and creak of a vehicle. She could not keep the heady excitement from filling her voice as she turned triumphantly to her maid.

"You see, Hettie, you were wrong. Everything is just as he promised."

The carriage, an open affair, was being pulled by

two strong horses. Marcus was seated in the back, and as the driver turned in at the gate and come to a halt beside them, he rose to his feet. He was smiling down at her. She found herself smiling up at him, seeing him silhouetted against the blue sky, tall and handsome and seemingly perfect.

My lover, she thought, with a wicked little shiver.

He jumped down, moving with his usual surety of foot.

"Mr. Worthorne," she said, holding out her hand and seeing it trembling, and hoping he didn't notice. "It is such a glorious day."

"The day isn't the only thing that's glorious." He took her hand in his, lifting it to his lips, and at the same time giving her a hot meaningful look.

Hettie sniffed.

"This is my maid and confidante, Hettie. I trust her completely," Portia said. And unspoken: She knows everything but she will say nothing.

Marcus gave her a understanding look, then reached to take Hettie's arm, moving her toward the carriage. "I'll help you up beside Zac. He won't bite," he added, glancing toward his grinning driver. "Or would you rather wait for your mistress here at the station, Hettie?"

"No, I would not," the maid said indignantly, not at all won over by his charm.

"Then up you go, *fraulein*."

"*Mein Gott!*" Hettie gasped, clutching at her hamper

with one hand and her bonnet with the other as she was lifted in his arms and planted onto the seat at Zac's side.

Marcus turned back to Portia. For a moment she thought he might lift her up in his arms, too, and despite her attempts to be calm, her heart beat faster. Perhaps he read her thoughts because he murmured "Later" as he took her hand, assisting her with all propriety into the carriage, before he leapt up beside her. "There," he said, as Zac flicked the reins, turning the equipage back into the lane. "We are all set."

"I can't quite believe I've done it," Portia breathed, gazing around from beneath the shade of her new straw hat.

Marcus leaned back, his arm resting along the seat behind her, tilting his body so he could see her face. He was wearing his lazy, sensual look, and it caused all manner of unfamiliar sensations to take flight within her. Most prominent was an ache of desire, and if they'd been alone she might even have climbed onto his lap, cuddling close while she pressed her lips to his. Never mind, she thought, reminding herself that there would be time for that. *Later.* Anticipation would help make the moment when they finally came together all the more exciting.

"All the way here I kept thinking someone would stop us." She could admit her inner fears now.

"You worry too much." His gaze lingered on her mouth.

"You don't worry enough," she retorted, gently turning the parasol so that the red trim danced in the sunlight.

He observed her, his body completely relaxed, his eyes narrowed and sleepy against the sun. "Why waste time on something that may never happen? My motto has always been to enjoy today and let tomorrow take care of itself."

"I'm sure Drake was thinking that when he gave up his game of bowls to sail out and defeat the Spanish Armada," she teased. "Or Lord Ellerslie, when he was in his tent with his maps and his men, deciding on his military campaign to outmaneuver Napoleon."

He grinned at her, unchastened. "Do you think of 'us' as a military campaign? What is your strategy for today, my lady? Are you going to make a bold frontal assault," his voice dropped, "or take me by surprise?"

She couldn't help herself, she had to touch him. She raised her hand, lightly stroking his strong, masculine jaw with her gloved fingertips. "I haven't decided. Do you prefer long protracted battles, or brief ones?"

"Both." Her fingers were still resting against his face, and he turned his head, took one of her gloved fingertips into his mouth and bit it gently between his strong white teeth. Then he reached up to capture her hand in his, turning it over to examine it with close attention. Her wrist was exposed between the fine pearl button of the glove and the lace trimming on her wide sleeve. A strip of fragile white skin with the veins close to the surface. He lifted her wrist to his mouth and pressed his warm lips to her, causing her to give an involuntary shiver of delight.

"There's really no need for us to do battle," he murmured against her skin.

"Oh?" she whispered.

"I surrender."

He looked up at her as he said it. Just for a moment, she believed she read sincerity in his face, as if he truly meant it. But the next moment he was smiling again, that lazy teasing smile that could cause her stomach to curl with desire but certainly did not inspire her with trust. No, she would never have allowed Marcus to lead an army into battle, or dictate government policy. He was a lightweight when it came to the bigger issues in life. Handsome and desirable and fun to be with, oh yes, but a lightweight nonetheless.

Abruptly and unaccountably depressed, Portia turned away, primly restoring her hand to her lap. "What made you choose this place to come to today?"

"I knew it as child." He straightened up, his teasing forgotten, and suddenly there was anticipation in every line of him. "Look!"

They had been climbing a gentle slope, and just as he spoke, they reached the summit. Portia, completely focused on Marcus, now noticed that the countryside had opened out. The hedges were gone and she could see across fields, with a marvelous view of wiry grass cliff tops dropping down into the calm, blue sea.

"Beautiful . . . " she breathed, wishing she could paint.

The road curved around, and then she could see even farther along the coastline, where the cliffs fell away and little bays were etched into their rugged faces. She had a brief glimpse of a small fishing village, huddled between the land and a stone-walled harbor, before the road wound inland again and was gone.

"Marcus, it is wonderful!"

He was pleased by her reaction, although he cautioned her with, "Not so attractive on a stormy winter's day, with the sea crashing in and the rain blowing sideways. But then again, wild weather has its own kind of beauty."

"Is that where we're going? That little village?"

"Yes. It's called St. Tristan."

Portia very much wanted to ask him more about his childhood. She already knew he lived at Worthorne Manor, but how did he come to know St. Tristan? But she bit her tongue. It was probably not wise to show too much interest, to dig too deeply. She didn't want him to discover that she had once been mousy little Portia Stroud, the vicar's daughter. She'd left that part of her life far behind, and Marcus was the last person she wanted to rediscover it.

Lady Ellerslie was how he saw her—a famous public figure, someone of stature. Besides, she reminded herself, this was a temporary affair between him and her. The less they knew about each other, the easier it would be to say good-bye.

Chapter 11

～∞～

The village of St. Tristan was every bit as pictur-
esque as it looked from the cliff tops. And, after
Zac set them down and trundled off in the carriage,
with Hettie peering back anxiously, Portia and Marcus
were finally alone to explore it together.

"Shall we?" he said, giving her his arm.

Along the waterfront, the people of St. Tristan went
about their daily tasks, which seemed to consist of fishing and everything that revolved around it. There were
nets to mend and boats to patch and the fish to clean.
Marcus explained that a catch had just come in, and the
part of it they could not sell to market, they would use
themselves, often salting it or smoking it for the winter.

Although Portia received a few curious glances, and
Marcus a number of smiles and waves, no one inter-
fered with them or appeared to care what they were
doing there. For Portia not to be instantly recognized
as the Widow of the Nation's Hero was so unusual that
at first she didn't know how to react, but in time she

began to relax and feel just like any other woman. It was similar to when she wore her veil; that heady sense of liberation.

They lingered to gaze at the boats bobbing at their moorings within the sheltered wall of the harbor. So small, some of them, and the fishermen so brave to set out to sea in such a craft. It must be a precarious life, she thought. Was that why the people went about their business with such seriousness? The boats and the nets they mended might mean the difference between living or dying.

With her hand resting in the crook of his arm, Portia was very much aware of Marcus at her side. One of the fisherwomen, expertly wielding her knife over the catch, looked up at his tall, handsome figure and gave him a little smile, as if she liked the look of him.

"Have you ever sailed?" Portia said, drawing his attention back to her, and feeling pleased when he turned instantly.

"I've swum and sailed," he replied easily.

"You can swim?"

"I learned in the lake at Worthorne Manor—my brother's estate. All the Worthornes swim like fish."

It was her chance to ask more about Worthorne Manor, to prevaricate and pretend she didn't know it very well, but she shied away. This wasn't a day to be serious. As they walked and talked and smiled at each other, she let herself enjoy the simple pleasure of being in his company without having to hide or pretend. The sense of lightness she had discovered while standing at

Little Tunley station began to build, until she thought she might actually float, with only Marcus's arm to anchor her to the earth.

What was this feeling?

It took her a moment to recognize it. Happiness. She was feeling happy.

Portia's appreciation of the simplicity of St. Tristan was not lost on Marcus. Just before she arrived, he'd had a moment—very uncharacteristic for him—when he began asking himself questions like: What if she hates it? A woman like Portia Ellerslie, used to a life with the wealthy and famous, a woman who breathes luxury, might laugh in his face when she saw what he had planned for her.

But the moment he saw her standing outside the station, like a vision with a parasol, his doubts vanished.

He glanced at her now. She glowed with joy. The chance to escape the life she led, even briefly, had lifted her spirits. What did that say about her current existence?

But he did not lecture or pry. Their conversation remained polite and meaningless, skimming over the top of deeper matters, and he kept it that way. She had not asked him any questions about himself, and he returned the favor. Neither of them mentioned what might happen next, or even whether there would be a next. For now it was enough that they were here, together.

Which was strange, Marcus thought, considering that

at the beginning of this affair he wanted her naked body in his bed and nothing more. When had his ambition changed?

"Are you hungry? Hettie has the picnic. Where is Hettie?" She turned about, searching for the carriage.

"Zac took her to prepare our luncheon. He'll be back in a moment to collect us and take us there."

The sunshine was in Portia's smile. "You've thought of everything, haven't you?"

"Of course."

No, he had no intention of telling her how much time and effort he'd expended on this trip to the seaside. Who would have thought that wooing a woman could be quite so exhausting? But this was Portia and she was worth it, he amended, watching her as she breathed in the salty air, tendrils of fair hair curling from beneath her hat. Oh yes, it was worth it. Marcus felt rather proud of himself for being so unselfish. Maybe he was turning over a new leaf?

Or maybe not.

His gaze dropped to the swell of her breasts beneath the high-necked bodice. He wondered if she'd be grateful enough to let him tumble her over the picnic luncheon, if he gave Zac the nod to distract the dragon.

Now *that* would be a perfect ending to a perfect day.

Luncheon was spread out upon a blanket on an isolated little beach along the coast from the village and hidden from view around a rocky point. Portia and

Marcus had to scramble down a cliff path to reach it, and by the time they arrived, Hettie had everything prepared and was guarding the picnic from any hungry sea gulls. Marcus could see that Portia was delighted. She sank down on the cushions Zac had carried from the carriage and cast an interested eye over the dishes.

There was cold roast lamb, pigeon pie, chicken mayonnaise, salmon, asparagus, and salad with boiled eggs. All of this to be followed by a gooseberry tart. There was champagne, too, which Marcus supplied and that had been cooling in the rock pools farther along the beach.

They ate hungrily, the sea air having increased their appetites. Portia gave up long before Marcus, but eventually even he'd had enough. He lay sprawling on his side, with his head propped up on one hand, eyes narrowed against the glare, watching her.

"How did you know it was going to be a fine day?" she asked him, sipping from her glass, her back still ramrod straight. "What if it was raining?"

"It wouldn't dare!" he said in mock outrage, and enjoyed the laughter dancing in her eyes.

"You must have thought about it, Marcus."

He hesitated, and then gave an uncomfortable shrug. "I thought about it far more than I like to confess to," he said, and the admission embarrassed him. Not because it was a weakness, but because worrying wasn't something he normally did. "I suppose we could have huddled under a tree."

She smiled as if his unexpected vulnerability touched her. It probably did. He reminded himself that he would never understand women.

"Didn't you say you used to come here as a child?" A moment after the words slipped out, she bit her lip, as if it was a question she had sworn not to ask.

"My aunt has a house near here. I used to spend holidays with her."

"You must have been company for her," Portia said in her best "opening a fete" voice.

He burst out laughing.

Portia's eyes widened. She looked as if she wished she could take the words back, or hit him with her parasol. "What did I say wrong?"

"I'm sorry. It's just . . . Minnie is one of those eccentric ladies whose hobby is traveling. A camel journey through the desert, an elephant through the jungles of India, or a canoe on the Amazon, it's all one to her. Intrepid and fearless are her middle names, and she certainly doesn't require the company of her feckless nephew to cheer her up."

"Ah, she is an adventurer like Lady Hester Stanhope." Portia understood now. "I would like to meet her."

He flashed her a sideways look. "You probably have. Minnie has been to Buckingham Palace. She'd recognize you in an instant, and then there'd be questions. Do you think it's a good idea, Portia? But if it is your wish—"

"No, no. You're right. It would mean more questions and someone may slip up." She smiled and took another sip from her glass, as if she didn't care, but there was something in her face that made him think she was disappointed.

Marcus looked over to Zac and caught his eye. Zac nodded and strolled up to Hettie, who was perching on a rock like a disgruntled pelican. Marcus watched them arguing, before Hettie was led away, still protesting, to fetch more champagne.

When they were out of sight, he reached over for Portia's glass and set it down. "You'll spill it." She laughed breathlessly as he tugged her down onto the blanket beside him. And then he was kissing her and it didn't seem to matter.

"Do we have time?" she murmured, already unbuttoning his shirt.

"Zac won't come back for a while yet."

"What if someone else comes by?"

"Worrying again?" he mocked.

As if to show him he was wrong, Portia sat up and took off her straw hat. She began to remove her pins, and her hair tumbled like golden honey about her shoulders. Gazing down at him with a little, wicked smile, she unbuttoned the high neck of her bodice. He reached to caress her, stretching up to kiss the hollow at her throat, enjoying the warm fragrance of her skin. She arched against him, her lips parting with a gasp, and her hair curled down her back and beyond her hips.

Marcus slid his hands down to her waist, spanning it with his fingers, and lifted her so she was astride him.

Her skirts billowed out over them, providing some modesty. "There, now," he murmured. "If anyone does come by, they still won't be able to see what we're up to." His warm hands slid up her stockinged legs, squeezing the bare flesh of her thighs. "Unless . . . unless you scream again, Lady Ellerslie. Are you going to scream?"

Her breath was ragged as his fingers moved upward, stroking her, teasing her, playing her as if he knew exactly what she liked. "I might." Her voice had grown husky. "And you?"

Her own searching fingers had found the hard length of him pushing against his trousers. She began to rub herself against him, eyes half closed, concentrating on the pleasure she was giving herself.

"Definitely," he groaned, and reached down to free himself.

She was already gasping and shuddering as he entered her, and he let her enjoy it. Then, when she was done, her head bowed, breasts rising and falling swiftly, her skin flushed, he began again. Slowly, exquisitely, taking her on the journey with him to Elysium and back.

When at last she collapsed, replete in his arms, he found himself watching her peaceful face with possessive eyes. She was *his*. No one else could make her feel like he did, not even the so-called Nation's Hero. His thoughts surprised and dismayed him.

What, was he jealous of a dead man now?

He was beginning to behave in a manner very

unlike his usual carefree self. Was he the same man who had shared his lover—one of the ballet dancers at a supper house in the Strand—with several of his Hussar companions and thought nothing of it? He could not imagine sharing Portia. At the very thought of it, rage flared up inside him and he clenched his hands into fists.

I would kill the first man who touched her, be he friend or foe!

Abruptly, Marcus stood up and began to strip off his clothing.

Sleepily blinking, Portia lifted her head, her hair tangled about her and her mouth swollen from his kisses. "What are you doing?"

"Swimming." He hopped on one foot, tugging off his trousers. He needed to dive into the sea and clear his head of these unfamiliar thoughts and feelings. He needed to be himself again.

"But Marcus—"

"Don't worry, I always swim when I'm down here." Naked now, he managed to grin in something like his old carefree manner, to reassure her, before he turned and took off down the beach, splashing into the water until it was too deep to walk, then throwing himself into the sea. The relief was instantaneous. In a moment he was powering through the sparkling water, leaving his troubles behind him, and with nothing in front of him but the broad horizon.

* * *

At first Portia didn't worry. She lay back down and tried to sleep. But something was niggling at her, preventing her from slipping away, and eventually she sat up, holding her hair out of her eyes so she could stare out to sea.

The sun was dancing on the waves, creating a blinding glare and making it difficult to pick out anyone who might be floating or swimming. Or in trouble.

She sat up straighter, shading her eyes with her hand.

How long had he been gone? For what seemed like endless moments she waited and watched, but Marcus didn't return.

She could bear it no longer.

She removed her shoes and stockings and stood up. The sand was hot against the soles of her feet, and squished up between her toes as she began to walk down the narrow little strip of beach—did it seem even narrower than when they'd first arrived?—to the edge of the sea. Lifting her skirts high with one hand, to avoid the wash of the waves back and forth, she shaded her eyes with the other and once more peered out over the water.

She couldn't see him.

This was ridiculous! Marcus was a grown man who could look after himself. Obviously he knew how to swim, or he wouldn't have dived in. But he was also impulsive and daring, and might do something on the spur of the moment that was unsafe.

She took a few steps one way along the sand, and

then turned and took a few steps the other. She glanced behind her, desperately searching for Hettie and Zac. Nothing. There was no one to help. No one but her.

Portia began to undo the fastenings on her bodice, tearing a shoulder seam as she hurriedly eased herself out of the tight garment. Then there were her skirts, and her petticoats. Somehow she climbed out of them, leaving them in a heap on the sand where they fell. Her stays followed, but she left her white silk chemise on, as a belated offering to modesty.

She waded into the sea.

It was colder than she'd expected, and the wash of the tide tugged strongly at her feet, but she kept going. "Marcus? Marcus!" Her voice seemed as faint as a sea gull's cry. Now the water was up to her waist, tangling her chemise about her legs and dampening the ends of her hair where it hung down to her hips.

Just for a moment she thought she saw something several yards away. A dark shape against the sunlight. A heartbeat later it was gone, and the smooth water stretched on, unmarked, to infinity.

"Marcus!" she cried, and took another step forward. Into nothingness. The sea bottom had fallen away, and she plunged down into deep, cold water.

There was a moment when she allowed herself to sink, the sky a blur of blue above her, the marine world silent and merciless about her. But she had not taken in enough air and her lungs were beginning to hurt. She needed to breathe, and soon.

Just then arms clasped her, strong and sure. She was being carried up toward the sky. And then her face broke the surface and she was gasping in oxygen through the wild tangle of her wet hair. It was Marcus who held her, one arm about her so that she was suspended without having to swim, while he smoothed back the heavy mass of her hair so she could see him and he could see her.

"What did you think you were doing?" he asked, his eyes very bright in his sun-browned face, his own dark hair slicked back like a seal's cap.

"What did you think *you* were doing?" Portia retorted, irritably rubbing at her stinging eyes—the salt, she told herself. "I was afraid you'd drowned."

"I told you, I swim like a fish."

"You told me, yes, but I didn't know if you meant it."

He kissed her cold lips. "So you came to save me?"

He was patronizing her. He didn't believe she could save him. He probably thought she'd panicked and run into the sea without giving a thought as to how she was going to accomplish his rescue.

Well, she'd show him . . .

Portia pushed away from him, taking him by surprise, and he let her go. With a single twisting dive, she plunged down into the water, down, down, into the silent green depths. Not so silent, though, that she did not hear him calling her name.

She ignored him, swimming on strongly for several more yards before she surfaced. When her head popped up, she spent a moment tidying her hair and catching her breath before she turned to look back at him.

Marcus was glaring at her as if he'd like to strangle her. He began to swim toward her, but he stopped before he reached her, keeping himself afloat.

"You can swim," he said accusingly, his eyes sparkling with anger.

Was he angry because she hadn't needed him to rescue her after all? How typical of a man!

"I learned to swim when Lord Ellerslie took us holidaying in Brighton. He preferred Brighton; he had happy memories of his days with the Prince Regent at the pavilion. He found that the seawater helped his rheumatism. While he was swimming in the men's area, I would go to the women's bathing sheds and ask the dippers to show me how to swim." Dippers, women able to swim, were employed to assist ladies into the water and to keep them afloat.

"You are full of surprises."

"Why didn't you answer me when I called? You heard me, didn't you? I know you did."

He gave a half smile. "I wanted to see what you'd do. The way you came to my rescue was very . . ." He shook his head and gave a shaky laugh. "Was very pleasing to my ego."

Portia considered him a moment with a searching gaze. "Then you weren't laughing at me?"

He appeared genuinely surprised. "No, Portia, I wasn't laughing at you. I felt humbled."

Then she was in his arms.

He was kissing her, and she was kissing him. He caught her around the waist, floating her to shallower waters, while their mouths clung and explored. Her chemise was no help to her modesty after all, clinging to her flesh as he cupped her breasts, rubbing her cold hardened nipples.

She gasped, turning into his arms, feeling his naked body against hers. She wanted him again. More than ever.

"*My lady!*" It was Hettie shouting from the shore.

Marcus groaned. "Ignore her," he said, nuzzling her throat, nipping her skin.

"My lady, your *clothes* . . . "

Something in her voice forced Portia's attention. With her hands resting on his shoulders, she raised her head and looked toward the beach.

Hettie was standing, her arms full of dripping, sodden clothing. Portia recognized the gray and white striped skirt. She tried to speak but instead gave a sort of wild shriek of horror.

"The tide is coming in," Marcus said, looking as if he might burst into laughter. "Portia . . . I'm so sorry."

It was his fault. If he hadn't pretended to be drowned, she would never have panicked and left her clothing where it could get wet. She would have put it somewhere safe, or never have taken it off at all!

"What am I going to do?" she wailed. "Marcus, what am I going to *do*?"

Chapter 12

Marcus had long lost the urge to laugh. How could he when Portia was so tragic? She huddled in the corner of the carriage, wrapped in the picnic blanket, while Hettie clicked her tongue and sent him malevolent looks and Zac stared stoically forward and drove on.

"Your aunt will help me?"

"Yes, she will."

"And she will tell no one?"

"I will swear her to secrecy."

"I shouldn't—" She stopped, but he knew what she'd been about to say. *I shouldn't have come.* The accident with her clothes, although potentially damaging to any woman's reputation, was catastrophic for Portia. The joy that'd shone from her eyes was gone as if it had never been.

What could he say? He felt helpless and annoyed. He wanted to make everything all right again, and yet that was not in his power. He did not live in the same world as Portia. To a man like him, who thrived on being in charge of his own life and what happened in it, the situation was almost unbearable.

His aunt, Minnie Duval, lived three miles from Little Tunley in what had once been the gatehouse to one of the county's great manors. The manor was gone, long abandoned and fallen down, but the gatehouse remained. When Zac drew the carriage up in front, his aunt was already making her way down the steps toward them. She was dressed in one of her outlandish costumes, an English wool skirt teamed with an Indian gold-frogged jacket that could have belonged to a warlord. On her head she wore a turban.

"Marcus," Portia gasped, as if she did not know whether to scream or laugh.

But it was too late to offer reassurances, Minnie had spied Portia and made a beeline for her.

"Dear me, you poor, poor child. Come with me at once and I will find you some dry clothes while the servants fill you a bath of nice hot water."

"Th-Thank you. I am very grateful, ma'am."

"Call me Minnie, please, everyone does."

"Minnie." Portia's smile trembled. "I think we might have met some years ago."

"I think we did," Minnie agreed expressionlessly, "but never mind that now. Let my nephew help you down."

Marcus clasped her about the waist, lifting her down to the ground with tender care, which Minnie pretended

not to notice. She slipped an arm about Portia and led
her inside. Hettie lingered, hovering at Marcus's shoulder like a bad omen.

"Say it, Hettie," he said wearily. "It's all my fault,
isn't it?"

"Yes! If Her Majesty hears of this, my lady will be
destroyed. The press will tear her to pieces, and as for
the public . . . " She shuddered. "They will never forgive her for doing something so outrageous."

"Then why continue with such a life? Why put
herself in the position of having to live up to others'
expectations?"

"Why?" Hettie glared, her plump cheeks shaking
and pink with a mixture of anger and sunburn. "Because she is Lady Ellerslie. She does not choose such a
life, she *is* that life."

"You make it sound as if she's been sentenced to
hard labor by the justices," Marcus mocked. "'I sentence you to be Lady Ellerslie for the remainder of your
natural life.'"

"Everything is a joke to you, sir." She said it sourly.

"Is that what you want for your mistress, Hettie? A
life where she's afraid to be herself in case it offends
someone?"

Something flickered in Hettie's eyes—doubt?—but
she refused to admit to it. "My mistress is a great lady,"
she said stiffly, and walked past him, following Portia
into the house.

Marcus decided he was weary of trying to make

Portia, and now her maid, understand his point of view. What was the use anyway? After today she'd never want to see him again.

Impatiently, he strode into the sitting room and poured himself some of Minnie's excellent brandy. The room was crowded with just about every memento his aunt had ever brought back with her from her travels, among them monstrosities like an elephant foot umbrella stand, beautiful ivory carvings, and erotic paintings illustrating the *Kama Sutra*.

When he had visited Aunt Minnie as a child, she kept the paintings modestly covered. But after he grew into a young man, Minnie announced that he was old enough now and if he didn't know what the paintings were all about then he should.

He smiled at the memory and what it said about his aunt's views on raising children. Some would declare her to be shocking, but he had loved her more than his own mother, and knew that his unconventional view of the world, and his easygoing attitude to life, could be traced back to her.

Minnie entered the room, as usual, by launching into immediate conversation.

"My dear boy, you look as though you've seen the sun rise over the Taj Mahal."

Marcus couldn't help but laugh. Sunrise over the Taj Mahal was one of his aunt's most exquisite memories, and she used the expression when she meant he was looking extremely pleased with himself.

"I am well, too, Minnie, thank you for asking," he teased.

"Why should I ask? You are always well . . . disgustingly so."

He bent to kiss her cheek. "Where is Portia?"

"I've left Lady Ellerslie in a nice warm bath. She fell into the sea, she says. An accident." Minnie gave him a searching look. "I told her I was certain you were to blame in some way. You always are. But she very loyally refused to give you up."

"It *was* an accident . . . sort of."

"Hmm."

"She was having a wonderful time. I swear I made her happier than she's been for years, Minnie! Until it happened."

"But does she make you happy, dear boy?" She gave him one of her intense looks.

"Yes," he said, then frowned.

"What is it?" She sank down into an enormous carved chair. The armrests were carved to represent lions' heads and painted in brilliant colors, and there was a canopy over the top to protect her from the hot Indian sun—or it would have if the throne were still in India. It had been a gift from one of the princes she met in her travels.

"Come, nephew," she said now. "Tell me all."

Why not? he asked himself. She was discreet. He had never been able to shock his aunt, and he didn't expect to do so now. And it might help him sort out his feelings to speak them aloud.

As Marcus told her his story, Minnie listened in silence, her turban slipping to one side as she rested her head on her hand. "So you see," he ended, "this connection between us was never meant to last longer than one meeting. Those were the rules . . . But I don't seem able to let her go."

"You can't change the rules?"

"I've already stretched them quite a bit."

Minnie smiled fondly. "I'm sure you have."

"She refuses to see this as other than temporary, no matter how I try and persuade her. She's stubborn like that."

"Or afraid," Minnie said softly. "She has a lot more to lose than you, nephew. Is she worth fighting for?"

He met her eyes, and she read the truth in them.

"Ah, then you must find a way to fight for her!"

All very well, Marcus thought, but what exactly was he fighting for? Portia as his mistress? Portia as his sometimes lover? Portia as his *wife*?

He shied away from that last one. Next thing he knew he'd be planning cozy domestic evenings, like Sebastian and Francesca, and dreaming of a nursery!

He shuddered, and quickly changed the subject. "I will have to beg your hospitality for tonight, Minnie. We have missed the train back to London. And besides, Portia can't travel in her present state."

"Of course not, and you need not ask, Marcus, you are always welcome here. I will go and ask Cook to water down the curry so it will go around."

Marcus grinned. "You are a wonderful woman, Minnie, I hope you know how much I appreciate you."

She made a soulful face. "You are the son I never had, dear boy."

He laughed, but teasing aside, he knew she meant what she said. Minnie was more like a mother to him than his own mother had ever been, mainly because he had hardly known her. Some would say his upbringing had been unorthodox, but Marcus was grateful for it. God forbid he should have turned out like the average Victorian gentleman, priggish and proper.

Thanks to Minnie, he saw the world as a much more flexible affair.

By the time Portia came downstairs the air was filled with a spicy, delicious scent. Some foreign dish, she suspected, after having met Minnie Duval. Minnie would be the last person to dine on plain roast beef and potatoes.

Marcus had been partially correct; she *had* made Minnie's acquaintance before. But it was at a formal function at St. James's Palace, not Buckingham Palace. Lord Ellerslie had still been alive then, and Minnie was attending with a group of Indian aristocrats and their wives. Minnie and Lord Ellerslie had spoken together but did not get on at all. India was a vast country and wracked by tribal wars, and Lord Ellerslie wanted to march in and force everyone to obey British law, while Minnie favored understanding the ways of the people and getting them to cooperate. Portia herself had barely spoken two words to Minnie, but she remembered her, and remembered her husband's scathing diatribe on her in the carriage on the way home. She hadn't been brave enough to disagree with him, though she wanted to. Minnie was small and well past middle age but was the most vibrant person Portia had ever met.

Recalling the Indian women in their beautiful and exotic saris, Portia looked down at herself. At the time, she had admired them and marveled over their strangeness, but never expected to wear something similar herself. She wondered what Lord Ellerslie would have thought.

The costume was actually very light and comfortable, apart from a disconcerting sensation of being half naked, even when she knew she was well-covered. No horsehair petticoats, no corsets, no flounces and buttons and hooks and gathers. The silk cloth, a beautiful shade of green with myriad colors around the borders, covered a narrow petticoat that tied at her waist, and a tight short-sleeve chemise that ended below her breasts. The green silk had been wound around her waist over the top of the petticoat, then tucked and twitched and pleated to fit. The remainder was drawn up under her arms and over the chemise to form a bodice, before a final swath of the cloth was wrapped over her left shoulder and allowed to hang down her back.

It was rather like a Roman toga, only far more beautiful.

Minnie's maid had fastened her hair up in an elegant knot, and she wore slippers. No stockings or gloves or stays. No wonder she felt underdressed.

"Lady Ellerslie!" Minnie said, spotting her hovering in the doorway. "You look very fetching, I must say." She straightened her turban and climbed down off an enormous thronelike chair with a canopy over the top, coming over to inspect her. "Beautiful," she pronounced. "Don't you think so, Marcus?"

"Deliciously so."

Portia gave a feeble smile, carefully avoiding looking at Marcus. "Thank you, Miss Duval."

"Minnie, please, I prefer Minnie."

Minnie . . . I am very grateful—"

"Oh pish. I would do the same for any creature in distress. I once saved a mule in Bengal, and I can tell you it was no easy matter to persuade the owner that I meant to have my way. Of course once I had it, I had to find somewhere—"

"Minnie," her nephew murmured, exasperated.

"Marcus tells me you won't be able to catch the train back to London . . . tonight. You'll have to stay."

"Have I really missed the train?" Portia said anxiously, turning to Marcus.

He nodded. He was gazing at her with that lazy, sensual look that made her want to wriggle about.

"Oh." Portia closed her eyes, overwhelmed by the consequences of Lady Ellerslie going missing and no one able to reach her. She would have to tell more lies.

Surely, on top of all of her other recent sins, this would see her damned?

Minnie was making impatient gestures at Marcus.

He cleared his throat, seeming to understand what his aunt was signaling to him. "You're not to worry," he said to Portia. "No one here will breathe a word, and we can always think up a plausible story if it becomes necessary."

"An outbreak of malaria," Minnie suggested.

"Perhaps not malaria," Marcus replied calmly, with barely a twitch of his lips. "Do we have malaria in England?"

"Cholera, then."

"Very good. We can use that."

Portia looked from one to the other, wondering if she'd strayed into a madhouse. She decided a change of subject was in order. "What *is* that delicious aroma?"

Minnie beamed. "Madras curry, my dear. I developed a taste for it when I was there in 'twenty-one. Have you ever tasted curry?"

"I believe I did have a spoonful once. It was a little hot."

"One needs a proper appreciation of Indian cooking to enjoy it. The hotter the better. Come along, Portia. I will see there is plenty of water on the table to quench any internal fires." Minnie trotted toward the door.

Marcus stepped in beside Portia, very close. "I like your sari," he murmured. "It looks much better on you than it does on my aunt."

"I feel underdressed."

"If you wore it at Buckingham Palace you might start a new fashion."

"Or be thrown out and barred entry ever again," she laughed, but her voice was shaky.

"Minnie always looks upon misfortune as a chance to experience life in a new and fascinating way."

"Does she," Portia retorted. "I'd prefer to avoid the misfortune in the first place."

"How very unadventurous of you," he mocked gently. "You should learn to live a little, Portia. Obviously you have led a very sheltered existence."

"I think you're right. Since meeting you I've come to realize how sheltered I am. But you see, I don't want to have adventures. I prefer my days to be without surprises."

Did she? She'd always thought so, until she threw caution to the winds and met Marcus at Aphrodite's Club.

"Right at this moment I just want to go home," she added, a little plaintively.

Marcus took her hand in his. "Well, you can't, so you'll just have to make the best of it. There are other women who would be overjoyed to spend the evening with Minnie and me."

"Then I must not be like other women."

He gazed down into her eyes. "No," he said, "you're not."

Portia couldn't help but smile. He really was very good at this.

Now he leaned closer, dropping his tone. "Forgive me."

Portia looked up at him, trying to read him. He seemed sincere, but it could all just be part of the game. Nevertheless, she couldn't blame him for what had happened. It had been her fault as much as his.

"I forgive you," she whispered.

After one taste of the curry, Portia reached for her water. It was so hot it made her cough and her eyes stream. Marcus pushed a plate of buttered bread toward her, giving her a sympathetic smile, but she noticed he tucked into his own dish without much trouble. He was probably used to it. Just as he was used to listening to Minnie speak about her travels to foreign places. But she found it all new and fascinating, and after a time became so involved in the stories that she forgot about the curry.

"But how did you manage it?" Portia asked. "Didn't your family worry?"

"Silly if they did. I was doing what I wanted to do."

"But . . . " Portia waved her hand, searching for inspiration. "What of your responsibilities?"

Minnie and Marcus both looked at her as if she was speaking Hindustani.

"Your responsibilities as a woman . . . a sister and

daughter. Your duty to your parents and your family. You must have thought of them."

"Not at all. My responsibility was to myself, to do as I wanted to and not to waste my life trying to be the perfect daughter and wife and . . . and aunt. I don't doubt I could have learned to embroider exquisitely and arrange flowers just as well, and pour tea without spilling a drop, but that wasn't what I wanted to do. Imagine waking up and being too old to fulfill your dreams because you put mundane matters first? How awful! And who would care about your disappointment apart from you? One must follow one's star, Portia, not turn one's back on it."

Portia realized again how alike Marcus and his aunt were. And the disturbing thing was, she envied them.

After the meal, they returned to the sitting room, and while they waited for coffee, Portia prowled about the room, inspecting Minnie's collection. The paintings of men and women in various bizarre sexual positions made her eyes pop. She fancied Marcus saw her looking at them, her head tilted to one side in order to work out whose leg belonged to who, for she heard him give a snort of laughter, but when she turned to look he was studiously examining his brandy.

"No, I never married," Minnie said, in answer to her question. "Never found the time. I had no desire to stay at home and have babies while my husband went out and had all the fun."

A shocking point of view, and yet Portia was not

shocked. Well, perhaps only a little bit, and it was a pleasant sort of shock. Minnie was being honest and outrageous, and probably stating what many other women didn't dare.

"You left a trail of broken hearts," Marcus said fondly.

"There was a boy, once, when I was a young girl." Minnie retorted. "But I think the broken heart was on the other foot."

"There was a boy when I was a young girl," Portia said, surprising herself. She didn't look at Marcus. She didn't dare, in case he read the truth in her eyes. "I used to watch him, secretly. He never knew. Once, in church . . . "

She bit her lip. Should she do this? What if he guessed who she was? In some odd, perverse way, perhaps she wanted him to know the truth. Or did she hope that realizing she wasn't the glittering creature he thought her would drive him away?

"I was to play the music for the Sunday hymns, and I was practicing. At least, I was supposed to be. But I happened to glance up and see him outside, going down the lane by the church. At that moment one of the village girls came up to him and began to flirt. I thought that if I went up into the tower, I would be able to see better what was happening. But I'd forgotten that there was bell ringing practice set down for that day."

Minnie clapped her hands with glee. "Do go on. What happened?"

"I think you can guess. I'd just settled myself nicely and was glowering at the pair of them, hating him for talking with another girl, even though I would never have approached him myself, and hating her for daring to flirt with my boy, despite the fact I had never publicly laid claim to him and never would. And then the bells began to ring. I was very nearly deafened. For an hour I lay there, my arms over my head, longing for it to end. By the time I was able to creep back down the ladder, I felt as if the bells were ringing permanently in my head. My mother wondered for days afterward why I did not answer when she called my name."

Minnie was laughing, but Marcus looked puzzled. "But why didn't you come down and explain?"

The two women exchanged glances. "Tell the village bell ringers that she was in the tower spying on a boy?" Minnie said as if he was lacking in wits. "How mortifying for her, nephew."

"I don't see why. The boy she was watching was obviously an idiot and she was wasted on him." He gave Portia his special smile. "I wish I'd been there."

She laughed. She couldn't help it. Marcus's brows came down, and eventually she had to stop because he was looking so cross.

"You're right," she said, her voice husky. "I should have come down from the tower and faced them. I should have told *him*. But I was young and unsure of myself. Not the woman I am now."

Minnie countered with her own story about a

youthful and unrequited love affair, and the awkward moment passed.

It was very late when Portia retired. She'd been smothering yawns, trying to stay awake, because she was enjoying their company so much, but at last she had to admit defeat. Once tucked into the elaborately curtained bed, the concerns that had plagued her earlier returned, and she thought she might spend the night tossing and turning. But thankfully, the sea air had tired her out, and very soon she was fast asleep.

It was one of the best and one of the worst days of her life.

Chapter 13

❦❦❦

"**M**arcus, she is a treasure." Minnie removed her turban and sat it on the table. Her grizzled dark hair stood on end.

Marcus didn't reply, staring into his glass.

"You know, I did not bring you up as a fighter so that you could give up when something was too difficult. I cannot speak for the Worthornes, but your mother's family, the Duvals, were made of steel. You did not know your mother very well, did you, Marcus?"

Marcus shook his head, leaning back in his armchair. "She seemed so distant when I was a boy, always concerned with other matters, and then she died."

"She and your father were very much in love. That surprises you, I see. My parents were against the match—they did not think the Worthornes were good enough, and your father had an unsavory reputation with cards and women."

Marcus sat up.

"Yes." Minnie nodded. "Hard to imagine, isn't it?

Once he reformed, he went all the way and became quite an austere man. But in those early days your mother was determined on him. It was him or no one. Eventually our parents gave in and let her have him, but she fought hard for her happiness, believe me. And they were happy. Perhaps a little selfish in that their love for each other took precedence. Not that they didn't love their children, but they were so wrapped up in each other they sometimes forgot to show it. A pity your mother died before you ever really knew her, Marcus, but then that meant *we* got to know each other."

"I can't claim to be a neglected child where you're concerned," he agreed, reaching for her hand.

She grasped his fingers, but her voice grew serious again. "My point is, your mother fought for what she wanted. You come from a long line of fighters. The earliest Duvals were robber barons."

"Robber barons?" he teased. "And you see me as one of them?"

"You're a Duval, aren't you? These were men who took what they wanted and would not be gainsaid. They even kidnapped women from their neighbors and married them; not that they stayed unwilling for long."

"Highly illegal, surely? Or highly romanticized in the retelling."

Minnie ignored his practical response. "I have always suspected you needed to find yourself in a crisis to learn what you were made of."

"Aunt Minnie . . . "

"My dear boy, as much as I love you, I believe you are a little aimless, if not to say feckless. You must search for direction in your life. Look for a guiding star. Who knows, this woman might be your star."

Portia, beautiful Portia, a star shining in the night sky. Was it possible he could win her if he set his mind to it? He was arrogant enough to think he could. But did he want to? Up until now he had never expected to find one woman he wanted above all others—he was a man who had never known what it was to fall in love.

"Marcus, the most important thing we can gain from our lives is not wealth, or grand palaces, or fabulous jewelry. It is love, and without love we are nothing." Her eyes were teary, as if she was remembering someone somewhere from her colorful past. A secret robber baron of her own?

Marcus didn't want to know, nor did he want to discuss his inner feelings with Minnie. He turned to comedy.

"But surely, Aunt, the most important thing in life is a good tailor?"

She threw her turban at him.

Portia was dreaming of swimming, but this time the sea was warm and soft as velvet as it brushed against her skin and she went diving into the green depths.

"Portia, my beautiful, beautiful Portia."

His voice was like the silky water, and she turned toward him. The dream became real, his arms about her and his lips on hers. Marcus, the man and the dream, warm in her arms.

His body pressed to hers. "Marcus?"

"Yes, yes, it's me."

"I thought I was dreaming." The old familiar dream back again. Teasing her, but never satisfying her.

"You're not dreaming."

She arched against him, feeling him inside her. Oh yes, this was real, real as her dreams had never been. He was moving against her, hard, passionate, as he did everything. She cried out softly, her face pressed to his shoulder, but he didn't stop. The pleasure hit her solidly, making her want to scream.

He took her mouth, stifling her and reaching his own peak. It was perfect, as the dreams had never been, because they had never been real.

The waves took her, rolling her over and over, and she fell asleep in his arms.

The next morning, Portia was up and dressed and already waiting when Marcus came down to breakfast. She was impatient to get away, and after a fond goodbye to Minnie, there seemed nothing to keep them.

Portia knew she wouldn't be able to completely relax until she was on the train to London. The ride in the carriage seemed so slow, Zac and Hettie sitting in silence in front, while Marcus seemed far too close to her in the back. His hand was resting behind her, and every time the vehicle swayed, he brushed her shoulder. Her nerves were so tightly strung it made her want to wriggle away. Or scream at him.

Or throw herself into his arms and kiss him.

But last night had been perfect, and she knew it would be impossible to improve on that.

"I should have thanked your aunt," she said, to stop her thoughts.

"You did."

"I should have thanked her again."

He was silent. While she was highly strung, Marcus seemed almost sullen. There was a brooding quality about him, as if he was locked in his thoughts. She opened her mouth to ask him what he was thinking, but she was afraid of his answer and what it might lead into, so she closed it again. There wasn't time for discussions about what had happened and why, and what might or might not happen in the future. She had a train to catch.

Suddenly, she saw the sea, blue and sparkling in the morning sun. An image came to her of Marcus in the water, tanned and sleek, smiling down at her in his arms, both of them as slippery as seals. Another memory to mull over at the next tedious dinner at the palace, she thought, stretching up to gaze at that little patch of blue until it disappeared behind the trees.

If he noticed, he said nothing, and it was in silence that they finally drew up at the station.

Just as the train whistle blew shrilly in the distance.

They hurried through the archway, and Portia could

see that there was no one else on the platform. The stream from the locomotive was already rising into the sky, and although it was still some way off, they could hear its noisy chugging approach.

"It will stop, won't it?" she asked, struck by the horrifying thought that the train might rattle right by her.

"I sent Zac down earlier to arrange with the station master for the train to stop," Marcus said. "I thought there might be some difficulty, but it seems that your name was enough to sway matters."

Portia gave a relieved sigh. "Thank you. You must think me a useless creature, but I'm not in the habit of making my own traveling arrangements."

He gave her a little bow.

She supplied her own answer. *No, I think you far from useless, I think you the most beautiful and fascinating woman I've ever known!* She hadn't been fishing for compliments, but still it wouldn't hurt him to offer her one or two. Had he lost interest in her after last night? Had he decided she was too much bother?

"You'll be home in time for luncheon," he said, watching the train approach.

"Just in time to answer a great many questions."

"Your friend begged you to stay overnight," Marcus said with a shrug. "She has been ill and you couldn't say no."

Portia tilted her head. "I wager you even have a name for my fictitious school friend."

Marcus smiled, and although it was a subdued smile,

it was the first one he'd given her all morning so it was worth having. "Dorothy Mickeljohn."

Portia nodded gravely. "Good old Dorothy. What is wrong with her? I'm afraid I've forgotten that, too."

"Scarlet fever as a child weakened her constitution. She's a great reader, though, devours a book a day, and enjoys music. You told her all about Jenny Lind. She was in tears."

"I feel as if I know her," Portia murmured. "How do you do it?"

"A wild and unfettered imagination," he replied. "I was caned for it many times at school, but they never beat it out of me."

"My lady?"

A little girl was standing before her on the platform. Her dark hair was tied neatly back with ribbons, and she was smiling shyly and clutching a hastily assembled bouquet of flowers. The station master and his wife hovered behind her, beaming with pride as they watched their child perform a wobbly curtsy.

Portia bent down with a delighted, "Oh, how pretty!"

"They're for you," the little girl said shyly.

"And what is your name?"

"Daisy, ma'am."

"Then you're a flower, too. You're certainly as pretty as one."

Daisy swayed closer, her voice dropping confidingly. "Are you the queen?"

"No, but I know her. Should I give her your flowers?"

Daisy gave it some consideration. "No, my lady, they're for you."

"Thank you. I shall take them home with me to London."

The train had slowed as it approached the platform, and the station master hurried to do his duty, while his wife recovered her daughter and hastened her away. It was nearly over. Portia turned and looked at Marcus.

"Good-bye," she said, holding out her hand.

He raised it to his lips.

She expected him to insist on another meeting, or at least to mention it. Of course, she'd have to turn him down. If she'd learned one thing from this disaster it was that she must put a stop to their affair. Now and forever.

"Portia . . . " He was looking deep into her eyes, and she realized then that, perversely, she wanted him to ask. She wanted him to want her. Even though she would turn him down.

The train with its line of carriages had shuddered slowly to its unscheduled stop. Hettie was already hurrying toward their carriage—not private this time, but first class. Portia began to follow her. She thought he'd stop her, call out . . . but he just stood and let her go. She still hoped he'd stop her with a word as she climbed the steps, but nothing.

Hettie fussed about her, getting in the way of the

window. By the time she'd sat down and Portia was settled in her own seat, the flowers still clutched in her hand, the platform outside was empty.

Marcus was gone.

The train jolted forward, hissing steam, and they were on their way back to London.

"Thank goodness for that!" Hettie said.

"Yes, thank goodness," she murmured.

She had been bursting to get onto the train and get home. She told herself that she should be vastly relieved. But instead she felt as if all the color had gone from her world.

Marcus didn't go straight back to Minnie's house. He told Zac to drive him to the cove, and once there he stripped off his clothing and swam. He swam until he was too exhausted to think. To ask himself why he hadn't done as Minnie said and fight for the woman.

Instead he'd let her go.

He'd seen the longing in her eyes, that and her determination to make this their final meeting. She craved his touch as a laudanum addict craved his little blue bottle. If nothing else, she was in lust with his body and his skills as a lover. He could have used that physical need to persuade her to see him again—he was arrogant enough to believe he was capable of it—but he hadn't.

Marcus knew it was because he was afraid. Portia meant more to him than he'd ever expected her to—

more perhaps than he meant to her—and he wasn't sure what to do about it. He'd set out to Aphrodite's that evening for a good time, not to find a lifelong partner. He wasn't sure of the direction of his own life, so how could he burden himself with someone else on the journey? Someone to care for and to love. Sebastian was right—he was drifting—and he didn't know what to do about it.

He looked around him, treading water, catching his breath.

He'd swum out a long way and needed to turn back. It wasn't as if he could escape the world forever; it would always be waiting for him. Even if now it was a world without Portia.

Slowly, Marcus began to swim toward the shore.

Chapter 14

Portia had barely taken a step inside the house in Grosvenor Square when she was besieged.

"My lady!" Deed, with his wig askew, appeared to have sustained a severe shock, but whatever he meant to say was lost in a terrifying shriek. Her mother was standing at the head of the grand staircase.

"Portia! Portia, my child! Terrible news . . . *dreadful* . . . "

Portia's heart leapt into her throat, choking her. For one dizzy moment she thought this was all about her and Marcus, that someone had discovered the truth and now it was all about to come out. Lurid broadsheets on every street corner blaring the news in appalling detail. Important people, people she'd come to think of as her friends, snubbing her. The images formed with terrifying speed. Victoria, her face a mask of distaste, saying, *You allowed yourself to give way to* lust, *Lady Ellerslie? What sort of message does that send to my nation?*

Portia swallowed. "What is it?" She managed to find her voice at last.

"There has been an attempt to assassinate the queen," her mother burst out dramatically, and sagged against the banisters.

Servants rushed to aid her, but Portia did not move. She was rooted to the spot, overwhelmed by the unexpected turn of events.

"Is she . . . ?" she whispered.

"No, my lady." Deed was beside her, watchful, as if he feared she might faint, too. "Her Majesty sustained a knock on her head from the brass end of a gentleman's cane. She was leaving Cambridge House, after visiting her uncle the duke. After the attack she stood up in the carriage and assured the crowd that she was unhurt. Very courageous of her it was, if I may offer my humble opinion."

Portia gave a shuddering gasp. "Oh, I'm so glad."

"She sent a servant to fetch you!" her mother said, having recovered enough to speak again. "What a time to choose to visit a nonentity in the country! And to stay on overnight without telling anyone."

"Dorothy had been ill. She begged me—"

"I don't care! I felt extremely foolish when I could not explain to the royal messenger where you were."

"I will go to the palace instantly," Portia said, hurrying to the stairs and stripping off her gloves as she went. "Have the carriage brought around!"

There had been five previous attempts upon Victoria's

life, the last as recently as one year ago, when a pistol was fired, but thankfully was loaded with no more than gunpowder. It had greatly alarmed the queen, however, perhaps more than the other attempts, when the pistol had been loaded and either missed its mark or misfired. Victoria always showed a brave face to the public, but Portia knew that in private she would be upset. And furious that anyone would want to harm her. As she hurried into her rooms, she wondered whether this time it was a plot to topple the monarchy, or just another deranged soul.

Hettie helped her change. "It is too dreadful for words," she murmured.

"But she is safe, that is the main thing," Portia said, unpinning her hair. "We must be thankful for that."

"I did not mean Her Majesty the Queen, *lieben*. I was thinking of what might have happened if she had sent someone after you and found you and that man."

"They wouldn't have been able to find me."

"And is that in itself not suspicious?"

"I would have thought of something," Portia said, hurrying to dress.

"You would tell lies to the queen?" Hettie retorted. "This is what comes of mixing with such persons as Marcus Worthorne."

"As I recall, you thought it amusing to tell lies to Victoria the last time."

Hettie gave her hair a vigorous brushing and began to pin it back up. Portia hoped she would now drop the subject, but it was not to be.

"He is no good. He cares only for himself. He is like a . . . a gigolo. He will abandon you when he is weary of you, I know it, and soon."

Portia turned to her with a cool stare. "I believe he has. Wearied of me, I mean. So you need not worry anymore."

"It is only that I worry for you—" Hettie began, but Portia turned away.

"See if the carriage is ready," she said, her voice still chilly. "I will be down in a moment. I must see if my mother is recovered."

Swiftly, Hettie left her alone.

Portia stood before her mirror, inspecting her appearance. She was pale, and there were weary smudges beneath her eyes, but these could be explained away by the shocking circumstances that greeted her on her return. And they *were* shocking. When she'd looked up and saw her mother and thought Victoria had been killed, she received a very severe jolt indeed.

It was enough to bring her to her senses without Hettie's nagging.

There were more important things in the world than Marcus Worthorne. She had a role to play, a duty to fulfill, and it was time to put aside her selfish desires of the flesh and concentrate on doing that duty.

Her mother had taken to her bed with a dose of laudanum. She was already half asleep.

"Mama? Are you feeling better?"

Her mother's eyes opened, the pupils large and dark

from the drug. "I'm weary," she murmured. "Shocking news . . . "

"It is. I am going to the palace now."

"Sometimes I get so confused. I couldn't remember where you had gone when they asked me. I tried but I couldn't remember. It was Deed who told them."

"It doesn't matter, Mama."

Her mother squeezed her hand. "I did not mean to be cross with you just then. You're a good girl, Portia. You've always done as you were told."

"Have I?" Her mother meant it as a compliment, and it should be so—a dutiful daughter was a noble thing—but Portia wondered if Minnie Duval would see it that way. If Minnie had been a dutiful daughter and always done as she was told, would she ever have left the country for her marvelous adventures?

"I told your father, when I heard Lord Ellerslie was staying with my friend: Just give the old man one glimpse of our sweet daughter and our fortunes will be made. There's nothing like a vision of spring when you have your foot in the grave. And he fell for you, didn't he? My beautiful, dutiful daughter."

Portia didn't want to hear this, not now. She moved toward the door, but again her mother's slurred voice stopped her.

"You have a touch of the sun, Portia, and your hair smells of the sea. Have you been to the seaside? I thought your school friend lived near Oxford?"

Trust her mother to remember the details now!

"That's right, Mama. Dorothy lives in Oxford. You must be dreaming." Another lie. But her mother was already asleep, her mouth ajar, her breathing thick.

Portia loved her, she knew she did, but just now it would be quite easy to hate her.

Victoria was pacing up and down, angrier than Portia had ever seen her. The swelling and bruising on her forehead, and the discoloration around her eye, were growing more evident by the minute. "How dare that creature strike at me in such a cowardly way! An unarmed woman! That he should strike at *any* woman is disgraceful, but his queen . . . I will not have it . . . I will not!"

"As the carriage passed through the gates at Cambridge House," the prince said, "the crowd came around her in a rush. The man who did this was among them. It was not just my dear wife in the carriage, there were also Eddie, Alice and little Albert. We must thank God none of our children were killed." The prince was pale and clearly suffering from shock, but as usual his voice had that reasonable calm that Portia so admired.

"Do you know who the man was, Sir?" she asked.

"We have discovered his name. He is Robert Pate, and he has lately retired his commission from the Tenth Hussars. He will not speak about his reasons for what he did."

Portia expressed her relief to find the queen safe, if not entirely well. It was obvious that Victoria's anger was sustaining her. The queen had shown her the bonnet that took the brunt of the blow from Pate's cane, and admitted that she was suffering from a headache.

"If these creatures had some plan they wished to carry out, some plot that we could discover and tear apart, so that this did not happen again," Albert said. "But they seem to be disturbed in their minds, and any plot they have is a fantasy of their own making."

"So Pate acted alone in this?"

"He has given his name and the fact that he was a soldier but no more. He will not tell us why he did what he did. Some imagined slight to himself or his family . . . ?" Albert pulled a face. "His mind is deranged, or that is what he wants us to think."

"If dear Lord Ellerslie were still here, Portia, he would have rushed instantly to my side," Victoria said with quiet venom.

"Your Majesty, I apologize. I was—"

The queen waved her hand. "It does not matter. You will never have to suffer such attempts on your life as I do. You cannot comprehend such matters, but your dear husband would have understood. He risked his life every day for me."

"Your Majesty—"

"I think I will go and lie down now. That is all, Lady Ellerslie."

Portia curtsied, telling herself that Victoria didn't mean to be cruel—she was upset, and rightly so—but still it stung. She caught Albert's eye as she said her farewell to him, and he shook his head slightly, as if to assure her the words were not meant. He understood Portia's position better than anyone; his own life was also lived in the shadow of his spouse.

But there was a difference. Victoria was alive, breathing and warm and loving him. Portia was alone, and right now she felt it more than ever.

Arnold made his way up the carpeted stairs of a nondescript house in Hackney. There was a closed door at the top and he knocked in a particular manner before opening it. Four faces turned to him silently, the room full of cigar smoke.

Food had been served, and the remains of that, and half-drunk bottles of wine, littered the table.

"He was arrested," one of the men said quietly as Arnold took his seat at the head of the table. "Should we worry?"

"Why? Already I am hearing he is simply some wretched soldier with scrambled brains. And we know he will not tell the truth. He will not break the oath."

"How can you be sure?"

Arnold poured himself some of the wine and took a gulp, pulling a face. "I am sure. I know Robert well. He believes as we do. He has been watching the queen for some weeks now in preparation for our attack. I can only think that, seeing her so close before him, he lost control. He struck out at the thing he hated the most. But he will not talk." He took another sip of the sour wine. "It's inconvenient, though, that this has happened now."

"Inconvenient?" one of his companions snorted. "I would call it more than that!"

"I don't think it is as serious as you imagine. There will be increased nervousness for a time, but that will pass. In fact it may work in our favor. No one will be expecting another attempt so quickly."

The men exchanged glances. He knew they had been discussing the plan before he arrived, perhaps doubting his right to lead them, but he pretended not to notice. His confidence was supreme.

"So you still intend to go on with it?"

"Of course." Arnold raised a surprised brow. "Robert would want us to continue with our work. We will succeed." He raised his glass, and in the candlelight, his pale eyes held the glitter of a fanatic. "The queen must die!"

With a shout, his companions raised their own glasses in response.

Arnold nodded, looking to each one, testing each man's resolve, and then he leaned forward. "That is our goal, my friends, and we must never forget it. For when I deal her the death blow, our cause will become more important than all of us. The country will finally begin to take notice. The people, the true English people, will realize the justice of what we have done. England for the English!"

Again the shouts of response as his companions stood and stamped their feet. Soon, Arnold thought, dizzy with triumph. Very soon.

When Marcus finally returned home, it was to be greeted by Minnie with the news that there had been yet another assassination attempt on the queen. The butcher's boy had just called with the latest. Marcus listened to his aunt's expressions of outrage and bewilderment in silence, but in his heart he knew that this would affect Portia deeply.

She would see it as a failing on her part that she was not there when it happened, even though she could have done nothing. She would see him as a conflict to her duty, and although she might wish to see him again, the duty would win.

Even if he approached her again, begged for another meeting, she would take this opportunity to end it between them. Utterly and irrefutably.

Their temporary affair was over.

Chapter 15

Since the assassination attempt on Victoria, it seemed to Portia that she had not had a moment to herself. The queen was more demanding than ever, as if punishing her for not being there on the day it happened. She spent every moment on tenterhooks, awaiting a summons, and when it didn't come, worried she might have missed it.

Consequently, she felt limp, her head aching, and at night she wanted nothing more than to lie down and sleep. But even that was denied her, because when she tried to sink into blessed oblivion, there was someone waiting for her in the shadows.

Marcus.

It was as if he was there, in her bed, smiling his lazy, sensual smile. She wanted him with a fierceness that unnerved her, she ached for him. And while night after night he still came to her in her thoughts and her dreams, he wasn't really here.

She hadn't heard from him. Not even a letter she

could tear up and return to him. Not even his uninvited presence at the latest opera or ballet. He had vanished as if he'd never been. And although she refused to admit it to herself, she missed him dreadfully. Not just for his body and his kisses. She needed him to make her laugh, to allow her to see the ridiculous side of life.

And now the statue of Lord Ellerslie, commissioned by the queen when he died, was finished. It stood on a plinth at the entrance to Green Park; Lord Ellerslie in his great coat, his shoulders in their characteristic stoop, as if he were contemplating some invisible battlefield.

It was as if he had never died, she thought, knowing she was being unfair and unkind, and yet unable not to feel suffocated by the memory of a man she'd hardly known. But the statue had to be unveiled, and she knew she had to be there, beside the queen, in her role as the angel in widow's weeds.

Oh yes, she knew what they called her. She had once been flattered by it, but now found it a sign of how little the public understood her. She was no angel, she was a flesh and blood woman, and she made mistakes and felt sad and happy and afraid. Why wouldn't they let her be herself?

And why did it matter to her these days so much more than it used to?

Marcus stood at the head of the causeway and gazed across the flat Norfolk landscape at Duval Hall.

The house seemed to crouch on its island, as if it might spring at any moment and capture anyone foolish enough to be within reach. He could never have imagined such a place, and he knew that if he had come here at any other time, he would have been horrified and probably turned around and gone straight back to London.

But not now. At this moment he was at rock bottom, and not even a building as hideously deformed as Duval Hall could drive him away.

Looked at in a practical and less fanciful light, the house *was* run-down and in need of repairs, but the basic structure was solid. It was very old, and had been added to in such a hotchpotch of styles over the centuries that it was difficult to know what architectural era it fell into. The hall stood on an island, or what became an island at high tide, when the waters of the sea came seeping in over the marshes and cut off the causeway. At low tide the marshes were laid bare, and the causeway could be used to travel back and forth to the house.

It was more like a ship than a house, really, and the wall that surrounded it resembled the hull. At night, with the sounds of creaking timbers and the wash of the waves, he could imagine himself out at sea. Yes, the house was a wreck, just as his brother had warned him, but it was salvageable. And he'd developed a fondness for it that seemed bizarre in the circumstances, or perhaps it was just that it was *his*.

As for his tenants and the people of the nearby village, they had been overjoyed to see him. It was many years since they'd had anyone of Duval blood in residence at the hall, and they treated him like a prodigal son. At first their enthusiasm amused him, but as the days wore on and he sensed their genuine liking for him . . . Well, he began to enjoy it.

Marcus Worthorne of Duval Hall. It had a ring to it. And the people here were desperately in need of a good landlord. Uncle Roger's land manager had done little more than drink all the best wines in the cellar. When he'd heard Marcus was coming, he fled with the blacksmith's pretty daughter to parts unknown.

Marcus could see why he might wish to make himself scarce.

The marshes had once been separated from the encroaching sea by fortifications that held back the tides. They were then drained by a system of channels and sluice gates so the land could be reclaimed and used for farming. Now, the waters had retaken much of the pasture, and repairs were needed to regain man's upper hand over nature. A great many repairs.

It was certainly not a project for the weak. Any sensible man would sell it and take what he could get, or else run back home and forget all about it.

Perhaps, Marcus thought, he wasn't a sensible man.

Since arriving here, he had walked for miles, following his tenants and the smaller farmers who were his neighbors, paying attention to what they had to say. He sat down with them at their tables and ate their food and drank their ale as if he were one of them. He laughed with them and laughed at himself when they gently teased him for his London ways.

By the time he was ready to return to London, he felt like one of them.

But it wasn't only repairs and a possible future he'd been thinking of as he walked his land. He'd been thinking of Portia, too, and all Minnie had said to him. He'd known as soon as he heard about the queen that Portia would make her choice; duty would be the winner, and he would be the loser.

That was because she'd been taught to put her own personal happiness last.

He stood at the head of the windswept causeway, the smell of the salty marshes filling his head as the birds wheeled and shrieked.

If he wanted Portia enough to fight for her, then he had to have something to offer her. After all, he was setting himself up against the Nation's Hero, and although such audacity would be frowned upon by the queen and the country, Marcus knew he could make Portia happy if only she would let him.

But she was a great and wealthy lady. He could hardly expect her to agree to throw in her lot with a man who had nothing to recommend him but a great technique in lovemaking. At least Duval Hall gave him a home, and in time it would give him an income. Somewhere to bring her to live; for them both to live.

Because he knew now what he wanted. He'd come to terms with it here in faraway Norfolk. He had missed London, but not as much as he'd expected. Duval Hall offered him challenges that were new and exciting, and he could see a future for himself here. But there was one thing he missed that could not be substituted or replaced.

Portia.

He wanted her, he needed her, and if necessary he would fight for her.

One balmy midnight, several weeks after the assassination attempt on the queen, Portia went sleepwalking. At least that was what she told herself; it was too humiliating to admit that she might have done such a thing while she was even fractionally in her right senses.

She'd gone to bed early with a headache and feeling slightly out of sorts—the unveiling of Lord Ellerslie's statue was to be held in the morning—and then at the stroke of midnight she lurched out of bed with only one thought.

I must see him.

Grabbing her cloak, she scrabbled around on the floor for her slippers, finally finding them and pulling them on. She caught a glimpse of herself in the mirror—pale and wild, her loose hair hanging to her waist—and drew the hood of the cloak over her head. Turning quickly, she almost fell over, and had to rest her hand against the door a moment until the room stopped spinning.

Outside it was quiet, the landing light turned down low. She headed down the stairs. She had forgotten how many bolts secured the front door and fumbled with them, making far more noise than she meant. The top one was more difficult than the others, and she pulled a chair over and stood upon it, wrestling with the mechanism until it finally sprang open.

Upstairs there were voices. She thought she heard her mother's in the aftermath of some dream. Hastily, Portia pushed the chair out of the way. She felt like a prisoner escaping her cell. Her heart was pounding. She flung the door open.

Warm night air rushed in, and she took deep breaths, clinging to the iron railing as she began to descend the steps to the street. She was on her way across the square when she heard Hettie's frantic cries in pursuit.

"My lady? My lady, where are you going? It is the middle of the night!"

"I'm going for a walk," Portia replied, but her steps faltered. The square was empty, the flickering gaslights giving the familiar place an eerie feel.

"A walk?" Hettie had reached her, her voice stifled by her attempt to be discreet. "*Lieben*, you are in your nightgown!"

Portia stopped and looked down at herself. Hettie was wrong. Her cloak hid her night attire, and the hood covered her hair and helped disguise her identity. No one could see who she was. What did it matter whether she was in her nightgown? Marcus certainly wouldn't care. He'd laugh and take her in his arms and make her forget with kisses from his wonderful mouth . . .

But it did matter. Of course it mattered. Everything she did mattered to someone.

She heard her own voice, impatient and petulant. "For heaven's sake, Hettie, can't I go for a walk? Surely I am allowed that?"

Hettie took her arm firmly but gently. "But where are you walking to, *lieben*?"

"I . . . Nowhere."

Hettie knew at once. She frowned. "You know you cannot go to that man. It is all over. If you turn up at his door in the middle of the night, he will laugh at you. He will send you away and tell all his friends."

Would he really send her away? Portia knew she had been final in her good-byes. There could be no room for second chances, and she'd given him none. He probably hated her now, or worse, had forgotten her completely and was besotted with someone else.

She shuddered.

Hettie was right. She could not do this. She was no longer Portia Stroud, the vicar's daughter. She was Lady Ellerslie, with a position to maintain, not to mention her dignity. This was a moment of madness and she must crush it.

Slowly, chin up, she made her way back into the house. Deed had been peering out of the doorway, and now he closed the door behind her. She heard a shuffle from the corridor as several servants spied on her from the kitchen stairs before her faithful butler shooed them away. It was clear that even her own household thought she was losing her mind.

"Hettie . . . " she whispered, suddenly appalled.

Hettie understood at once and slipped an arm about her waist, murmuring soothingly. "You are not yourself," she said as they climbed the stairs. "I will fetch the physician."

"No, please, I don't want any more fuss."

"Portia? What is happening? Has there been more bad news?"

Dear Lord, now her mother was awake, a shawl thrown over her nightdress, her graying hair loose about her shoulders, her eyes wide and fearful. She couldn't deal with her mother just now.

Hettie took charge. "I think I should send for Dr. Bryant, Mrs. Stroud. Lady Ellerslie is not herself."

"Yes, yes, if you think it best," her mother said. She came and pressed her palm to Portia's forehead. "She is very flushed."

"I want to go back to bed," Portia protested, turning toward her bedchamber. They followed.

"I will fetch you a sleeping draught," her mother announced, something of her old self in her voice. "You must not go wandering about in the dark, daughter. The woods are dangerous around Worthorne Manor. Sometimes there are Gypsies, poaching, and if you were to fall into the lake, who would save you?"

Her mother was back in the past again. "I don't want

a sleeping draught, Mama, you know I abhor laudanum." Portia climbed into her bed and lay back, closing her eyes and wishing they would leave her alone.

"I think your mother is right," Hettie said. "We cannot risk you going out into the street."

"No laudanum."

"Then it is the doctor, *lieben*," Hettie announced triumphantly.

"Oh, very well. Not that he will thank you for getting him out of his bed for nothing."

But Dr. Bryant didn't seem to think it was nothing. He examined Portia and asked her a great many questions. In the end his diagnosis was a slight fever, although he wasn't satisfied that was at the heart of her problem.

"I am more concerned about her state of mind," he said to Mrs. Stroud, while Portia lay with her eyes shut and pretended to be asleep. "She isn't a young girl anymore, and she has no husband and no children. Sometimes when a woman hasn't fulfilled her proper function, she can become melancholic. She can suffer from hysteria. Have you noticed any outbreaks of temper? Screaming fits? Crying?"

Portia clenched her fists and bit her tongue. Hysterics? She'd show him hysterics if he didn't get out of her house now. She could barely wait until he had left the room before she sat up and burst out with, "I never want that man in my house again!"

"But Portia—"

"No, Mama, I mean it. Surely there is someone younger? More progressive? Someone who does not believe women are put on this earth to breed like cattle?"

Her mother appeared bewildered. "But Dr. Bryant was recommended to you by Her Majesty herself."

"I don't care! I don't want him. I can't believe he would think such things, let alone speak them aloud!"

Hettie and her mother glanced at each other, and she knew they were thinking that the doctor was right. It only infuriated her more. But even in the midst of her anger she knew that Dr. Bryant was only saying what most men, and women, believed. Perhaps it was the contrast between the doctor and Minnie Duval that was making her so angry.

Minnie had rebelled against the attitudes to women, refusing to allow herself to be pushed into the narrow confines of what was expected of her. Portia admired her for it. She envied her. Hearing Dr. Bryant spouting his own beliefs had only made the difference between her own life and Minnie's more stark.

"I wish I had never met him," she whispered.

"Him?" Hettie repeated.

"I wish I had never been to Aphrodite's Club. I wish I could be comfortable, without any doubts, just as I used to be."

"You will be comfortable again," Hettie promised her. "Try to sleep, my lady. Come along, Mrs. Stroud, you should be in bed yourself. It is very late . . . or very early. My lady has a statue unveiling to attend in the morning."

"Statue?" Their voices were fading.

"Lord Ellerslie's statue, remember?"

"No one told me about that!"

"Oh, Mrs. Stroud, of course they did . . . "

Portia had almost drifted into sleep when she was awoken by the touch of a cool hand on her cheek. She struggled to open her eyes. Her mother was peering down at her.

"Mama, what are you doing up again?"

"Hush! I've brought you a cup of milk," she whispered. "It will help you to sleep. Remember, I used to bring you warm milk when you were a child? And I would sing to you. Do you want me to sing to you now?"

Portia's eyes filled with tears. It had been so long since her mother had been her old self. Some days it seemed as if she was becoming a half-familiar stranger. She dreaded the moment when her mother's mind would fail her completely, because she knew now that it could only be a matter of time before that happened. And then who would remember her first steps, her first words? Her life before she became the possession of the nation?

"Drink your milk," her mother said, pressing the cup into her hands. "Don't spill it, now."

Her emotions blunted her natural instincts, and it wasn't until she had drunk the milk down that she noticed the satisfied expression on her mother's face and knew she'd been duped.

"You didn't!" she gasped, thrusting away the now empty cup. "Mama, please, tell me you didn't . . . "

"You need your sleep." She sounded hurt. "Mother knows best, Portia."

"How much laudanum did you put in?"

"Not much, just the usual draught. It will help you to sleep, and in the morning you'll be better, you'll see."

Portia groaned. "We are unveiling Lord Ellerslie's statue tomorrow! I am to go to Green Park with Victoria and Albert . . . everyone will be there! Lara will be furious with me if I don't do everything I ought. Oh Mama, how could you! Hettie!" she wailed.

By the time Hettie was sent for and came hurrying into the room, the awful drugged sensation was already enclosing her, like a sheep's fleece. Hettie's plump face was tilting oddly and blurring at the edges. Portia tried to lift her hand, but it was too heavy.

"I must be there tomorrow. Please make sure I wake in time, Hettie . . . "

"It was for her own good," her mother was saying sullenly.

"How much did you give her, Mrs. Stroud?"

"Just the usual draft. It isn't safe in those woods, you know."

"I know. My lady? My lady, it will be all right. I will see that you are awake and ready in time. My lady?"

But her voice was fading, and then there was nothing.

* * *

Hettie sat by the bed for a long time, watching over her sleeping mistress. Mrs. Stroud had not given her as much laudanum as she had feared, but nevertheless she was concerned enough to stay and see that all was well. With luck, the effects would have worn off by morning. They could send excuses, citing fever, but Portia would be distraught if it came to that. These days she was afraid to say no to anything the queen said, but to say no when it was a memorial statue to her own husband . . .

Hettie shuddered at the consequences.

It was all the fault of *that man*. Getting her clothing wet and stopping her from catching the train, causing a rift between her and the queen. Hettie didn't trust him, and despite what she'd said to Portia, she wasn't satisfied that he was gone for good. He was bound to be plotting some new mischief.

The way he'd looked at Portia that day by the seaside! He'd wanted to possess her completely, and he was the type who was used to getting what he wanted. Selfish, spoiled, and completely without scruples. He could destroy Portia on a whim and then claim it wasn't his fault. And now he was interfering with her mistress's sleep, enticing her out into the night like some sort of . . . of demon.

Hettie's expression grew grim.

The lingering presence of Marcus Worthorne might require her to take serious steps. She'd never thought she would go behind Portia's back, but now she was beginning to think it might be necessary if she was to save her mistress from destroying herself utterly.

Arnold Gillingham had spoken to her not long after the soiree given by his wife. Hettie, surprised that a gentleman would seek her out, was at first suspicious when he began to speak about Portia and how they must all do their utmost to "look after her."

"It is in all our best interests," he'd said, his cold blue eyes boring into hers. "I want you to know that if you ever feel it necessary, you can come to me. I am fond of Lady Ellerslie, and I would not want to see her in any bother. None of us would want that."

Hettie had pretended not to know what he was talking about, thinking to herself that she could never be so disloyal. But she remembered it now with a sense of relief. Perhaps Arnold was right. Perhaps there would come a time when it was necessary to ask for his help. Perhaps she would be grateful to do so.

And that was Marcus Worthorne's fault, too.

Chapter 16

The crowd was immense, spilling over from Green Park into the Mall and St. James's Park. There was a holiday atmosphere, with bunting and streamers and children waving little union jacks. The people of London had come out on this bright summer day to pay their patriotic respects to their dead hero, and to gawp at the royal couple and the "widow."

Marcus used an ungentlemanly elbow to force his way through the onlookers until he was no more than a few rows back from the dais that had been set up to accommodate the royal party.

Once again Martin O'Donnelly had proved invaluable when it came to information concerning Lady Ellerslie's whereabouts.

"She'll be there," he'd stated. "The statue is in memory of the late Lord Ellerslie. How could she stay away? Besides, the queen takes her everywhere these days. Won't let her out of her sight."

Marcus said nothing, mulling over his words.

"Excuse my impertinence, sir, but why don't you call on her in the usual fashion?" Martin's bright eyes were full of curiosity.

"Because I don't want to speak to her, I want to see her," he said quietly. "And I want her to see me. After that I'll know what I have to do next . . . or if there is to be a *next*."

Just when he thought they were never going to arrive, the royal carriage drew up, flanked by equerries. The queen was plumper than ever after her last pregnancy—how many little princes and princesses was it now? Marcus wondered as he watched her lean upon her consort's arm. He supposed he could see the attraction. They certainly looked a contented couple; a picture postcard for domestic bliss.

And then he forgot all about the queen as there was a sentimental "Oohh" from the crowd.

Portia had stepped down from the carriage and was walking toward the dais. She was elegantly beautiful in her gray silk dress and matching bonnet, her somber outfit a foil for her bright hair. The angel in widow's weeds. But Marcus knew better. Portia wasn't an angel; she was a temptress. Or she could be, if she would give herself permission to please herself.

There was much fussing about on the dais as the royal party and their attendants arranged themselves on the chairs provided. The statue's creator gave a speech—some famous chap, although Marcus couldn't remember his name—and London's Lord Mayor, re-splendid in robes and the gold chain of his office, also spoke for an inordinate amount of time.

"Load of waffle, if you ask me," someone muttered behind Marcus. Several frowns were sent his way by a well-dressed group at the front of the crowd. A baby began to cry.

Marcus was watching Portia. She was wearing her usual half smile—her public mask. Beautiful but a mask nonetheless. He wondered what she was thinking behind it. What was she feeling? Was she missing him as much as he was missing her? Could he change her mind if he let him get near enough?

If he hadn't been watching her so closely he might have missed the way her fingers trembled as she reached up to tuck a stray wisp of hair beneath her bonnet. His gaze sharpened and he noticed the pronounced shadows under her eyes. And her pallor; there was not a shred of color in her cheeks. She stared down, as if withdrawing into herself.

What had happened to his beloved in the time he'd been away? This was not the Portia he'd left at the station in Little Tunley. This was not the woman who swam with him in the sea and made love to him so openly and freely beneath the sky.

The speeches over with, the queen rose, casting a sharp glance back to Portia, who, taken by surprise, stood up abruptly. She swayed. Horrified, Marcus watched her lose her footing and begin to fall. Her head lolled back, her lashes fluttering, and she reached out for help.

There was a rush of blood to his head. "Portia!" Before he knew it, he was pushing through the crowd, fighting like a madman to get to the dais.

One of the queen's attendants had seen Portia fall and was supporting her.

"Portia!"

At the sound of her name, her head came up and she struggled to right herself. She was already searching the sea of upturned faces.

"Portia!"

She found him. Her gaze locked with his and he saw her lips move. "No!" she said. But it was too late. He'd reached the five steps that led onto the dais and there was no going back. He ran up them. Someone grabbed at his arm, trying to stop him, but he pulled angrily away, reaching for Portia.

She was there, and he drew her into his arms, gazing down into her face, which was perfectly white. Her eyes were as blue as the sea at St. Tristan, but as dark and troubled as that sea had been calm. The others, the royal party and the strangely silent crowd, ceased to exist.

"Marcus, you should not be here. I told you it was over. This is wrong." Her voice was hardly more than a breath.

"It doesn't feel wrong to me." He squeezed her fingers in his, raising them to his lips. He wanted to kiss her mouth. He thought about it, but there wasn't enough time to do more than think.

There was a scream and then angry shouting. The crowd about the dais surged forward. Several of the queen's guard surrounded him. Before he knew it, he'd been restrained by a great many hands and was being roughly pulled away.

"You monster!" the queen cried. She was glaring at him as if he was a rapist, or at the very least an assassin, and he realized—as someone called for his arrest—that was exactly what they believed him to be. Above the hubbub and confusion he thought he heard Portia's soft, "Oh no!" and then an authoritative voice ordered again, "Arrest him!"

Marcus fought hard but was quickly overwhelmed and dragged backward down the steps, sustaining a bruise or two. The police had him in custody now, and no matter how he tried to explain himself or demand that they release him, they would not listen. The crowd encircled him threateningly, waving fists and parasols, calling him names and screaming for his blood.

"Get him away from here," the police constable shouted, "before they tear him to pieces. We don't have enough men to hold them back."

Marcus was hustled into one of their horse-drawn prisoner wagons. The door was slammed shut, enclosing him in semidarkness. He could still hear the voices outside. There was thumping on the walls and someone demanded he be hanged for laying a hand on "our Portia."

It was insanity. The British public imagined he had tried to harm their darling and they wanted his blood.

No amount of explaining would change their minds at the moment; they were beyond reason.

At last the wagon began to move. A relieved Marcus slumped, covering his face with his hands. He felt bruised and battered, both in body and in pride. If he had ever doubted Portia's popularity, he was convinced of it now. She was held very high. Which made it even further for her to fall.

Perhaps he should take her at her word and vanish from her life forever. But despite what had just happened, he had no intention of giving up.

Portia was shaking. Someone had helped her back onto her chair and one of Victoria's ladies-in-waiting was vigorously fanning her. She'd very nearly fainted. It was the laudanum. This morning she had still been feeling woozy and wooly-headed, but had no option but to do her best to rise and make her appearance at the palace.

By the time several domestic crises had been gotten through involving the royal children, and Prince Albert was dragged away from his plans for next year's Great Exhibition, Portia wanted to go home again. But she couldn't, so she mentally gritted her teeth and settled into the royal carriage as they set off for Green Park.

Lara and Arnold were already there, the former's eyes misty and her lip trembling. This was a big occasion for her, and Portia was glad she had not spoiled it. Arnold was more pragmatic.

"Who'd have thought the old man would get his own statue," he drawled. "Still, he'll probably be forgotten in a hundred years."

Portia had stared at him. "Why do you say that?"

"My dear Portia, it is the villains whom history remembers, not the heroes."

"There is no inscription," Lara interrupted. "I thought there would be an inscription. A quote perhaps from one of his diaries."

"'Where are my bloody boots?' He was fond of saying that," Arnold murmured.

A moment later the ceremony began.

She'd never imagined, never in her wildest dreams, that Marcus would be there.

"I am all right," she murmured now. Then, in a stronger voice, to convince herself as well as the group around her, "I promise you, I am all right."

"He tried to attack you!" Victoria was outraged.

"No," Portia insisted. "No, Your Majesty. I—I know him, a little. He saw that I was about to faint. He wasn't attacking me; he was coming to my aid."

Victoria's eyes narrowed suspiciously.

"I think she is right, Your Majesty," someone ventured. "He seemed most concerned to see that Lady Ellerslie was unwell."

"What is his name?" Victoria was looking at Portia.

"Mr. Marcus Worthorne, Ma'am. His brother is the Earl of Worthorne. You may know him. The earl's wife is sister to Lady Montgomery."

Victoria knew the connection, but she was still not impressed by the interruption to Lord Ellerslie's ceremony.

Lara wasn't either. She clicked her tongue, peering over someone's shoulder, her expression telling Portia everything she needed to know about her stepdaughter's opinion of her stealing the limelight on this day of all days.

"Strange way to come to anyone's aid," the queen said, "leaping over the barriers and pushing aside innocent bystanders. Is he deranged, Lady Ellerslie?"

Portia bit her lip. "No, Ma'am. Just a little impetuous."

There was a murmur of amusement. Someone chuckled. The queen was not amused. "The police will get to the bottom of it," she said, as if that was the end of the matter. "Now, do let us get on! Give me the scissors, if you please, and I will cut the ribbon. Unless another of your impetuous acquaintances wishes to join us on the dais, Lady Ellerslie?"

Portia wisely kept silent.

The opening was swiftly performed, and not to be outdone by her stepmama, Lara leaned against Arnold and genteelly shed a tear or two. The statue, which was very lifelike, was admired and applauded. A few moments later they left to the cheering of the crowd and shouts of "Bravo, Lady Ellerslie!"

It was touching to be their heroine, but not when it meant Marcus—no matter how foolishly he had acted—was the villain.

Portia glanced at Victoria as the carriage bowled along, wondering whether Her Majesty was seriously displeased or simply annoyed. Well, there was nothing to be done about it now, and besides, there were far more urgent matters to be dealt with. As soon as she arrived home she must send someone to the police to explain. Did she know anyone in authority who could pull strings?

Why had he done it? What was he doing in Green Park? She didn't believe he was there because he had an interest in the late Lord Ellerslie's statue. No, he'd come to see *her*.

The arrogant, impetuous fool!

But oh, he had looked so good. She'd forgotten how handsome he was . . . No, that wasn't true. But she *had* forgotten the intensity of his physical presence, the way it took hold of her until she ached to throw her arms around him and, in front of everyone, kiss him wildly.

How Lara, and the queen, would have loved that!

Portia shuddered at the thought of the press's interpretation of such actions: righteous fury at her lack of self-control, the perceived betrayal of her dead hero husband . . . Public opinion was a fickle thing, and although at the moment they loved her, they could tumble her off her pedestal in a flash if she upset them.

Marcus must not seek her out again, she thought. She must get word to him . . . write to him. No, no, a letter was not enough. She must tell him face-to-face. She wiped her damp hands upon her skirts, still feeling light-headed. She would go to him and speak to him in person so there were no more misunderstandings. She'd thank him politely for coming to her aid but assure him she was perfectly well and his assistance was no longer required.

Would he believe her?

He must. She would have to ensure that he accepted her decision once and for all. The thing was . . . Portia sighed; she was not sure she believed it herself. Suddenly a life without Marcus in it seemed bleak indeed.

Chapter 17

The police station to which they brought Marcus was housed in a narrow building off Piccadilly. They kept him in a cramped room belonging to the officer-in-charge, who was busy elsewhere, with a constable on guard near the door in case he decided to make a run for it.

They seemed to think he was a desperate criminal, and Marcus supposed that at the moment he resembled one. There was a bruise on his cheek and another near his eye and several on his shins from the dais steps, which meant he limped. His coat sleeve was torn at the seam, hanging untidily down his arm, and he was missing a couple of buttons. Apart from these minor physical injuries, he was suffering from some emotional hurt—to his pride, mostly.

From masterful lover to miserable convict in one fell swoop.

The day hadn't turned out anything like he'd visualized it.

"So, little brother," said a familiar voice.

Marcus's head came up and his eyes filled with relief. "Seb! About time."

The constable watched them impassively.

"I came as soon as I could," Sebastian replied mildly, strolling into the room. "It's not every day my brother is held by the police for causing an affray in a public place. Well done, that must be a first for you."

"A ridiculous mistake," Marcus burst out, unable to restrain himself. "I wasn't going to hurt anyone. As soon as I touched her the crowd went berserk. They were literally baying for blood. I think the police brought me here more for my own safety than anyone else's."

"Of course, that must be it," his brother said dryly.

Marcus felt his momentary animation giving way to gloom. He surveyed his drab surroundings with a grimace. "Are you going to get me out of here?"

"I'm doing my best, Marcus. Be patient."

A gentleman appeared in the doorway and murmured something to the constable, who left. Middle-aged and flabby about the waist, he looked as if he had not slept for many hours, but when his tired eyes met Marcus's, his expression was sharp and intelligent.

"This is Chief Inspector Jack Fellows, from Scotland Yard," Sebastian said. "Jack, this is my brother, Marcus."

Chief Inspector Fellows gave him a little nod. "Well, Mr. Worthorne, you've certainly caused us some aggravation. That mob were all for marching down here and tearing apart the station to find you, but we managed to persuade them not to. Mind you, we had to call out over a hundred of our men to stop them. It was almost a riot."

"If I could have been allowed to explain—"

"They wouldn't have listened. They haven't forgotten the attack on Her Majesty by that lunatic with the cane. The ordinary Londoner is beginning to think there must be dozens of these monsters roaming the streets, searching for respectable women to do harm to. Mind you, the newspapers aren't helping. The masses are ripe for a rumpus, and today you gave them the very trigger they needed when you grabbed hold of Lady Ellerslie. You're lucky you weren't torn apart."

"I didn't 'grab hold' of her. I resent the implication."

"Marcus," Sebastian warned him. "Remember where you are."

"You have caused the constabulary considerable disruption and expense," the chief inspector continued. "And we saved your skin!"

"Apologize, Marcus," Sebastian growled.

Marcus sighed. What was the point in arguing? He needed to get out of here now. "I apologize, Mr. Fellows, for any disruption I may have caused, and I am grateful for being arrested in order to save my skin."

The chief inspector smiled. "I'm glad to hear it, Mr. Worthorne. I do understand that your intentions were to assist Lady Ellerslie, and a statement to that effect has been given out to the newspapers. Let's hope they print it in the evening editions and the public believes it. I wouldn't want you to be the victim of any more mob violence. In the meantime you are free to go."

"Free?"

"You are not under arrest, sir. We have spoken to Lady Ellerslie and she confirms what you told us. We are letting you go, and your brother has offered to take you safely home."

Marcus rose to his feet.

"I hope you have learned your lesson," the chief inspector added.

"Learned my lesson?" Marcus glared at him. "I didn't do anything wrong."

"Marcus," his brother warned sternly, before turning with a charming smile to the policeman. "Thank you, Jack. I appreciate your help."

"My pleasure, Mr. Thorne," Fellows said, using the sobriquet under which Sebastian had been known before he resumed his proper title and status in the world. He nodded at Marcus. "Watch that one. Bit of a firebrand, I'd say. Needs something to keep him occupied."

Angrily, Marcus strode past them and out of the door before he did something he, and Fellows, would regret.

Outside, it was growing dark. Not knowing how long he would be, and not wanting to draw attention to them, Sebastian had sent the carriage away. The two brothers walked briskly, both eager to get home, although for different reasons. Marcus imagined Sebastian was keen to see his wife, but Marcus himself needed to wash and change and set out as soon as possible for Grosvenor Square. Even if Portia refused him entry, he wanted to try and see her.

He didn't know exactly what he was going to say to her. He was working on some ideas, but it was difficult to concentrate when Sebastian kept interrupting his thoughts.

"I hope you know how many strings I had to pull to get you out of there."

"Thank you, brother."

"Just why have you taken to attacking famous ladies in public places, Marcus? Not your usual style."

Marcus shot him a frowning look. "She was about to faint. I went to her aid. I would never hurt her."

"Yes. That's what she told me when I spoke to her earlier."

"You saw her?" Marcus stopped and stared at his brother in amazement.

"What did you think I was doing all this time? I knew if I was to save my little brother, I needed Lady Ellerslie on my side. She was just about to send her lawyer to you, by the way, but I persuaded her that might just make things worse. A hammer to kill an ant, etcetera. And the gutter press would soon latch onto it, asking questions it would be better not to ask."

Marcus nodded but wasn't really listening. She'd been going to send her lawyer? His predicament mattered to her, then. The knowledge was balm to his lowered spirits.

"How was she?"

"A little flushed, but that was after I'd kissed her . . . "

Marcus swung around. "What!"

" . . . hand."

Sebastian smiled at the expression on Marcus's face, and then laughed. He laughed until the tears ran down his cheeks. Marcus was silent throughout, with a long-suffering glint in his eyes.

"I'm sorry," his brother gasped at last.

"Very funny," Marcus said coldly.

Sebastian's humor left him. "She's out of your league," he said. "I'd set my sights on someone less elevated, if I were you."

It was Marcus's turn to laugh, though with a bitter note. "You don't think I'm good enough for her then, Seb?"

"On the contrary, I think you're every bit as good as her, but they won't let you have her. You saw what happened when you touched her. She's the sacred widow, Marcus. They'd rather she died tragically from grief than you have her all flushed and happy with your baby on her lap. They want a symbol to worship, a memory to treasure, not a real flesh and blood woman. She's out of your reach, yes, but not because of *you*. Because of *her*."

"Thank you for your advice, brother, but I prefer to make my own mistakes."

"Go for a baronet's daughter. An innkeeper's wench. Why look to the only woman you cannot possibly have? That's just perverse."

"You did."

"Blast and damn it, Marcus! You and Lady Ellerslie are in a situation that can only end in grief. You're younger than me, and I've always watched out for you. If you think I am being insulting then I am sorry, but my first instinct is to protect my brother."

At last Marcus relaxed and smiled. "I'll bear it in mind for the next time I'm arrested."

Sebastian swore again, but there was no time to say more. They were home.

Francesca was waiting in the hall. "Oh Marcus!" she cried, throwing her arms about him.

He gave her a hug. "I'm fine, Fran. The police were most hospitable. And Seb pulled some strings, apparently, which he'll never let me forget."

Francesca glanced lovingly across at her husband, who was removing his hat and gloves.

"We were so worried. I could hardly keep still, and Lady Ellerslie kept peeping at the mantel clock whenever there was a lull in the conversation—"

"Lady Ellerslie?" He cut her short, his gaze focused hard on hers.

"Didn't you tell him?" Francesca turned to Sebastian in surprise.

"Tell me what?" Impatiently, Marcus looked from one of them to the other.

"That Lady Ellerslie is waiting to see you in the library," Francesca answered, her eyes wide with curiosity.

Marcus looked toward the library door.

"She's in disguise," Francesca added with a little smile. "Incognito. In case anyone sees her. Sebastian will try and play everything down, say you hardly know each other, that you just happened to be in the crowd when you saw her faint and so on. A misunderstanding now happily put to rights. He says you'll be forgotten by tomorrow."

"Back to being a nobody," Marcus said levelly.

"Marcus, you know you could never be that!"

"Francesca, don't encourage him," Sebastian growled. "And as for you . . . " He shot his brother a penetrating look. "Go and speak to Lady Ellerslie, and stay out of trouble."

Portia was staring at the first edition copy of *Clarissa* she'd discovered in the bookshelves and trying to settle her nerves, but the heroine's willingness to die rather than live with shame had begun to grate on her. Besides, she had so much to think about.

Marcus's brother, the Earl of Worthorne, had persuaded her to let him handle matters and told her he was well qualified to do so. He'd inspired trust in her and a sense of confidence; both of which she found sadly lacking in his brother. And yet they were very alike.

"I must see Marcus," she'd said to him, trying to keep the wobble out of her voice, assuming her usual calm poise with difficulty. The incident on the dais had rattled her—she was still light-headed and shaky.

"Do you think that's a good idea, my lady?" Sebastian's dark eyes were remarkably penetrating.

"There are things that must be said."

The earl had looked at her a moment with an expression that was almost pity, then bowed his head in acquiesce. "My brother has a remarkable ability to attract ladies. I wouldn't want you to think . . . "

I wouldn't want you to think you are the only one.

Portia managed a little smile. "Don't worry, I won't let my partiality for him blind me to his faults. I have more to lose than him."

Sebastian seemed to want to say more but changed his mind. "What did you have in mind?"

"I'm not sure." She'd waved her hand vaguely. "I could send a hired coach perhaps? Or take a room incognito at a waterside inn?"

Sebastian smiled. "A hired coach at midnight by the river? You and my brother are well matched, my lady, when it comes to romantic fantasies. No, I think it would be best if you came to my house and waited there. My wife Francesca will keep you company until I can bring Marcus home."

Nervously, Portia had agreed, but she'd worn a bonnet with a thick black mourning veil to disguise her identity. The press already knew about Marcus's arrest, and although they weren't suggesting there was anything romantic between them, she didn't want the possibility to occur.

Portia closed the book with a snap. Clarissa lacked

courage, she decided; Minnie could have taught her a thing or two. She set the book aside just as she heard *his* voice out in the hall.

She was about to jump up and wrench open the door when she stopped, reining herself in. And then what? Fling herself into his arms? Declare to the world that she was completely lost to good sense?

No, no, that would never do. It was over and she was there to tell him so.

He mustn't know how many hours she had spent torn between conflicting emotions. She was a grown woman of poise and experience, yet her life was ruled by the opinions of others.

Put like that, she sounded as weak as Clarissa, but when you considered who those *people* were—Queen Victoria and Prince Albert, the population of London— it was never as simple as it sounded. She had made her choice long ago to shoulder the responsibilities that the title Lady Ellerslie gave to her. To throw that all away for a man who had so little to recommend him would be the act of an imbecile.

She made herself hard and cold and practical. Marcus might be handsome, he might make her body sing with desire whenever she came close to him, but that wasn't enough. It *must* not be enough.

Then why were her eyes stinging with tears?

Out in the hall he spoke again, his words muffled and indistinct, and then she heard steps approaching. *His* steps. She recognized them. Despite all her resolutions, her breath quickened and her pulses began to pound.

The door opened and there he stood, rumpled, one of his sleeves torn, his hair messy, a bruise on his cheek, and his eyes blazing.

"Lady Ellerslie." His voice was full of suppressed passion.

A lesser woman might have swooned.

But Portia was strong and determined. "Mr. Worthorne," she said, beginning her rehearsed speech. "I came here to thank you for—"

"You could have sent a letter." He was looking at her as if he'd like to throw her onto the rug in front of the fire and ravish her.

She regathered her defenses, knowing she was flushed, forgetting that he could not see her face through the veil.

"I wanted to see you . . . *thank* you, to your face. You were very kind and everyone assumed the worst." She cleared her throat when he didn't answer. "It was the least I could do."

He still did not answer, and she was finding it increasingly difficult to meet his gaze, again overlooking that he could not see through her veil.

"Please, aren't you going to sit down? Are you hurt? You look as if you might be? Marcus, please—"

He flung himself suddenly down into an armchair. "There's nothing to concern yourself about. I'm a little bruised, that is all. How long have you been here?"

"An hour or two. Lady Worthorne has been very kind."

"You must have been very eager to see me to wait so long. I wonder why?" He sounded angry.

"Marcus," she said, clenching her hands together. "I think you know why. I wanted to persuade you . . . to convince you that whatever was between us truly is over. What happened today must never happen again."

"Well I'm sorry if I inconvenienced you, my lady, by coming to your rescue."

"You know what I mean. Why are you making this so difficult?"

"Why should I make it easy for you to tell me not to see you again? Have you found someone to replace me? Is that why you're so determined to be rid of me? A handsome Coldstream Guard who can service you whenever you wish and will never touch your heart, or a member of the royal household under strict instructions to keep Lady Ellerslie happy and away from the likes of rakes like me?"

She flinched.

He shook his head and rubbed his hand over his face. "Forgive me. I'm sorry. I'm in a foul mood. Perhaps I'd be more amenable if I could see your face under that accursed veil."

Portia lifted her veil and fixed it over the front of her bonnet, taking her time, trying to regain her sense of calm. His words had stung, but he was upset and she thought she could forgive him his bitter, hurtful tongue.

"I had to wear the veil," she explained levelly. "I could not afford anyone seeing me entering your house."

"Of course not. How terrible if the mob thought you cared about a man who was *alive*."

Marcus moved restlessly in his seat. He knew he was being difficult and rude, but couldn't seem to help it. Seeing her here, hiding her face, preparing to tell him yet again that he wasn't to see her, had fired his already frayed temper to the breaking point.

Eyes narrowed, he watched her summoning up her polite public mask. God damn her, why would she not argue with him? He wanted to see her passion and her temper; he wanted to see that she cared.

"Your sister-in-law tells me you have been away. Did you know of the recent assassination attempt on the queen?" she said calmly.

"Yes, I've kept up with the news. Even Norfolk has some contact with the rest of the world."

He could see that she wasn't listening; understandably, she was focused on her own problems. But he *wanted* her to listen. He wanted to tell her about the things he'd done, the thoughts he'd had, and his plans and visions for the future. Because he now had a future, something that he'd never imagined the first time they came together, and he wanted her to hear about it. Ever since he gazed across the causeway at Duval Hall—his house—he'd had this burning urge to share everything with her.

And now she wasn't even listening.

"I was visiting my property in Norfolk," he said anyway. "It is called Duval Hall."

"Oh?" Now she was staring at her hands.

"I have hopes of making something of it. In time. The hall will need repairs—there's an enormous glass window that has been broken . . . partially broken, anyway. I have arranged to have it repaired. And the farmland must be drained and reclaimed. Hard work, you might say, for a gentleman of leisure, but I'm willing to give it a go."

And he laughed, because he was embarrassed and hopeful and longing for her approval.

She didn't answer. Again he could see she wasn't listening. His life was nothing to her. She moved among the highest in the land and he was but a younger son with few prospects. He might be a good lover—he *was* a good lover—but there was nothing more he could offer her, nothing more she wanted from him.

The realization chastened him. A lesser man would have stormed from the room or burst into tears. Marcus did neither. Instead he began to plot and plan how he could use the one thing she needed from him to win her over.

Her desire for his lover's expertise had drawn her back to him several times already when she'd tried to end it. If he couldn't win her with his prospects, then he'd bind her to him with his body.

With a self-mocking smile he left his chair and went

down onto his knees before her. She jumped. She hadn't expected him to do that. He reached for her hands and grasped them firmly in his, stopping her from rising. She was rigid. He understood then just how edgy she was in his presence, and how cleverly she had been hiding it. Beneath her mask she was awash with feelings.

Good.

"Marcus, I can't—"

"I was nearly killed for your sake today," he said, and watched her face pale. "I put my life at risk for yours. Some women might find that heroic, Portia, not to say erotic."

"I—I'm sorry for what happened to you," she said in a low voice, looking into his eyes in such a frank and serious way he wanted to tumble her on the sofa. He resisted, for now.

"Are you?"

"They had no right to arrest you. I tried to tell them, but I couldn't make myself heard. I don't think they would have listened anyway. They were determined to turn you into an assassin."

"I suppose I was lucky the equerries didn't run me through with their swords."

She shivered and her calm seemed to desert her. She drew one of her hands from his clasp and reached out, as if to smooth back a lock of his dark hair, before changing her mind and curling her fingers into a fist. She wanted to touch him but was denying herself the pleasure. Well, he would see about that.

"Why were you in Green Park?" she asked urgently. "I don't understand how you came to be there."

"I wanted to see you. Are you well? I cannot tell you how I felt when I saw you faint." He rested his hand upon her knee.

Her breathing grew unsteady. "I—I was a little faint, but I am much better now. My . . . I took some laudanum, to help me sleep, and the effects lingered longer than I expected." She shook her head impatiently, as if she wished she had never mentioned it.

"Why can't you sleep?" he murmured. Whether intentionally or not, she had swayed closer, and he leaned forward and pressed his lips to her cheek, and then the corner of her mouth. She was trembling. His mouth hovered over hers, teasing, wanting her. "I can help you sleep," he whispered, and boldly his hand slid up under her skirt.

At first, her gaze locked with his, she didn't seem to know what he was doing. "It—It was an accident," she said. "My mother gave me the laudanum. I don't normally take it."

She gasped and stiffened. His hand was gently brushing the side of her knee through her stocking, and she seemed to have only just realized it. Her eyes widened. He kissed her before she could think of protesting, and kept kissing her. She gave a sigh as he pressed her back into her chair. His hand was resting on the warm, smooth skin of her thigh now, and he felt her quiver, wanting him to touch her and at the same time afraid of losing control.

Poor Portia. It must be difficult for her in the circumstances, he thought, wanting to break with him forever and yet addicted to his touch. He smiled, nuzzling her cheek, her throat, before returning to her mouth.

His fingers found what they were seeking. She was moist and hot, and she moaned softly. He used his thumb on the eager little bud, sliding his fingers inside her. She melted around him.

"I missed you," he said.

"I—I missed you," she managed. There was a pink flush in her cheeks now and she was biting at her lip to stop herself from making the sort of sounds she usually made, in case someone heard her. "Someone will come, Marcus."

"No one will come. Do you want me to stop?"

He began to remove his fingers.

"Oh, please, no . . . "

She was kissing him desperately. He returned to his ministrations, using all his skill, leaning away from her so he could watch her face. The mask was gone now, well and truly.

"Don't worry," he murmured into her ear, "I won't stop. Not until . . . " One last firm stroke and she reached her peak. Her body clenched, spasming, and then she went limp, her breasts rising and falling beneath the tightly buttoned bodice.

He sat back on his haunches to look at her, ignoring the ache in his groin and the obvious effect she was having on his anatomy. She looked adorable, flushed and replete, her half-closed eyes drowsy and dazed. She sighed and her mouth curved into a smile.

"Let's say good-bye properly," he said evenly. "At Aphrodite's Club. One last time." He'd taken advantage of her weakness. He'd played her perfectly. She couldn't deny him.

"We've said good-bye, Marcus."

He laughed. "You're not serious? Portia—"

"I am serious."

The flushed, sleepy expression was swiftly replaced with one he knew all too well.

"I know you want me. I want you."

"I won't deny that. I can't." She turned her face away. "But we cannot continue to meet, Marcus."

"I'm not suggesting we do. I'll be returning to Norfolk, my lady, and you'll never see me again."

Ah, he had her attention now.

"You're going away?" Doubt filled her eyes. "But . . . I don't believe you."

"Do you want me to promise?" he mocked. "Well, I will. My life is in Norfolk now, and that is where I will stay. If I do visit London, I doubt I will be moving in the same circles as you, Portia."

"You really are leaving for good?"

"Yes." The lies fell easily from his lips; he reminded himself that they were in a good cause. "So you see, this really will be our last good-bye and then we will part forever. That is what you want, isn't it, Portia? Never to see me again?"

"Yes." She stared at him a moment more, and he could see the raging doubt and longing in her face, warring with each other. Then she spoke quickly, as if afraid of changing her mind. "Very well, Marcus. One last time. One final good-bye."

He hid his smile of triumph and bent to kiss her fingers.

"One final good-bye, Portia. Let us make it something to remember, hmm?"

She flipped her black net back over her face and rose to her feet. "I look forward to it," she said, as if arranging to take tea and scones. He wanted to take her by the shoulders and shake her until she screamed and struck at him, as she had that time in the Campaign Room, but instead he bowed politely and watched her go.

There would be time yet to make her see sense, and he did not intend to give up.

Chapter 18

Hettie stood irresolute in Curzon Street, looking up at the Gillingham residence. They were home. She had seen them return from some outing or other and go inside. Perhaps they were preparing to retire? She shouldn't interrupt them. She'd come back in the morning.

But Hettie knew she had to do something to save her beloved mistress from herself. She was at Aphrodite's Club right now, losing her soul and everything else to that wicked man. And Arnold had told her to come to him if she was ever in need of his help.

She'd truly thought she could extract Portia from her mess, but matters had gone beyond her ability to mend them. She was sorry she ever agreed to be her mistress's accomplice—she had actively encouraged her!—by arranging that first visit to the club. Since then Portia had fallen more and more under the spell of Marcus Worthorne, and no matter how often she said it was over between them—"This time it really is, I promise!"—she kept going back to him.

Hettie felt sick with guilt. She was, in a sense, betraying her mistress, but what else could she do? She cared deeply for Portia and was desperately worried about her. If Portia were found out, she'd be ruined, her life in tatters. Hettie couldn't have that. For it all to end in scandal and ignominy? No, that would never do.

And, a little voice whispered in her ear, *what will happen to you, Fraulein Hettie?*

It was true, she wasn't getting any younger. Soon it would be time to step aside for someone more spry, someone more up-to-date with the fashionable changing world Portia lived in. Hettie knew she also had to think of herself and her own retirement. She would not allow herself to consider this as a betrayal; it was a practical solution.

The Gillingham's housekeeper gave her a superior look, but she recognized Hettie and didn't quite dare send her away. After leaving her waiting a moment in the kitchen, she returned. "Mrs. Gillingham will see you."

"But I wanted to talk to *Mister* Gillingham," Hettie protested.

"I can't help that. He's out and Mrs. Gillingham says *she* will see you. Well, make up your mind. It's late and I want to go to bed."

Hettie realized she had no choice.

Lara Gillingham was dressed in a yellow and green patterned dress with a plunging neckline and lace-trimmed sleeves. Jewelry sparkled at her throat and her hair was entwined with pearls. Hettie noticed that her eyes were particularly bright. Too much wine, she thought scornfully, but kept her manner respectful as she made her curtsy.

"You have come from Lady Ellerslie, Hettie? Why did she not come herself? She is well, isn't she? The Green Park incident was a week ago. I thought she was recovered from all the unpleasantness."

"Yes, ma'am, she is recovered. It isn't that."

"Then what is it, Hettie?"

Hettie bit her lip and looked awkward. It was an act, of course, but she had decided upon a certain way of playing her part to Arnold, and now she would have to convince Lara.

"I am concerned about Lady Ellerslie, ma'am. I don't know what to do, and I thought that you could help."

Lara's attention was caught and she leaned forward. "What is it?"

"My lady is most beloved by the people, ma'am. It'd be a shocking thing if she were to do anything that might put their love for her in jeopardy."

"Why would she? What on earth could possibly cause her to jeopardize her position? Hettie, tell me at once!"

Hettie assumed a pensive pose. "She is lonely, I think, and that can make any woman vulnerable to the manipulation of a clever man—"

"Portia has a man!" Lara shrieked, then clapped her hand over her mouth.

Hettie was beginning to have serious doubts about

coming here tonight, but it was too late. She must make the best of it, and pray that it did her mistress some good. Portia could not be in any worse straits than she was right now.

"I am very concerned that she has fallen under this man's spell," she said, sticking to her script. "If he makes her forget her position, and her family and friends do nothing to save her, then it will not be just her reputation that suffers. Will it, Mrs. Gillingham?"

Lara stared at her. "Then we must stop her. Immediately. Before this stain spreads to all of us."

"Yes." Hettie tried not to breathe a sigh of relief.

"And no one must know. Dear God, imagine if *the queen* found out . . . "

Hettie did not think it necessary to answer that. Lara Gillingham finally understood the full gravity of the situation.

"Where is Portia now?" she asked, eyes sharp and narrow.

"She has gone to meet him, ma'am. But she will return home before too long. She never stays away for the whole night, except—" She stopped herself, biting her lip. Best not to mention St. Tristan, it would only complicate matters.

Luckily, Lara didn't seem to notice. "Thank you, Hettie, you have acted correctly in coming to me, and I won't forget it. Like my father, I reward loyalty. And say nothing to anyone else, especially not to Lady Ellerslie. I will deal with the matter from now on."

"Very good, ma'am. You will not tell her? That it was me who . . . who . . . "

Lara arched an eyebrow. "I will be as discreet as necessary, Hettie."

Was that a yes or a no? Hettie didn't have the courage to ask her a second time. She had to hope that Lara told Arnold and he took over "the matter." Arnold had promised discretion. That was what had drawn her to this cause of action.

As Hettie left the room she told herself she was relieved it was all out of her hands. But she wasn't. Guilt was already niggling at her, making her feel squirmy and uncomfortable. She hadn't realized that Lara would be quite so gleeful at Portia's expense, and if Portia found out who had told . . . her mistress would never forgive her.

Hettie had been her personal maid since she married Lord Ellerslie. The queen had a hand in getting her the position—Hettie was from Saxe-Coburg, where Victoria and Albert's own family originated. But that was a long time ago. She considered herself English now, and Portia was her family. And now she had betrayed Portia, even if it was for her own good.

She didn't know if she was going to be able to live with that.

Portia was lying in Marcus's arms. The passion, the wild attraction between them, was still there, and there was no point in denying it. If the feelings had faded, even a little, she could have believed their affair was dying a natural death. But it wasn't. As soon as he kissed her, Portia knew matters were as intense as ever.

She should have been disappointed, but she was glad. Glad! Even though her passion for him would make her life miserable when he was gone.

Marcus stroked her cheek. "You are very pensive, my lady."

She shifted her head so she could look into his eyes. He was watching her from beneath half-closed lids, as if he had a secret. "Is that a bad thing?"

"Sometimes it isn't wise to think too much. Act on your instincts, that's my advice."

"Is that what you do?" She shifted in order to see him better, but couldn't read his face.

"Of course." He smiled, then bent to kiss her in the sensitive area beside her ear, and she lifted her shoulder to try and protect herself from his teasing.

"I thought God gave men and women the ability to think and reason to lift them above the animals. Isn't that what we're taught in Sunday school?"

He widened his eyes. "Are you calling me an animal, Portia?"

She giggled—she couldn't help it. He seemed to have the uncanny ability to make her laugh when she least wanted to.

"If I am a beast, then it is you who turn me into one."

She gasped as he flung himself on top of her, subduing her with his strength. Gentle strength. As if it was his desire to show her how much stronger he was, and at the same time to teach her that he would never use his superior strength to harm her.

"Ask me," he murmured, nuzzling her temple, her hair.

"Ask you what?" she said breathlessly, as if she couldn't feel him hard against her thigh.

He kissed her, drawing out her soul. "Ask me," he said again.

"No." Her lashes fluttered.

"Portia," he whispered, his mouth hot against her breasts, his body heavy and desirable upon her.

"Marcus—" she began, then stopped. What was the use in fighting it? This was their last time together, and she wanted him, needed him. She might very well love him.

"Marcus?" he prompted her.

"Please, please, Marcus, make love to me."

With a growl, he complied.

Afterward, she felt him watching her intently from the shadows of the bed as she began to dress. She turned to smile at him as she slipped on her petticoats, tying the ribbons about her waist. She felt weary, emotionally exhausted as well as physically, and did not want to think about tomorrow, or the next day, when he would be gone. Forever gone.

"Marry me," he said.

She froze, not sure she'd heard him correctly. It was so ridiculous, so preposterous and unexpected. They

were saying good-bye. He couldn't have asked her
to—

"Marry me, Portia."

She tried to tie the ribbons, but her fingers were
shaking so much that she gave up and reached for her
scarlet dress. "You know that's not possible," she said,
her throat tight, her voice husky.

"Why not?" he demanded arrogantly. "I need a wife.
It's time I married and had an heir."

Portia shot him a look. "Oh, *you* need a wife, do
you?"

"Of course it wouldn't be the same as it is now. We'd
be able to sleep in the same bed without having to get up
and go our separate ways. That would be a novelty."

"Marcus, we made an arrangement. You knew at the
beginning it was impossible to have more than this. We
can't suddenly change things just because you decide
you need a wife."

"I told you about Duval Hall," he went on, sounding
more pompous with every moment. "I own it. We can
live there. It's in Norfolk, of course, but it's surprising how fond I am of it already. At least you'd be able
to live your own life without having to ask the queen
every time you want to change your bonnet. Damn it,
you could even go bare-headed if the mood took you."

"No, I'd be asking you instead."

"Are you saying I am a tyrant?"

"Just selfish and bossy. You haven't a clue, have you?
You don't put yourself into my place because you can't.

Suddenly you have a house and you decide you need a wife and nothing else matters to you. You think you can remake the world the way you want it. Well you can't, Marcus. We had an arrangement and now it's over. This was the last time, remember? You promised me. And this time I mean to hold you to your word."

He was on his feet, snatching up his clothing.

Portia climbed into her dress, shimmying it up over her bosom and slipping her arms into the narrow sleeves. By the time she'd finished with the fastenings, he was straightening his jacket and smoothing the cuffs. He ran a hand through his hair. Despite her annoyance with him, she couldn't help but look. What woman wouldn't want to wake up every morning to Marcus Worthorne? Sit down to breakfast with him and know he'd be there again tomorrow? And how dare he make such an offer to her in that offhand way when he knew it was impossible for her to accept it?

"You know my life is not my own," she said quietly. "For once try and understand."

Marcus bent to pick up her veil from the floor, running it through his fingers. "I do understand, Portia. You're frightened to have your own life because then you might actually start thinking about what makes you happy instead of pleasing everyone else."

"You mean like you?" She sat down to draw on her stockings.

"Well, pleasing me would be a big part of it, but I think you'd find some satisfaction in the arrangement."

"You are impossible, Marcus!"

Portia moved to find her shoes, but he was too quick, kneeling down to slip them onto her feet so very carefully, as if they or she were made of glass. His tenderness was so unexpected that it took her aback. She wanted to rant and rave at him, but when he looked up at her with his knowing smile, she couldn't. He was doing it on purpose, of course, to disconcert her even more than he had already.

Or to make her cry.

"Would I make a lady's maid, do you think? Would you employ me? You could keep me in your boudoir for whenever you needed me."

"You're far too dangerous for a lady's maid," she retorted, forcing strength into her voice. "Dangerous for the lady's peace of mind, that is."

He handed her the veil.

Portia placed it over her head. "There," she said brightly. "No one will know me now."

"Wouldn't want anyone to know you'd been spending your time with a nobody."

She was shocked by his casual bitterness. Could she have hurt his feelings by refusing him? Did he care that much? But no, it wasn't possible. It had been a whim on his part, not meant to be taken seriously, and he must have known she'd say no. Besides, Marcus was far too confident in himself to be hurt by anything she said.

He must have read her thoughts in her silence. "I'm not used to women being embarrassed to be seen with me.

Most of them quite like it. I wager if I asked any one of Aphrodite's pretty protégés to marry me, she'd say yes."

"Then ask them. You say you need a wife. Ask one of them."

It sounded like a dare.

"Perhaps I will," he said slowly, watching her as if he could pierce her veil. "I'll be sure she isn't famous, though, with a family of leeches battening onto her and the whole of England telling her they love her when they don't even know her. In short, I want a nobody like myself."

"You seem to think I don't understand what it is to go about unrecognized," she said quietly, "but I was a nobody, too, once."

Marcus looked at her a moment in silence, and for one breathtaking moment she thought he might remember her from the days at Worthorne Manor. But of course he did not. The vicar's daughter was long forgotten, replaced by hundreds of other more accommodating women.

"I wish I had met you when you were a nobody," he said. "I think I would have liked you better then."

Fury heated her cheeks. How dare he! It was unforgivable. She clenched her hands into fists. He hadn't given her a second look when she was the vicar's daughter, stammering her way through a sentence whenever he spoke to her, hiding in the church tower to watch him flirt with someone else. It was the mysterious and famous Lady Ellerslie who had captured his attention; her very unattainableness made him want her.

Her anger made it so much easier for her to leave him.

"I'm glad we had this conversation. I didn't realize until now just how shallow and vain you were," she said with stony quiet, rising to her feet. "You don't care how much I risked coming here tonight, do you? It means nothing to you because the only thing you care about is yourself."

"Of course! That's why I was arrested, for thinking of myself."

His mockery was beyond bearing. Why had he brought that up? She wanted to detest him and he was twisting her words.

"Some of us have more important things to do than satisfy our own base desires. But you don't understand that, Marcus. If you want something, then you take it."

He didn't answer her.

"Well, don't you?"

"I want you, Portia. That's the trouble. I want you, and you can't see how happy I could make you. You'd rather stay miserable."

"Arrogant, insufferable—"

"Yes, all that and more. But I can change—I have changed. Give me a chance to show you how happy I can make you."

She stared at him a moment more and then with a cry of exasperated disgust flung open the door and walked away.

* * *

Marcus leaned on the jamb and watched her pass through the salon like a whirlwind in scarlet. He'd upset her; he'd shaken the foundations of her narrow little world.

Well, good.

He wanted to go after her and show her what a real argument sounded like. He wanted to pull off her veil in front of everyone and say: *Here she is, and she's mine!* But he didn't, he couldn't.

He'd asked her to marry him and somehow it had come out wrong. He hadn't planned it, but seeing her, touching her, being with her, he hadn't wanted the moment to end. The words had just come out, and as soon as they were in the air between them, he knew it was a mistake and wanted to take them back. He'd done it all wrong, let his frustration overcome his good sense. For a man who prided himself on his ability as a lover, he had really made a mess of his marriage proposal.

He could see why she was angry and upset, but he had a right to feel that way too. Marcus Worthorne, the man with no direction in his life, with nothing to hold onto, had turned himself around for her. Everything he did now, he did with thoughts of Portia and what it would mean to her. To them. He was working toward them all the time.

He thought women were intuitive. Then why, he asked himself angrily, couldn't she understand that?

Chapter 19

 ❯❯❮❮

Portia, weary and heartsore, entered what she thought of as the sanctuary of her home in Grosvenor Square, and found she had stepped into the midst of a maelstrom. Deed's face, the first thing she saw, and which she used to monitor the level of trouble brewing deeper within her house, was twitching nervously.

"What is it, Deed?"

He gave her a pleading look. "Mrs. Gillingham is here, my lady."

"Lara? At this time of night? This is becoming a habit. What does she want now?"

"And *Mister* Gillingham."

"Good Lord." She sounded faint. "Both of them?"

"Yes, my lady. They wanted me to convey to you the urgency of their desire to see you as soon as you returned."

"*Urgency*?" Portia looked down at herself. She was respectably covered by her cloak, but beneath that she might as well be naked because she was wearing the alluring scarlet silk. She did not for a moment suspect this visit had anything to do with her whereabouts tonight—they probably wanted to ask her another favor—but neither did she want them asking any awkward questions.

"Tell them I'll be down soon, Deed," she said over her shoulder, heading for the stairs. "Give them refreshments. Lara particularly likes the macaroon biscuits. That should keep her busy."

The words were barely out of her mouth when, ominously, she heard the click of the drawing room door opening.

"Ah, Portia, there you are." It was Arnold, sounding as mild and unruffled as ever. "Do come in here. We wish to speak to you about something rather important."

Portia turned and forced a smile. "Arnold! What a nice surprise. Deed did mention you were here. If you'll excuse me for just a moment, I need to change."

"But, Portia, we wish to talk to you now."

Still polite, still mild, but this time Arnold had a chill in his voice that reminded her of a frosty morning.

"*Now*," he repeated as she hesitated. He held the door wide and stepped aside, waiting.

It was her house. She knew she could refuse. But refusing would create its own set of problems. Portia decided it was best to acquiesce. She would keep her cloak on and get it over with as quickly as possible, then pleading weariness, would retire to bed.

"Very well," she murmured through stiff lips, and passed by him into the drawing room.

Lara was seated on the straw-colored sofa, her back very straight. There was a strange look in her eyes. "Portia," she said in a harsh voice, "how could you?"

Portia understood then it was far worse than she had imagined. Lara's look was one of revulsion, and that meant they knew where she'd been and perhaps even who she'd been with.

In a moment of panic she turned for the door, but it was too late. Arnold had closed it and was standing in front of it, his handsome face without a flicker of compassion or understanding.

"What are you doing?" she asked him, chin up, eyes flashing. "This is my house and you have no right—"

"This is my father's house," Lara corrected her angrily. "And we have every right. We are here to bring you to your senses, *Stepmama*."

"My senses? I don't know what you mean?" But she did, and behind her angry front, in her heart, she was afraid.

"You will ruin us all." Lara had risen to her feet. This was her moment of revenge for all the perceived wrongs Portia had done her, and she was making the most of it.

"I've ruined no one. What are you talking about?"

"I think you know," Lara said, and her face looked swollen with gloating. "You've fallen from grace, Portia."

"Have you been drinking?"

Lara rushed at her. Before Portia could react, she had pulled aside her cloak. Lara shuddered dramatically at the flash of scarlet silk. "A scarlet dress for a scarlet woman," she intoned, voice trembling with loathing and excitement.

"Do not touch me."

"Oh, I'll touch you!" Lara cried, tearing at the cloak. "I'll touch you, all right," she said, tugging at the ties that held it about Portia's shoulders. "Take it off, take it off, and show us all what kind of woman you are. You should never have married my father. You did not deserve a man like that."

After a brief struggle the cloak fell to the floor.

She might as well have been naked, Portia thought, but stood stiffly, her chin up, as if their opinions meant nothing to her. "I will not forgive you for this," she said with quiet dignity.

Lara stared at her, eyes bulging, as though she had swallowed a whole fig. "Arnold," she gasped. "Tell her . . . tell her . . . "

In contrast to his wife, Arnold was perusing Portia as if she was a banquet that he wasn't certain he wanted to partake of. She remembered that for all his indolence, Arnold loathed weakness in others. And he would consider her feelings for Marcus a weakness and despise her for giving in to them.

"Lara is correct, Portia. You will ruin our family if this goes on. The queen will send you away. You know she cannot abide immoral behavior. A whiff of adultery and you will be banished to some godforsaken Scottish castle, or worse . . . to the colonies."

"How can I commit adultery when my husband is dead?" Portia mocked him.

Lara gasped in shock, hand clutched to her throat, but her eyes were glittering with excitement. "You brazen creature! Is that all you can say? What about my father's memory? His good name?"

"He lives on in the hearts and minds of the people," Arnold reminded her, as if she needed reminding. "They will never forgive you if you betray him. Can you live with that, Portia? Can you look all those who love you in the eye and tell them you no longer care? And for what, a tumble with a man like Marcus Worthorne?"

"You don't know—"

"Of course I *know!*" His face twisted in disgust. "He's been sniffing around you for months. That little note at the opera, and the tryst in the Campaign Room—did you think I didn't know about that?" he said with a flash of amusement at her ignorance. "His heroics at the unveiling of Lord Ellerslie's statue. No gentleman would behave in such a way, bringing shame and embarrassment to you and your family. I thought you'd come to your senses then, but obviously you prefer cavemen to gentlemen. The time has come, Portia, to put an end to this nonsense once and for all."

"I don't know what you're talking about," Portia said stubbornly, her face white. She didn't know whether she was humiliated or furious, or both. What he had

said was true, but it was a truth stripped of all the goodness and warmth and joy. It was Arnold's view of the
world, and it chilled her to the bone. "Get out," she
demanded. "Get out now!"

"Oh? And what will happen to your dear mother?"
Arnold went on evenly.

"What do you mean?"

"Well, I would imagine you would not want to risk
anything happening to her, Portia. You've managed to
keep the truth hidden very well, until now. What if it
is discovered that she is going slowly mad? I've heard
about her antics. She'll have forgotten her own name
soon. What will people say if she hurts someone?" He
smiled.

"My mother would never hurt anyone!"

"Wouldn't she? I know some very good doctors who
would disagree with you and insist on locking her up."

First shock and then fury seethed within her. Any
thought she had of trying to reason with him vanished
in an instant. "You can't do that. I won't let you."

"But Portia, how can you stop me? Especially if you
are embroiled in a scandal and the queen sends you
away? Your mother will be left behind with us."

He was threatening her! Arnold, whom she'd always
thought of as a colorless and bland personality, was
threatening her. Did he mean it? She looked into the
pale ice of his eyes and knew that he did.

For a moment she felt like crumpling, sinking down
into one of the overstuffed chairs, but she wouldn't do

that. They had no right to threaten her. Her life was her own, no matter how they tried to manipulate it.

"You are wrong," she said. "Whatever I do or have done has nothing to do with you. You have no right to talk to me as if I was a child, and I forbid it."

"You forbid it?" Lara said. "You, the parson's daughter? No, Portia, it is Arnold and I who will give the orders here. We will make certain you are obedient, Portia. From now on there will be no breath of scandal attached to your name."

"What?" Portia managed a laugh. "Don't tell me you are going to be my prison guards?"

No one else laughed.

"We're moving in with you for a little while," Arnold informed her in that chilling tone of voice. "Just to keep an eye on things. You have been unwell, dear Portia, and naturally as your loving relatives we are concerned for your well-being."

"My mother—"

"Your mother is a crazy old woman," Lara said with scorn.

"As I said, I know several very prominent doctors," Arnold went on. "A word in the right ear, Portia, and I could create enough doubt for questions to be asked at the highest level."

Lock her up.

"That would never happen. I would not let it." But she was feeling all the frustration of a mouse caught in a trap.

"Oh dear me, yes, Portia, it would. And it will if you do not do as you are told from this moment on."

This time she didn't answer, although she was certain he read her feelings in her eyes.

"Ah, you want to kill me, don't you? You're showing more spirit tonight than I've seen in you for a long while."

"Arnold, let her go," Lara said sharply.

Arnold paused, just to defy her, and then shrugged and stepped away from the door. "Go to bed, Portia. We will see you in the morning."

Portia looked from one to the other. Lara didn't return her gaze but stared fixedly at the drawing room clock, while Arnold kept his rigid smile. She supposed she could continue to argue. She could rant and rave like a madwoman, demanding they leave her home, but she was beginning to see that such tactics were useless.

Arnold meant what he said. He would have her poor mother locked up. Men had the power to do such things and she couldn't pretend otherwise, as much as she wished it so. The day was yet to come when in England women were treated as equals to their menfolk.

The only way out of this was to be calm and reasonable, to convince them they were mistaken about her unreliability. She must show them that she was as eager as they to be seen as the perfect Lady Ellerslie. And then, when they relaxed their guard . . . then she would send them far away from her house and those she loved.

"As you wish," she said lightly, rising to go to the door. "Good night."

But as she climbed the stairs she felt the hot sting of tears in her eyes. Tears of anger and hurt and misery. How dare they! All her life she'd been told what to do by others, and she'd done it, but this time . . . Yes, she knew she shouldn't have seen Marcus again, but she needed him. He helped make her feel alive. It was one thing for her to tell herself she was doing the wrong thing, it was another to be told by Lara and Arnold.

By the time she reached her bedchamber, the tears were pouring down her cheeks. Hettie was waiting for her, and when she saw that dear familiar face, she went into her maid's plump arms.

"There, there, *lieben*," Hettie soothed. "It's for the best."

It didn't occur to Portia to wonder how Hettie knew; Hettie always knew. Instead she asked herself how something that hurt so much could possibly be for the best. She knew her duty, she knew what was expected of her, and she had chosen that life over Marcus. Wasn't that enough? Did they have to punish her as well?

"Come now, let's get you into bed," Hettie was saying. "Everything will seem brighter in the morning."

"They are going to stay here."

"Oh dear," Hettie said, but continued to undress her, finally tucking her into her bed. "I'm sure once they see it really is over they will leave you be."

Portia closed her eyes, and after a moment the light dimmed and Hettie left her.

It really is over.

The words echoed in her head. She felt as if she had lost a part of herself. *Marcus is gone forever.* There was a sort of grief tearing her at insides, making her want to scream. With a cry, she turned over and pressed her face into her pillow, muffling the sounds coming from her throat. At last, exhausted, she fell into sleep.

Arnold could see that Lara was full of grim self-righteousness. He left her to enjoy it, and going to the table, poured himself a large brandy. Portia always kept the best brandy, just like her late husband, unlike the shoddy stuff Lara thought would do.

The affair with Marcus Worthorne had come to light much sooner than he would have liked, but he was confident they could keep it under wraps. At least for now. In fact it was imperative they do so, because of his own plans. He needed Portia to remain on good terms with the queen so he could use her to get close.

Poor Portia. That defiant, guilty look in her eyes. Her stubborn determination to deny all. She really was a magnificent woman. Still, he had no time to admire her. She was a tool to be used in his plot to kill the queen. Arnold did not experience emotional attachment—he did not allow himself to do so. He had given his life to his vocation, to his father's dreams of an England for the English, and win or fail, he would never be diverted from that road.

Chapter 20

Marcus had no intention of respecting Portia's decision. But there were things he had to do, and he wanted her to suffer for a little while at least. Before he acted, he wanted her to understand just how much she wanted and needed him, and, more important, to regret turning down his proposal.

So one week went by and then two, and though he felt as if he couldn't wait any longer, he did. He waited.

A few times he went up to Duval Hall, to oversee the repair of the window and the hiring of men to work on repairing the dikes and draining the land. Any money Uncle Roger may have had was spent before he died, but Marcus had a little of his own, left to him by his father, which he had invested quite sensibly. He wasn't as feckless as Sebastian believed.

So he worked and he planned and he waited.

"Are you still interested in Lady Ellerslie, Marcus?"

Francesca's bright voice brought him back from mulling over his bacon and eggs and coffee. He gave her a bleary look. Last night he had been out with some of his old comrades from the Hussars, which meant plenty of drink and dancers.

One of the dancers, he recalled, had been a sweet-faced woman with blue eyes and a rather engaging laugh . . . He sat up. Had he taken her to bed? Marcus grappled with his illusive memory. No, he thought, relieved. No, he hadn't. He remembered now. He'd bored the poor girl to tears with his declarations that there was only one woman in the world for him.

"Marcus!"

He jumped.

"I was speaking to you."

Marcus blinked. "What were you saying?"

She looked at him in despair. "I said, one of them goes everywhere with her. It's very odd. In fact it has been remarked upon. There were some of those scandalous little broadsheets being sold on the street corners yesterday. I kept one to show you."

She was on her feet, rummaging about in a drawer, and then handed him a dubious looking sheet of paper. His eye was caught by a rather good cartoon, although the ink had smudged.

He peered at it more closely.

A blond woman with a pained and haughty expression stood in a drawing room, while a man and a woman in police uniforms were handcuffed to either side of her. He recognized that woman's large nose and the man's flop of hair. It was meant to be Lara and

Arnold Gillingham. And there, seated on her throne behind them, was the plump little queen, her chin resting on her hand as she gazed pensively at a portrait of the late Lord Ellerslie.

"Read it," said Francesca impatiently.

"'The prisoner is here to see you, Your Majesty./ Good, good, not enjoying herself too much, I trust?/No fear of that, Your Majesty.'" Marcus blinked. "What is this? Good Lord, I said something like that!"

"They go with her everywhere—the Gillinghams, I mean. Perhaps she's ill. I thought you might know."

"*I* don't, but perhaps *they* do," Marcus murmured.

Suddenly he could feel the blood begin to pound through his veins, as if his determination, in limbo for weeks now, had returned to life. He straightened in his chair, staring about him, while Francesca observed him with amused concern.

"Where's Seb?"

"He's at Worthorne Manor. You know that, Marcus. He said good-bye to you yesterday."

"Did he?"

"He told you to stay out of trouble."

But Marcus wasn't listening. He looked down at the cartoon again, and his instincts told him that it was Portia who was in trouble. It was time to throw himself onto the dais again—metaphorically speaking—and this time he wouldn't allow anyone to stop him.

"Marcus, what *is* the matter with you . . . ? Marcus!" she wailed as he shot to his feet and hurried from the room, his coffee cup left teetering. His footsteps pounded across the hall and the front door slammed.

Apart from the evening meal, Portia found it easier just to keep to her room. If she went downstairs, she had to share the house with Lara and Arnold, and although she had brazened it out at first, playing the heroine, now she was weary of Lara's venomous stares and Arnold's superior smiles.

It wasn't that she cared what they thought of her, but she was angry that they should think they could treat her this way. Oh, she understood that they believed she would bring disgrace on them and were looking out for their own interests. They saw her as the golden goose, and couldn't afford to let her run off with the gander. But they had no right to bully her and keep her prisoner in her own home, and worse, accompany her everywhere she went. There seemed no escape, but at least she could close the door to her bedchamber and pretend to be alone.

And now her mother, whom she was trying to save from a terrible fate, had taken to coming downstairs and sitting with them after dinner. "So nice to have these little family gatherings," she said to Portia, clinging to her arm. "It reminds me of when your dear father was alive. Was he your father? I can't remember . . . "

"Can't you, Mrs. Stroud?" Arnold said with that nasty smile.

"Did these family gatherings include lessons on morality?" Lara added, forcefully dissecting her chicken pie.

Portia didn't find much joy in dining at home anymore, but her pride forced her to continue doing it. Besides, she didn't want them to become suspicious. She'd been working on a plan to spirit her mother away, but she needed an accomplice and as yet could think of no one she trusted enough to resist Arnold's threats and to keep silent.

Apart from Marcus.

She sighed; she could hardly ask him. Especially as she had not seen him since the night they said good-bye at Aphrodite's. Their last night. He could be anywhere now. He'd promised he was going to Norfolk to make a life there, and she had believed him, but that was before he asked her to marry him. Deep down, Portia wondered whether she ever truly believed he was going away for good. Perhaps it had suited her to believe, so she could use it as a sop to her conscience and agree to one more night in his arms.

She still dreamt of him. It was worse than ever. She wondered if she would ever forget him or whether she would carry his touch, his kisses, his smile with her to her grave. When she remembered how she'd told him to marry someone else if he wanted a wife, she shuddered at her own hasty words. Marcus with another woman was beyond bearing, and yet she couldn't have him herself. She *couldn't*.

Abruptly, she rose and went to stand at her window,

looking out. She was due to attend a function tomorrow night—a grand ball at St. James's Palace—and she should be planning her outfit. Once upon a time she would have looked upon such things as of the utmost importance. She'd felt it was her duty to represent her husband to the best of her ability, that everything she did reflected upon him and his memory. Now, all she could think of was Arnold and Lara and their treatment of her, and the undeniable fact that she was a prisoner.

Even Hettie wasn't the same, although she could not put her finger on exactly what was different about her faithful maid. But she had noticed the way Hettie watched her, as if waiting for something to happen.

She remembered all the times she had spent with Marcus, but in particular remembered that day at St. Tristan. There was a golden glow about the memory, like a heavenly experience, and she wished she could run down the stairs and out of the house and catch the train to Little Tunley. She wished it was possible to go back in time.

Perhaps, just perhaps, if she had her choice over again, she might stay at St. Tristan and never come back.

"I have sent the lavender shot silk to be pressed," Hettie said, bustling into the room. "The one with the *à la grecque* neckline and three flounces on the skirt. It is elegant but quite plain for a ball dress, and Her Majesty always admires you in lavender. You should wear it to the grand ball, my lady."

"She thinks it makes me look sallow," said Portia wryly.

Hettie smiled. "You're very beautiful, my lady. Even queens are women, underneath their crowns."

Portia sat down before the mirror, while Hettie picked up the wreath that was to sit on her hair. The hairdresser would come, and her fair tresses would be caught up in elaborate twists of curls to one side, while at the back it would be plaited and held off her nape with jeweled combs.

"Victoria professes to love me, but I don't think she does. Not really. It was Lord Ellerslie she loved. I am a reminder of him, and she sees herself as the guardian of his memory."

Hettie's eyes were downcast as she concentrated on her task, trying the wreath in various positions. "You have never spoken like this before, my lady."

"I have never felt like this before."

"Don't let the Gillinghams hear you, *lieben.*"

Portia used her key to open her ebony jewelry box inlaid with mother of pearl. "Don't worry, I will mind my tongue." She chose her favorite black mourning locket with a silhouette of Lord Ellerslie upon the front and a lock of his hair inside. "I want Mrs. Stroud to take a holiday."

"Oh?" Hettie raised her eyebrows.

"For her own sake she needs to go away. If only she had kept in touch with the people she knew before, when we lived in the New Forest, but she dropped them all when we came to London." Her mother had been so full of Portia's triumph, she believed herself above her old friends. Now she was in need of them and it was too late. Even if they could help her, Portia doubted they would. There was Great-aunt Cecily, of course, who lived in Cambridge. Cecily would enjoy taking Mrs. Stroud in, if only to be able to constantly remind her of how far she had fallen. Portia knew her mother would not enjoy such reminders, but could beggars be choosers?

"Cambridge might be somewhere safe," Portia murmured to herself. "I wonder if it is possible . . . ?"

"Is *Frau* Stroud in need of somewhere safe?" Hettie whispered, meeting her eyes in the glass. "Why? I don't understand."

Portia hesitated. But despite her strangeness of late, Hettie was still one of the few people she loved and trusted. Briefly she explained the threatening conversation she'd had with Arnold and Lara the night they'd found her in the scarlet dress.

"*Mein Gott*! I did not know. I am sorry, *lieben*, I did not know . . . "

"Why should you?" Portia sighed.

"Deed would help us, my lady," Hettie said thoughtfully. "He does not approve of the Gillinghams. And your mother's maid is very loyal. Once we have got her out of the house, we could take her to this safe place in Cambridge."

"Yes, Hettie, you are right. I will speak to Deed. We

must be ready. If a chance presents itself, then we must act without delay. It might be the only one we get."

"We should have a sign, my lady. A word that will tell us both that the time to act has come."

Portia thought for a moment. "It must be something that cannot be mistaken for anything else." And then, "I know. Sari!" she announced with a conspiratorial smile. "I will say 'sari' and you will know that our plan is about to commence."

It felt good to have a plan, to be doing something at last. She would save her mother from Arnold's spite, and then she would set about saving herself.

Marcus was walking. He'd been to Half Moon Street, where the Thorne Detective Agency was located, and the stroll had done him good, blown away the cobwebs. He had much to think about.

In fact, he felt more invigorated than he had for weeks. Alive. He hadn't realized how far he'd sunk into gloom until now. Although he'd refused to accept Portia's decision, he allowed himself to lose his impetuosity. He hadn't exactly fallen into a sulk, but was only human and wanted her to suffer for hurting him. Now he understood that he had been waiting for something to happen, some trigger to set things moving once more.

He wanted her. He needed her. He might even love her, although, never having been in love, he couldn't be sure of it. Was that why he had asked her to marry him in that uncharacteristically clumsy manner, because he was in love with her? Well, whatever the reason for his bizarre behavior, he knew one thing. She was in need of his help and he meant to rescue her.

Martin O'Donnelly, when they spoke a moment ago, had eyed him with a wariness that made him wonder if he looked as wild as he felt. But as usual, Martin had come up with the goods.

"The Gillinghams are living with her," he said. "It could be due to concern for her health, but I don't think it is. Mrs. Gillingham has been heard to say some very unkind things to her stepmother."

"I can imagine. Find out her engagements for the next few weeks, Martin. I may want to bump into her—accidentally of course."

"The Gillinghams always accompany her, sir. You may find it difficult to get close without them overhearing."

"I'll worry about that." He frowned. "Gillingham. The name seems strangely familiar to me. Was there some scandal long ago?"

Martin smiled. "It just so happens I know all about that, sir. Mr. Arnold Gillingham's father is the one you're thinking of. He was a scholar. Believed in the purity of the English race and that all our current problems stem from 'contamination' of that purity, as he put it, sir. Anyone from the Normans onward were interlopers in his eyes." The detective's Irish accent seemed to grow stronger, as if in protest.

"I do remember, Martin. He did something unforgivable, didn't he?"

"He insulted the king. Called him a German something or other, and said he had no right to sit on the throne of England. He was banned from court, sent into the country. Evidently, he went completely mad. He died while trying to chase off some Italian stonemasons who were repairing the local church, insisting they were contaminating good English architecture. Arnold Gillingham is the son of this man, and according to gossip, has much the same sympathies. Word is, he will only employ servants with what he considers 'proper' English names, which meant he had to sack his French cook."

"I see. No wonder I don't like him."

"Not many people do, sir."

"Then the sooner I get Lady Ellerslie away from him, the better, Martin," Marcus said with a smile. "She'll be so grateful she might even decide to stay with me. Does that sound like a plan?"

Martin wisely did not voice the doubts that flickered in his eyes. Indeed, Marcus didn't want to hear them. Recklessly, he was set on his course, and nothing was going to stop him.

Chapter 21

Dressing in the lavender shot silk for the grand ball at St. James's Palace took ages, but by the time she was finished, even Hettie, who was as particular as she about these matters, nodded her approval. "You look *elegant*, my lady," she said impulsively. "You look like your old self."

Portia smiled, turning from side to side and examining her reflection in the long mirror. The dress was very wide in the skirt and relatively plain, and although the *à la grecque* neckline was low, it was not immodestly so. Her new slippers were a little tight but she would not be dancing, so it hardly mattered. Yes, she looked well enough, but as for her old self . . .

"I don't feel like my old self, Hettie. I feel like a ghost of my old self. Something seems to be broken inside me."

"Time is all you need," Hettie reassured her anxiously. "Everything will settle down, in time."

"I hope you're right. I keep asking myself why I am

still here. All the little things I took pleasure in now seem like chores. Perhaps I am losing my mind like my mother, and Arnold will have me locked up."

Hettie was growing agitated, as if the conversation had taken a turn she did not like. "Lady Ellerslie, you will be late."

"And I mustn't be late, must I? There are too many people who will be displeased with me. I must be a good little general." She was being strange and bitter, and Hettie went to move away from her. Portia clasped her maid's hands and tried to reassure her with a smile. "Forgive me. I hardly know what I am saying. Thank you for making me look elegant."

Hettie nodded, the tension leaving her. "It is my pleasure to serve you, my lady. I will come with you to the coach, in case you need help arranging your skirts."

Portia put on a brave face, but at the head of the stairs she almost turned and ran when she looked down and saw that Arnold was waiting for her. She was weary of this; the sooner it was over with, the better. Still grasping one of Hettie's hands, a sudden thought occurred to her, and she took a chance. "Hettie will come with me tonight," she said loudly. "There is really no need for you to bother yourself, Arnold."

"It is no bother," he insisted with his cold smile.

"Nevertheless, Hettie will come. I may need help managing my skirts and she will be much more useful at that than you."

Their eyes met, Arnold's watchful, and then he

smirked. "As a matter of fact I have another engagement, Portia. I was about to tell you I thought you were well enough to go on your own, but now you've put it into my mind you're right; Hettie can go with you."

If it was a victory, he'd taken it away from her. She felt she should be angry but she was just relieved that she'd be spared Arnold's company. And then she realized.

This was their chance. This was the moment they had been preparing for.

"Fetch your cloak, Hettie," she instructed, turning to face her maid, her face stiff with the effort to appear unconcerned. "The carriage will be here in a moment. Don't forget my sari."

Hettie's startled eyes fixed on hers. "Yes, of course, my lady. I will not forget."

Now it was up to Hettie to put their agreed-upon plan into action.

Slowly, Portia descended the staircase, careful in her voluminous skirts, telling herself that she must not give herself away. Sometimes it was as if Arnold could read her mind . . .

"Where's Lara?" Portia asked.

Arnold was leaning negligently against the newel post, still watching her. "I believe my wife is instructing your cook in the correct way to serve the soup. Don't worry, when you've come to your senses, Lara will come to hers."

"Will she?" Portia lifted an eyebrow. "I think she is enjoying herself far too much."

He laughed. "She *is* crowing a little loudly, isn't she? You can't blame her for making the most of the opportunity; she's hated you for years."

Portia gave him a curious look. There was something about him she had never liked. A slyness. As if he knew things, or thought he did, that others didn't. She opened her mouth to tell him exactly what she thought of his behavior toward her, then remembered that he could change his mind and come with her after all, which would ruin everything. She remained silent.

But he knew. "You loathe me, don't you, Portia? That's because I am better than you. Although I am a close observer of men and women, and it never surprises me how low they can sink in the sewer of greed and desire, I do not indulge in such depravity myself."

"Oh, are you above all that?" she mocked.

"I am," he replied without any irony whatsoever.

"I don't believe you."

His eyes went cold. "You will understand one day, Portia."

"My lady!" Hettie hurried down the stairs with her cloak, looking flustered.

Portia looked up into Arnold's eyes. "I will never understand you, Arnold, and I do not want to. I despise you."

She turned away before he could answer, moving toward Deed, who had just appeared from the depths of the house to take his place by the door. "Deed," she said in a low voice, "you have your instructions? I believe this is the evening we previously discussed."

"I remember, my lady. Miss Hettie has already mentioned it to me. And may I just say, it has always been my greatest pleasure to serve you, my lady."

Aware that Arnold was watching, she nodded, as if their conversation was nothing out of the ordinary. "And the coachman is aware of his orders?"

"He is, ma'am. All is in hand."

Behind him, Arnold had straightened and was now watching her leave.

She no longer had to wonder whether he hated her. It was written in his face.

With a shiver, Portia hurried toward her coach.

"Sshh, ma'am, you'll wake everyone up," Mrs. Stroud's maid whispered, one strong arm about the older lady as she helped her down the back stairs.

"But where are we going?" Mrs. Stroud wailed. "It's dark, look, I can see the stars."

"Well, you're going on holiday, ma'am, aren't you lucky? Mr. Deed has arranged for the coach to come and fetch you in the mews at the back. Won't that be nice? And then you're off."

Mrs. Stroud thought about that. "I'll miss my dinners with what's-his-name," she said. "And my daughter . . . is she coming, too?"

"Some of the way, I believe."

"Can't I say good-bye?"

"No. It's a secret, you see. No one must know."

"Ah." Mrs. Stroud put a finger to her lips, her shawl

slipping off her shoulder. She was still wearing her nightgown under a hastily donned dress, and her gray hair was plaited for bed, with a nightcap jammed on top. The maid had brought a rug for warmth and given her charge a dose of laudanum to "send her off" for the journey.

Lady Ellerslie wouldn't approve of that, but Hettie had told her to do it all the same. They couldn't risk her having one of her screaming fits, or running back into the house for some reason or other just because she'd got some mad notion into her head.

If Arnold caught them, they would all suffer. They were terrified of him, even Deed. There was something not right about his eyes. No, all in all, Mrs. Stroud was the lucky one.

Hettie had followed Portia outside to the Ellerslie coach, her voice breathless with fright and excitement.

"Mrs. Stroud be will waiting for us in the mews at the back. Her maid and I had to bundle her up and she's still half asleep, but she'll be there, *lieben*."

"Then we must fetch her, and when you have set me down at the grand ball at St. James's, you will take her on to Cambridge. I will ask to borrow one of Victoria's coaches to return me home. With luck, Arnold will not find out she's gone until tomorrow at dinner, and by then she will be safe. I don't care what he says to me, I will not tell him, and I will insist it was all my idea—as indeed it was."

"I wish you could go, too, my lady, and escape the Gillinghams. I don't like to think of you facing Arnold alone. He will be very angry."

Lord, yes. She hid her shudder, speaking calmly.

"If my mother is gone, Arnold and Lara will not be able to threaten me with locking her up. They will pack up and return to Curzon Street. The sooner they are out of my house, and my life, the better," Portia added in a low, angry voice.

"I agree, ma'am." Hettie's reply was heartfelt.

"Once they are gone, Hettie, I swear to you I will never have them back! Never again will I harbor treachery in my own house."

They fell silent, each thinking their own thoughts. The coach was traveling along the quiet street that ran out of the square and was moving slowly, ready to take the turning into the mews, when suddenly there was a clatter of horses' hooves and a loud shout. The vehicle lurched and came to a stop. Outside there were voices, and movement on the box where the driver was seated.

"What is it? Have we had an accident?" Portia said, trying to see out of the window.

The door was flung open and a masked intruder climbed up into the coach. The door closed behind him with a sinister thud.

For a brief moment the lamp illuminated him.

He wore black, every inch of him, only his eyes showing through the small square between the scarf tied about his mouth and nose, and the hat jammed on his head. Even so, there was something familiar about him. And then he leaned over and blew out the lamp and it was pitch-dark.

"Out. You. Servant," he growled.

"Good God!" Portia sounded more angry than afraid. He was ruining their plans. "Do you know who I am?"

"I won't leave my mistress," Hettie burst out.

The man groaned. "Nothing is ever simple with you, is it?"

"Marcus?"

"Of course," Marcus said softly. "I've come to save you, my lady. Whether you like it or not."

She shook her head vehemently. "No, Marcus, no! You don't understand! I will be ruined!"

"Exactly," he said. "You need to be ruined. It's the best thing for you."

"You must not!" she cried, her voice rising. "My mother. They will harm my mother."

There was a moment when no one spoke. She could hear her own breathing, harsh and strained. And then he said, "Your mother? Why should they harm your mother?"

It was Hettie who answered.

"Mr. Arnold has threatened to put my lady's mother into a . . . a place where they'll lock her up."

"Yes," Portia whispered, "it's true."

"So you're telling me I can't kidnap you because it

would mean your mother will be punished?" Incredibly, he laughed.

"They're using her as a sort of hostage to my good behavior," Portia said. "I've been trying to think of some way to get her out of Grosvenor Square, They watch us all the time. Tonight is the first time Arnold isn't accompanying me, so we planned to make the most of it."

"You could have asked me to save her," Marcus said mildly. "I'd have done it."

"Would you?" She tried to see his eyes but it was too dark. "Never mind, we have made our own arrangements."

He reached out and opened the coach door. "Come on, we have to hurry. I have another coach waiting on the other side of the gardens."

"No, I told you, I can't. My mother is waiting. We are going to pick her up in the mews and my coachman is taking her on to Cambridge."

"Cambridge? Why Cambridge?"

"My great-aunt lives there."

"They'll know that, won't they? They'll have her back within hours. No, I'll rescue your mother. I'm much better at it than you. But you must come with me."

"I'm going to a ball at St. James's," she wailed.

"And very beautiful you look, too."

Portia shot him a desperate look as he reached for her arm, assisting her down to the ground in her voluminous skirts. This close she could feel his warmth, smell his masculine scent, and as usual it was having its effect on her. Despite the situation she found herself in, she was glad to see him. Not because he said he would rescue her mother, but because he was Marcus.

"You promise you will help me if I come with you? This isn't a trick?"

"I promise." His eyes slanted wickedly as he smiled beneath his disguise.

"You're as bad as Arnold," she murmured.

"I'd be insulted, if I believed you meant it," he said mildly. "He's the villain and I am the hero. There is a vast difference. Do *you* promise?"

Did she have a choice? She did. But the need to say yes was overwhelming. "Oh . . . very well! But what of my own coach? They can't go back yet, Arnold will know."

"I'll send them to the ball anyway, in case someone notices. If the coach is there, it will appear that you must be, too."

Portia marched toward the dark bulk of his coach, her lavender skirts belling around her, her too-tight slippers pinching.

Suddenly, Hettie's steps came pattering behind them and she tugged at Marcus's cloak. "Take me!" she pleaded.

He turned to stare at her. "Certainly not."

"But I must come. My lady needs me. How will she manage without me? I—I have to come with her. She will be cross if you leave me behind, and you don't want her to be cross."

"Bloody hell," he muttered, trying to free himself from her frantic grip.

"Let her come with us," Portia called from the coach. "Arnold will punish her if I'm not here."

"Please, Mr. Worthorne, I have to come, too."

He threw up his hands. "Get in, then, but I'll have no complaints from either of you."

When they were both seated in the coach, he gave the driver his altered instructions and they set off. The mews were reached by a lane behind the Ellerslie house, but Marcus had told his coachman to stop at the head of that lane. Now he climbed down, peering into the shadows.

"She's waiting down here?"

"Yes."

"All right, but if you disappear while I'm gone I will find you and kidnap you all over again," he said threateningly.

Portia shrugged, hiding the insane urge to smile. "I have no intention of going anywhere."

He waited a moment more, as if expecting more resistance, and then with an exasperated curse strode off into the darkness.

While he was gone, Portia gave some thought to her situation. Bizarre as it was, it seemed to her that being kidnapped was actually the best solution. Hadn't she just been thinking how she wished she could run away? Concerns for her mother had prevented her, but if Marcus would deal with that, there was nothing to stop her. Apart from her own sense of duty.

If Marcus kidnapped her, the choice between duty and escape was made for her. There would be nothing more for her to worry about. Apart from what he might do next.

She could hear her mother's complaints getting closer, interspersed by Deed's reassurances and Marcus's low rumble.

The coach door opened and her mother peered up at her, wrapped in a shawl and still wearing her nightcap. Her eyes were wild and accusing.

"Portia! This gentleman says we are going for a ride in his coach. What on earth can he mean?"

"He means what he says, Mama. We are all going on a holiday."

"In the middle of the night?" But her mother allowed herself to be assisted into the coach.

"The middle of the night is the best time to start a holiday," Portia said brightly. "Then when you get there, it will be a nice surprise."

Her mother settled into a corner, while Hettie made a fuss, tucking a rug about her and murmuring reassurances; her eyes began to close. Then the door was slammed and Marcus flung himself back in his own seat as the horses moved forward with a jolt. A moment later the vehicle was rattling out into the busy London streets.

Portia waited until she could bear the tension no longer. "Arnold wasn't—"

"No, he wasn't. He isn't. He is completely unaware that we are gone. Your butler seems to be very competent. By the time Arnold *is* aware, it will be too late, the trail will have gone cold, and he will have absolutely no idea where to find us. Any of us," he added with a significant nod toward Mrs. Stroud.

Portia pondered this. "Good," she breathed.

"I'm glad you approve, my lady."

Her slippers were too tight and she eased them off under cover of her lavender skirts. What would Victoria think when she didn't arrive at the ball? How shocking! There would be a scandal. Would they suspect Marcus? Would they think she had run away with him like some naïve young debutante? She hoped they did not. And yet the very idea of running away with Marcus gave her a shivering sense of excitement.

As if he'd read her mind, he said, "You have no control over what's happening to you, Portia. You're being kidnapped, remember."

Again she found the notion oddly comforting.

"Where are we going?" she said after a moment.

"Duval Hall," Marcus replied.

She'd heard the name before, but couldn't think where. Maybe Minnie Duval had mentioned it—the family home? She allowed her eyes to close. Marcus was seated across from her, watching over her, and he would take care of everything. Portia felt safe for the first time in weeks.

* * *

Arnold expected to find the household sleeping when he finally came home around two o'clock the following morning. Instead, lights were blazing and Lara was up and smelling of sherry.

He'd spent a productive few hours with his friends, while he ate a good dinner and enjoyed a cigar with his brandy.

"I need to be very close to her when I pull the trigger," he'd told the conspirators. "There's no point in lurking in Hyde Park or hiding in a crowd of nannies and children and hoping for a lucky shot. I want to be certain."

"Are you able to get that close to her?"

He thought of Portia. "Yes. Yes, I will be able to get close enough."

Their glances reflected a mixture of admiration and fascination. Arnold was so certain in his own mind that he was doing the right thing, they thought him courageous and reckless beyond their understanding. But he knew that the queen must die. One could lobby and make speeches and write letters for a lifetime and get nowhere, but this action would blaze a trail around the world, and the assassin and his cause would be instantly famous and never forgotten. His father, if he were still alive, would have been proud of him. His father had always been his model and hero, and those who had scorned him and sent him away because of his beliefs would be sorry.

He had lifted his glass. "To the cause!"

They lifted their own, echoing him.

And now Lara was babbling at him about Portia and her mother missing. Eventually he got the story from a very worried-looking Deed.

It seemed that after Portia went to the ball at St. James's, Lara had retired. The next thing she knew, one of the housemaids was shaking her and saying that Lady Ellerslie hadn't come home and neither had her maid. And then, when they looked in on Mrs. Stroud, thinking she might know what had happened, they found that her bed had been vacated and she was gone, too.

Arnold knew he'd been outwitted. He wondered how, a short while ago, he could have been king of the world, and now . . . he would be a laughingstock among his fellow conspirators. Or worse, they would consider him a danger to their plans!

He would not have it.

Arnold swore that Portia would pay for this. No matter how long he had to wait, he would be patient and find her. And then, by God, she would be very sorry.

Chapter 22

Portia was dreaming again. She was in a boat sailing on the blue ocean beyond St. Tristan. The sky was bright above her and someone was holding her in his arms and she hadn't a care in the world. It was only when the boat hit a hole in the road and rocked dangerously that she realized she was actually in a coach traveling through the night. Running away from everything she'd become with the man she hardly knew. The man who was her lover, or had been before they said good-bye.

She sat up, wide-awake.

Marcus was *kidnapping* her. He'd admitted it. He was acting against the law of the land. If Arnold found out, if Victoria found out, he'd be arrested and taken back to London. What was the sentence for something like this? Years in prison, at the very least, if the public did not tear him apart first for daring to lay a hand on their angel in widow's weeds.

What had she been thinking of to let him do this?

"Bad dream?"

He was awake, too, leaning back in his corner, legs stretched out and head tilted to rest against the padded leather. He looked sleepy, as if he was barely awake. The dawn light was slanting through the window, shining across his handsome face and tussled dark hair. He looked so perfect that for a moment she couldn't speak. She wanted to remember him like this; her unreliable, reckless, untrustworthy hero.

The temptation was to climb onto his knee and wind her arms about his neck and kiss him. To forget everything but the physical excitement he created in her. She glanced at her mother and Hettie, both sleeping, to reassure herself she wasn't alone with him. Just in case she did something silly.

"You can't do this." That was better. She sounded firm and determined; a woman in charge of her destiny.

"Can't do what?" He didn't seem in impressed with her tone.

"Kidnap me."

"I already have." He closed his eyes again and folded his arms. "And I'm enjoying every moment of it." One eye opened. "You were fine with it a moment ago, why have you changed your mind?"

"I was thinking—"

He groaned.

"Marcus, the consequences are too grave. Remember what happened when you climbed onto the dais at Green Park? And this is so much worse. I can't let you take such a risk with your life and your freedom. I don't know how I ever imagined it would be all right to allow it."

"Portia, Portia . . . " he sighed. "That is why you are being kidnapped . . . abducted . . . whatever you want to call it. So that whether or not I take a risk isn't up to you. I'm not one of your responsibilities or your charities. Please, don't waste your guilty conscience on me. You didn't ask me to take you away from London, I did it all by myself, and I'll face up to any repercussions, all by myself."

"But Marcus—"

"Do you want to be kissed?" His eyes were wide open now and the devil was in them.

"What do you mean?" she whispered uneasily.

He unfolded his arms. He sat up.

"No, no, I don't want to be kissed!" she said, shrinking back and drawing her cloak tightly around her, as if it would protect her.

He looked into her eyes a moment more, and whatever he saw in them made him smile in that arrogant, male way. "Then hush," he said gently, "or I will have to ravish you."

Marcus was pretending to sleep. It seemed the easiest option. If she saw he was awake, he'd be peppered with questions and recriminations from his lady love. He'd tried to reason with her. After all, he had saved her mother, and as the considerate kidnapper he was, he was bringing her maid, despite the fact that it made it very difficult for him to seduce Portia.

But she wouldn't listen.

Until he threatened to do to her the very thing he was longing to do. Kiss her.

He smiled.

"I saw that," she said triumphantly. "You're not asleep at all."

"We'll be changing horses soon."

"Aren't we going to stop anywhere for longer than a few moments?"

"Obviously you don't get kidnapped very often, Portia. It isn't usual for kidnapper and hostage to stop for a nice meal and a bed at an inn during their flight."

"They will come after me," she insisted raggedly. "You don't know what Arnold is like, how single-minded he can be when it comes to getting his own way. You'll be thrown in gaol."

"It won't be the first time," he reminded her.

She stared at him. "Why are you doing this, Marcus? You agreed it was over between us. We said good-bye."

"I changed my mind," he drawled.

"You must let me go. Please. If we're found together, they will arrest you. They may even hang you!"

There was such anxiety and desperation in her voice that he was moved. But he wasn't about to change his mind. "Portia—"

Then Hettie piped up.

"What's there to go back to, *lieben*? The Gillinghams? The queen? They do not love you. But this one . . . this one *does*."

"Hettie," Portia groaned, "you wretch. Whose side are you on?"

"I am on your side," Hettie said firmly.

Momentarily outmaneuvered, Portia huddled in her corner and stared out of the window at the countryside slipping by. After a time Hettie began to snore gently.

"You'll be safe with me," Marcus said at last. "Hettie is right. I love you. I must. I've never felt like this before, not for any of the others."

"You're outrageous!" she gasped. "How many others?"

"Portia, I can make you happy. It's true you will no longer be the apple of the people's eye, but you'll be mine."

"I am wearing a ball gown, Marcus. I am wearing a locket containing my dead husband's hair. I have no luggage and no money. You can't take someone off the street without a hairbrush and a change of clothing and expect them to be happy."

"What locket?" he demanded, ignoring the rest.

She lifted it from between her breasts. He stretched out his hand, frowning. After a moment's hesitation, Portia undid the clasp and held it out to him.

She expected him to examine it and give it back, but instead he sprang across the intervening gap and snatched the locket, releasing the coach window just enough to toss it out.

"That's one less thing you have to worry about," he said triumphantly, his face a wicked smiling mask.

"Oh, Marcus!" Her voice shook with tears.

He groaned, and reaching out, lifted her into his arms. She squeaked, but he settled her onto his lap despite her voluminous skirts and the miles of shot silk. Her elaborately dressed hair tickled his chin. She didn't struggle, perhaps she was beyond it, but neither did she lie trustingly against him as he wished. Instead she sat stiffly, unwillingly, refusing to yield.

He spoke gently, holding her hands tightly in his. "Portia, he's gone and you're with me. I want to spend my life with you. Doesn't that mean more to you than a society that worships a lock of hair from a dead man, even if he was a hero? It's bloody morbid, Portia. You're young and beautiful; you should live your life to the full."

"With you?" she asked, blinking, trying to pull her hands away.

"Of course with me! Who else?"

"They'll find us."

"By then it'll be too late," he said smugly. "You'll be compromised."

"Marcus, you don't know what you're doing. You can't just act as you wish. There are rules. There are *laws*!"

He did know that. He understood the dangers of his actions and he accepted them. She was worth any risk. And like his aunt Minnie, he was an optimist who believed that if you trusted in yourself and your instincts, things had a way of sorting themselves out. He did trust in himself, he always had. Why couldn't she do the same?

"Why is my daughter sitting on that man's lap?" They'd woken Mrs. Stroud and she was staring at them with wild eyes.

Hastily, Portia slipped back into her own seat, her face bright red, expecting recriminations. But her mother had already forgotten.

"Where are we?"

Portia reached across to pat her hand. "We're nearly there," she assured her, relieved, and then went very still as it occurred to her that there was something very wrong indeed. Her head turned sharply and she stared at Marcus. "We should have reached Cambridge by now."

"We're not going to Cambridge. I told you that wouldn't do."

"Then . . . "

"We're all going to Duval Hall, you and your mother and your maid, and me."

"Duval Hall?" Mrs. Stroud demanded. "Where is that? Do I know it?"

"It's home," Marcus said with satisfaction and pride. He grinned. "We're going home."

Marcus's home was a flat, bleak landscape, much of it marshy with occasional sheets of still water. Hun-

dreds of birds filled the gray sky, and she could smell
the sea. It seemed alien and vast and empty of human
life, and yet strangely beautiful.

A house stood on an island before them. It looked as
if it had been formed from the land itself, a hotchpotch
of styles, some of them quite ancient, with a wall enclosing them all.

"Duval Hall," Marcus said with pride. "My home."

There was something very sinister about Duval Hall.
In fact it looked rather like a prison, Portia thought.
Had he brought her here to this place to lock her up?
She turned to her mother, intending to reassure her as
much as herself, and found Mrs. Stroud gazing about
with bright eyes, showing more interest than she had
during the entire journey.

The coach rattled across the stone causeway,
through the open gate in the wall, and into a cobbled
courtyard.

Inside the wall it was not so bleak, and the shelter it
gave allowed for a garden where there were even mature
trees growing. They might have entered another world
from the flat emptiness of sky and land outside.

As they climbed from the coach, weary and rumpled,
servants came hurrying to greet them, their smiles shy
and curious. They were pleased to see Marcus, she
could tell. "Young master," they called him, and he
gave them instructions as if it was perfectly natural for
him to take charge.

It surprised her.

This close, she could see that the house was being repaired. There was scaffolding erected against several sections of the exterior walls, with piles of bricks and mortar and all the mess of serious work taking place. Fallen masonry and roof tiles lay about the yard. Several men had stopped what they were doing to stare at the new arrivals, particularly at Portia in her lavender ball gown.

A shaggy-coated dog came running, barking, and flung itself against Marcus. He laughed and rumpled its ears, looking very much at home.

But then, he had already said this was his home. Not the old manor house in the New Forest, not London with all its pleasures, but here, on the edge of the sea, on the edge of the world.

Suddenly, Portia felt as if she didn't know Marcus at all.

"Are you coming inside?" He was holding out his hand to her.

She looked around. Hettie was already leading Mrs. Stroud in out of the cold wind and the threat of rain. There was no option but to go forth into that great gloomy house. Portia lifted her chin, pretending she was not afraid, her public mask in place. She gave him her fingers and, lifting her heavy, wide skirts with her other hand, allowed him to guide her over the hard cobbles in her thin satin slippers.

She would have remained silent the whole way, but it was the puddles that undid her. No matter how she tried, it was impossible to avoid them completely, and when her petticoats dragged in the mud for the fifth time, she could no longer hold her tongue.

"I don't suppose you have a seamstress and a clothing emporium in the neighborhood?"

He looked blank, and then shrugged. "I'm sure we'll find something. Does it matter?"

She would have said something sharp, but they were inside the hall now, and she was surprised into silence. It was not gloomy at all. There was a huge stained-glass window looming over the staircase, and the light cascaded through in a brilliance of reds, yellows, and blues.

"My uncle Roger was an artist in his own way," Marcus said at her side, pleased with her reaction. "He designed the window and oversaw its creation and its placement."

Portia gazed up, wide-eyed, and could see angels cavorting. "What does it mean?" she asked in a reverential voice.

"This was his idea of heaven." He leaned closer, his breath warm against her cheek, his lips temptingly close. "There was a section that was broken when I came, but I've had it repaired. You might find it especially interesting. I'll show you . . . later."

"My lady?"

The soft voice at her elbow startled her, and Portia looked down to see a short, plump woman with graying hair.

"This is Mercy, my housekeeper and cook," Marcus said with a smile.

"Mercy," Portia said, "I wish I could say I was happy to meet you."

There was a hush and then Mercy laughed. "I said that meself, forty year ago, but I wouldn't leave now for any money. You'll see. This place grows on you, my lady. And the young master here has such plans. This old place had died along with Master Roger, but he's brought it alive again, truly he has."

Marcus wore a smug look, and Portia refused to meet his eyes, thinking that would only encourage him.

"I'll take my lady up to her rooms now, sir," the housekeeper said. "They've been readied to your instructions."

"Thank you, Mercy."

Portia could feel him watching her all the way up the stairs, but she didn't turn back. She had a feeling he would consider that another victory.

Her rooms consisted of a bedchamber and a sitting room, both of which were clean but looking rather shabby. Dark paneling covered the walls and the floor was uneven from age, but still it had a great deal of charm. There were several vases of fresh flowers—the sort of flowers one usually found in hothouses and not growing on the marshes of Norfolk.

"He had those brought in specially." Hettie was already there, warming the sheets with hot coals in a pan.

"Did he? They're beautiful." Tears again. She forced them back, telling herself it was because she was tired.

"The bedding is new, too. You can rest," Hettie said. "You must be very tired, *lieben*."

"He buys me expensive flowers but I have no nightgown. I have no clothing or luggage. I am a prisoner here. How can I rest?" And she would not cry, she told herself furiously. Under no circumstances would she cry.

"You can rest because you are tired," Hettie replied comfortably.

"And now you have turned against me, too. How could you? You used to be always telling me how much you distrusted him, how he would ruin me, how he was a selfish, self-centered rake with—"

"I've changed my mind," Hettie interrupted blithely.

"But *why*?"

Hettie just looked secretive.

With a groan, Portia allowed Hettie to undress her, stripping her down to her chemise and drawers. Obediently, she climbed into the bed and rested her head back on the pillows. The scent of the flowers drifted across her.

"Where is my mother?" she remembered to ask.

"She has her own rooms, my lady. She seems happy enough. I don't think she knows what is happening, not really, but she isn't concerned. She has already told me twice that she likes Mr. Worthorne. He has wicked eyes, she says, and then she giggles like a girl."

"Oh Lord," Portia moaned, "not another one," and turned on her side.

She heard voices and some hammering outside, on the other side of the house, and then birdsong. The light shone in dappled patterns through the velvet curtains. Soon her whirling thoughts began to settle. Marcus had kidnapped her, she reminded herself, and there was nothing she could do.

Her eyes flickered and closed and she gave a great sigh.

And slept.

Chapter 23

By the time Portia woke it was late afternoon. The house was quiet and there was a light spatter of rain against the small windowpanes. She stretched and climbed out of the big, soft bed. Her stockinged toes curling on the floor, she made her way to the window and drew the curtain aside to look out.

The world beyond was awash with water. The sodden marshes were ruffled by rain droplets, and the slate gray sky was glowering. It was a bleak prospect, and yet there was a glimmer of sunlight on the horizon, and a man in a narrow boat was slipping through the channel between the reeds. He threw out a fishing net to trail through the water, the smoke of his pipe hanging about him in a cloud.

It was all so peaceful.

She felt as if something inside her opened up and soaked it in. Gradually the rushing in her ears and the thumping in her chest and that faint nausea in her stomach began to disappear. London was far away. Even if she'd wanted to explain herself to the queen, she couldn't. Marcus had taken matters out of her hands and out of her control. This was his home, and no matter what he said, in essence she was his prisoner.

She should be furious—she *was* furious! She wasn't a woman who looked to be saved by anyone other than herself. But she was also strangely excited by the prospect of being Marcus Worthorne's captive. He'd never hurt her. He was probably planning to make love to her, if she agreed to it.

Her skin warmed, tingled, at the thought of him touching her.

So much for it being over. Portia knew she wouldn't be able to keep up that pretense for long. She wanted him as much as ever, and all the more for being starved of him for so many weeks. But she wouldn't just roll over and let him take her. She would hold out as long as she could, for the sake of her pride.

She was still gazing out of the window when Mercy brought her a tray and asked her if she wished to come downstairs. "We dine early here in the country, but there is time for you to explore," she explained. "Duval Hall is the sort of place you can live in for years and still find something you've never seen before."

"Is Marcus here?"

"The young master is about, aye."

The term they used for him had annoyed her before, but strangely, it now it made her smile. Portia stretched her arms above her head and yawned, apologizing with a grimace.

"You're weary, my lady. Happens to city people when they come here. They don't realize how weary they are until they stop."

"Yes, perhaps you're right. Things have been rather fraught lately."

"You have a sip of tea while I find you something to wear. Later on you can have a nice long soak in a hot bath."

It sounded heavenly. Portia's eyes blurred and she wondered why she was being so emotional. "Thank you. *Is* there something to wear? I don't have any luggage."

"Master Roger had a trunk of clothing belonged to his wife. They're very old-fashioned, my lady, but none of us here care about that. It's what's inside the clothing, here," she touched her heart, "that's important."

Was there a hint in there? That appearances weren't so very important at Duval Hall? In such a bleak, isolated place there would be no room for posturing and pretense.

The tea was hot and sweet, and she drank it down as she waited. The sound of a bell began to toll out across the marshes, but try as she might, she could see no church or tower.

"What is that?" she asked Mercy when she returned with two strong men carrying a trunk. "The bell?"

"There's a fog coming in from the sea. It's to warn

anyone out in their boats or with a way to go home to start out now. The tower is on the other side of the house, my lady, which is why you can't see it."

"A fog."

"We call it a sea fret here. Thick as smoke they are, sometimes, and easy to get lost in. Now, here are the clothes I told you about. I'll let you have a look through them while I go and find your maid for you."

The trunk was old and marked, and when she opened it, a strong smell of lavender wafted out. Inside, the clothing was folded and packed with care, and as she drew out the first dress—flimsy yellow muslin— she realized they were in the Regency style of around forty years ago. Like the sari she had worn at Minnie Duval's, these were clinging fashions with waistlines under the breasts and skirts that dropped to the ankles without any gathers or tucks, and without the need for more than one narrow petticoat.

By the time Hettie slipped into the room, she had almost emptied the trunk. "Look!" she cried in amazement. "There are shoes and bonnets, too, and stockings and these dreadful old-fashioned corsets, and some very beautiful cashmere shawls."

"Hmm." Hettie cast her eye over the clothing spread on top of Portia's bed. "Does any of it fit you, *lieben*? That is the important thing."

"I think so. Or if not, they will only need some minor alterations."

"What of the slippers?"

"They are a little big, but I found some boots with laces that will be useful."

Hettie nodded, beginning to sort through the clothing herself with a professional air. "You should wear this one today. I will see that the rest are washed and pressed."

Portia tried to read her faithful maid's face. "Is it very bad here, Hettie? Shouldn't we have come?"

Hettie smiled. "No, it is not bad at all. It is not London, certainly, but I can make do. Mrs. Stroud does not seem to mind."

"Where is Mother? I haven't seen her since we arrived."

"She is with Mercy in the kitchen."

"In the kitchen?"

"She seemed perfectly happy, my lady, so I left her there." Hettie handed Portia a chemise, silk stockings, and a paper thin petticoat. "Here, these should do. Will you dress now?"

"I heard the bell ringing."

"The fog is coming in. If you go up into the tower you can see it creeping across the sea like an enormous fleece of wool. I would not go out in such a thing," she added with a shudder.

The dress, a pale turquoise, made her eyes look green. Apart from the scarlet silk, Portia had not worn vibrant colors for so long that it was strange to do so now, even though technically she was out of mourning. It was only to please the queen that she had remained in half mourning for so long. The style of the dress, accentuating her bosom and then falling in a narrow skirt to her ankles, was flattering, if strange, to one brought up on tight waists and wide skirts with many petticoats. She felt uncomfortable yet daring, as if she was walking about in her underwear.

The boots didn't exactly go with the dress, but with some padding in the toes, they fit comfortably enough, and she had her own cloak to wear over everything, for warmth and modesty. Hettie found a brush for her hair, and as there was no hairdresser, styled it simply in plaits, using the jeweled combs to keep it up.

"I will clean the lavender silk," Hettie muttered to herself, frowning at the mud stains around the hem. "You may need it."

Portia laughed, surprising herself. "I somehow don't think Duval Hall hosts many balls, Hettie."

"But you may need it when you return to London," her maid retorted.

Portia sighed. "London seems far away," she said.

There was a moment when her emotions could have dived, as a wave of memory and anxiety threatened to swamp her, but she pushed the past aside and rose above it. She was here now and she'd make the best of it. She might even enjoy herself.

"Come on, Hettie," she said firmly, and held out her hand. "Let's explore."

Chapter 24

❦

Marcus was working on a sluice gate out in the marsh. It was rusted open and he and his men—he'd hired several big strong lads from the village—were trying to close it. If the water could be kept from flooding what had once been a rich and productive field, it could eventually be reclaimed. He could be growing crops here by next spring.

Satisfaction filled him until he felt puffed up with it, like one of those red-faced, booted landowners who boasted about the size of their turnips and whom he used to laugh at when he was a lad. The image of himself in such a guise made him smile. *I've turned into Farmer Worthorne,* he thought with secret amusement. Who'd have thought it? Sebastian would have one of his laughing fits. But Minnie would understand; she would see what had attracted him to Duval Hall and why he wanted to stay.

There were tall weeds and marsh grasses growing in the channel beyond the sluice gate, clogging it up.

Under the influence of his new enthusiasm, Marcus had stripped off his shirt, and taking up one of the picks, had been intent on digging them out. The cold air on his bare skin, the sheer joy of doing something physical and useful, had gone to his head. His men, amused at first, changed their minds when they saw that this was no token effort by a feeble London gentleman.

Marcus was in earnest, and they admired him for it. They redoubled their own efforts. He could at that moment have led them anywhere, he thought, and they would have followed him.

"Sir."

He looked up, squinting through the lock of hair that had fallen in his eyes. One of his men was pointing toward the causeway. Two women were making their way on foot across it; one of them was Hettie, and the other . . . He peered more closely. It was Portia as he rarely saw her, her fair hair coming loose from its pins, her cloak flapping out behind her and disclosing a dress the color of a tropical ocean. A dress that looked more like a nightdress.

As always when he saw her, he wanted her. He expected he always would. But he'd come to accept that it was not that simple after all. He had brought her here to Norfolk—for her own sake, he told himself—but now that she was here, he wondered what he was going to do with her. His plan had been to keep her here. He'd imagined, in his willful ignorance, that she would grow fond of Duval Hall.

And fall in love with him.

But now, thinking of her under his roof, he began to doubt.

Would she begin to hate him and long for London and her expensive life and her high society friends? The sorts of things he could not give her, would probably never be able to give her. Portia's life was as different from this as the sun and the moon, and now his reckless action had all the potential to become a disaster for them both.

But he wasn't going to give up yet.

He knew very well that there *was* something he could give her that she wouldn't get anywhere else. Something she craved. Perhaps he should take this opportunity to remind her of it, and what she would be missing if she went back to London.

"Best pack up now," he called to his men, handing one of them his pick and wiping his hands on his breeches. "You'll be wanting to get home before the weather closes in." The air was already beginning to feel clammy; the fog could not be far away. He picked up his shirt, dusting it off, and with a smile deliberately slung it over his bare shoulder.

His men glanced at each other. "Master, are you going up there like that? In front of the ladies?"

He raised an eyebrow. "Certainly. Do you think I'm overdressed?"

They chuckled like schoolboys. Marcus left them, climbing up the bank and onto the track above the channel. The causeway was not far away, and he strode toward it, and Portia.

There was a misty stillness to the air, and Marcus knew it would get worse as the fog rolled in. He was on the causeway now, his long strides eating up the distance. They had seen him approaching and were waiting for him to reach them. He cast an already knowledgeable eye over the tide and saw that it was a way from full yet, although in another hour or two it would be lapping at the place they were standing.

Portia stood very still. Not many gentlemen, he supposed, strolled into her presence wearing breeches and boots and nothing else.

"My lady," he said, giving her his most formal bow, and lifting his head, met her eyes.

They were wide. Her gaze slid over him, while behind her Hettie held up a hand to her mouth to hide a smile.

"Marcus, you are half naked!"

He was fully aware of it, and that there was mud halfway up his boots and smeared on his breeches. But then he'd been digging, not strutting down Bond Street, and he was not ashamed of it.

"My shirt was damp," he said nonchalantly. "I didn't want to catch cold."

She looked at him suspiciously. "And this way you won't?" She began to fumble with the ties of her cloak. "Take this and put it on. The wind is bitter."

He reached out and closed his hand over hers, stilling her efforts. "I don't feel the cold. I'm hot-blooded, or so I'm told."

There was a flicker in her eyes as if she was remembering things she'd rather not. She looked away so he couldn't see, clutching the cloak about her like a suit of armor.

"If you die of a cold, then you will cheat the hangman at least," she said shrewishly.

He laughed, knowing she was trying to distract him from the fact that his body was affecting her just as it always did. She was fighting herself, trying to pretend she didn't want him to swing her up in his arms and take her to his bed.

"I'm not going to die, Portia," he said, slipping an arm about her waist and pulling her to him. "I have a great deal to live for."

She went rigid, unyielding against him. Her eyes were like blue glass, cold and haughty, refusing to show her feelings, refusing to give an inch. After a moment he released her.

"What are you doing out here?" he asked, as if nothing had happened.

"We were exploring the hall," she said in a cool, unruffled tone. "We saw you from the bell tower and thought we'd come and see what you were doing."

"I'm trying to clear the channels so I can drain my land," he said. "But now the fog is coming in," he took her arm firmly in his, "so we'd better go back to the hall and take shelter. I wouldn't want you to wander off and get lost, my lady."

She looked around her and gave a shiver. "Is it always like this?" she murmured, and his heart sank. She hated it. She would never stay. Not if he made love to her every night and every day for the next ten years.

"No, it isn't always like this," he told her evenly, as if he didn't give a damn. They began to walk back in the direction she'd come, and Hettie fell in behind them. "Sometimes it's worse."

Portia didn't say anything to that.

Marcus glanced down at her dress, which he could see beneath her open cloak. It was old-fashioned, the sort of thing he could remember people wearing in portraits at Worthorne. At least he could see the delicious shape of her without all those blasted petticoats.

"Where did you find that? It suits you."

She brushed the thin cloth rather self-consciously. "Your housekeeper found it for me. It belonged to your uncle's wife."

"Hmm."

"Surely you don't begrudge me wearing it? It's your fault I am here with nothing but my chemise!"

"I don't begrudge you wearing it." He smiled into her eyes. "Actually, I was thinking that I'd have preferred to keep you without any clothes at all."

Her gaze narrowed; her mouth pursed. "Marcus—"

"And what did you think of my house?" he went on,

before she could roast him. He might as well hear all the bad news at once.

"Your house?"

"Yes. Don't spare me, I'd like to know."

"What does it matter what I think?" she said crossly.

He stared at her profile, trying to read her, but she refused to look at him. The misty dampness in the air had caused her hair to curl wildly, springing out of its pins, tickling her neck. He wanted to kiss her until she was willing in his arms, and he might have done so if the maid hadn't been lurking.

"Are you really going to live here?" she said abruptly, curiously.

"Yes, I really am."

Now she did look at him, her gaze sliding across his broad, tanned shoulders and lingering on the hair on his chest, trailing down over his flat stomach to the fastening of his breeches. For a moment she seemed to have lost the thread of her thoughts, her fingers tightening where they curved about his arm. She cleared her throat.

"But. . . what are you going to *do*?" she asked, sweeping her other hand around her at the marshes and the water and the sky.

She sounded bewildered, but he decided to carry on as if she was genuinely interested. Besides, he was dying to tell her what he planned, so he did. He spoke of reclaiming the land and repairing the walls and channels, of planting crops and bringing in animals, of being a proper farmer and landlord. He spoke of meeting his neighbors and having dinners and parties, and inviting his friends from London to stay—once the house was fixed—of an interest in local issues and even politics, if that was necessary to change things for the better. He could hear the passion in his voice and knew it was in his face, and that Portia probably thought him a first rate bore.

They had reached the wall that enclosed the house, and Hettie went in through the gate, leaving them standing together, alone. It was very still and quiet. The fog was beginning to creep like white fingers over the marsh, making everything eerie, deadening the world to a muted hush.

Portia seemed to be closer to him than she was before, and he wondered if she was nervous. He resisted pulling her to him again. "What is it like in the winter, when there's a storm?" she asked, as if the weather were her main concern.

"Frightening, so they say, but it would be invigorating, too, don't you think? I can hardly wait. I have a fancy to stand on the bell tower and let myself be lashed by the wind and rain from a North Sea storm."

She met his eyes and didn't look away. "You are the most unusual man," she murmured. "You kidnap me, and my mother. You bring us here where I'm sure no one will ever find us. And now you tell me you are going to spend the rest of your life here, digging ditches and fighting storms, when you're not overseeing justice as the local magistrate, or standing for Parliament. Surely you will miss London? What about your friends in the Hussars?"

"I'll still see them when I come to town, it just won't be as often. Anyway, I think I've grown out of drinking myself blind and ogling dancing girls." He laughed. "Don't frown, Portia. I know you find it incomprehensible, but I'm happy with my lot."

"I'm . . . I suppose I'm surprised, that's all. I did not think you were the sort of man to be satisfied with a life like this."

"A rascal and a waster?" he mocked, watching her.

"When I first saw you at Aphrodite's Club you were so at home there, so obviously a man of the town. I could not imagine you in any other setting."

She was being honest, and her opinion did not come as a surprise—he had known all along what she imagined him to be—but it was an opinion he was determined to change.

"I am a man who enjoys the good things of life," he said softly, "it is true, but I could not spend all my days and nights with nothing to do but live such an existence. I thought I could, but I know now I am not a man to be idle for long. I am looking for a challenge, and I think I have found it here."

"And women?" She spoke as if she was merely curious and did not care. "Will you be content with the village girls, or the . . . the vicar's daughter?"

Something in her face, in her tone, struck a chord.

For a moment he tried to puzzle out what she was telling him, but he could not. He reached out and cupped her face in the warmth of his palm. "Why would I want the vicar's daughter when I have you?"

Her breath caught, but whatever she was about to say was never said. He'd realized how cold her flesh was and exclaimed, "You're freezing!" Instinctively, he wrapped his arms around her, pulling her into his warm embrace.

He thought she'd protest and struggle, but instead she did the opposite. She burrowed into his chest, soft and yielding, her cold hands resting against his bare skin. "Oh Marcus," she sighed, her breath tickling his throat, "you don't want me. What use am I to you? You'd be better off with the vicar's daughter, or at least someone who will not bring you infamy and trouble."

Her unexpected response surprised him. "Portia? What is it? Tell me."

He was certain he felt her lips press against his skin. But the sensation was brief, and the next moment she'd pulled away, leaning back in his arms, her gaze fixed on his. "You seem to have found your life here, Marcus, but mine is in London."

"You're being suffocated," he said, angry, annoyed by her refusal to see what was in front of her. "I can't believe you want to continue to live like that, under Arnold's watchful eye."

"Whether I want to or not is not the point. I will have to go back. I will have to face the consequences of what I've done. There is Arnold and Lara to deal with, remember? I can hardly leave them in my home as if they are entitled to it and all my belongings. And there are people there who depend upon me and the decisions I make. Even if it means returning to disgrace, I will have to go back and deal with all of that and . . . and explain myself to the queen."

It was courageous of her, and he could see why she needed to return. Just not yet. And for God's sake not alone! She was cutting him out of her life . He tried one more time, as the clinging fog closed in on them. "Then we can face them together. You don't have to be alone, Portia."

"But I am alone," she reminded him quietly.

He took her arm again, and led her through the empty courtyard toward the front door of Duval Hall. "You forget. I kidnapped you."

"No. I asked you to take me away. And that is what I intend to say when I return to London."

She thought she could take the blame for his actions. Portia the martyr. He looked down at her and shook his head in disgust. "No. That will not happen. I forbid it."

He was regarding her with that familiar look. Portia wished he wasn't half naked. There he stood, feet apart, hands on his hips, his trousers clinging to him, while the skin of his chest gleamed with sweat and was streaked liberally with dirt.

She should have been appalled and disgusted. Any

other woman in her position would have been. But she knew she must be different because she found him tempting almost beyond her ability to resist. A moment ago, when he'd held her in his arms, she'd kissed him. It had taken an immense strength of will to pull away and put some distance between them.

It was her own fault. When she and Hettie had climbed up the bell tower to see the view, she'd spied him working with some of his men down on the marsh. Bare to the waist, swinging a pick like a navvy. Not like the sort of gentlemen she was used to at all.

The sight had made her heart begin to race wildly.

She'd heard of grand ladies who preferred to share their charms with servants and the common men of the streets, but she'd never thought she might be one of them. Or was it just Marcus who stirred her blood? He alone who made her legs turn to jelly?

His eyes, more gold than hazel, were warm and amused and staring into hers, seemingly reading her thoughts. "Portia, my love, you are my prisoner now. I may never let you go back to London."

Oh Lord. She should be furious with his arrogance. It was the sort of thing Arnold might have said. But it was different when Marcus said it, and her senses had never spiraled out of control when she was confronting Arnold Gillingham. If she was a lesser woman, she would have given in right now, handing herself over as his hostage, but Portia knew that would not be fair to her, or to him.

He had spoken to her of his dreams in a manner

that touched her heart, but he could not see that if he wanted to fulfill those dreams, he could not be saddled with her. Her disgrace, the scandal that would attach itself to them, would put a stop to any hopes he had of being well thought of here in Norfolk. People would look at him sideways and hurry on their way, and as for being elected to Parliament . . . it would not happen. He would end his days alone, ostracized and bitter.

He would hate her, and Portia could not bear that. Better to be parted now.

But she could see he had no intention of letting her go, and she would need time to persuade him it was the right thing to do. They needed to come to some sort of compromise.

"I will stay for a week."

"A year."

"A fortnight."

"A month."

"Marcus—"

They were interrupted. "Mercy says your bath is ready, my lady." It was Hettie, standing behind them, her hands primly folded. They hadn't heard her approach.

"We will continue this conversation later," Portia said, to let him know she wasn't about to give up and he hadn't won.

"By all means," he mocked. "As late as you like. Your room or mine?"

She climbed the stairs with her head high, refusing to respond.

Chapter 25

Portia felt completely relaxed. She'd bathed and Hettie had helped her dress in another of the old-fashioned gowns, this time a pale yellow with a matching long-sleeved jacket that fit tightly to her arms and shoulders and buttoned just below her breasts. With her hair curling softly around her face, she felt like another woman in another time.

It was so easy to slip into this fantasy Marcus had created for them both, where she was his willing prisoner and they would live here together, safe and happy, and no one would ever find her.

But her too-tight lavender slippers brought her back to reality. They pinched, they were uncomfortable, they were a reminder of the truth.

Mercy served them in the dining room. This was in the oldest part of the house, and was darkly paneled with a ceiling crisscrossed with heavy beams. It had an intimate feel. Despite the many candles burning in sconces, they were unable to keep the shadows at bay, and the fire crackling in the hearth cast a soft glow while Duvals peered down at them with Marcus's eyes. Portia thought she might have stepped into one of those outrageous and yet delicious Bronte novels.

This could be her life, she told herself in amazement. And she was turning her back on it . . . Just for a moment she wished she was someone else, someone who was selfish enough not to care that staying would destroy Marcus's chance for happiness.

"I don't think Mrs. Stroud was up to joining you this evening," Mercy said, as she kept an eye on the young girl who was doing the serving. "She was happy enough to take a tray in her room. Did you know she enjoys a game of chess, my lady?"

Portia blinked. "I did not even know she could play."

"It seems it was a favorite of hers in her younger days. My niece is giving her a game."

"She is forgetful sometimes," Portia began, then wondered why she could not tell the truth. Arnold was not here to punish her now. "Actually, she's very forgetful. All the time."

Mercy nodded. "I've seen it before," she said cheerfully. "Usually with the old ones, but sometimes it happens to the younger ones. It will get worse. One day she won't know who you are. You should make the most of her while she still does."

"My mother not knowing who I am?" Portia said when she and Marcus were alone again with the pudding. "It's a lowering thought."

"Are you close? I hardly knew my mother."

Portia smiled wryly. "My mother was the one who ran our house and our lives. My father either couldn't be bothered or he hadn't the strength to stand up to her. It was my mother who arranged for me to meet Lord Ellerslie."

"And the rest is history," he said grimly. "She has a lot to answer for."

"You don't know what I was like before," she murmured, grimacing.

"What were you like?" He was watching her over his wineglass, the candlelight in his eyes.

"Young and uncertain. Shy. The typical ugly duckling."

"And it took Lord Ellerslie to turn you into a swan? Somehow I doubt that."

"He helped me to become the woman I am."

"You underestimate yourself."

Do you remember poor little Portia Stroud from the vicarage? The girl who was so in love with you she could barely speak in your presence?

But she didn't say it, she couldn't bring herself to do so. And what would he think of her if she did? He was enamored of Lady Ellerslie not Miss Stroud. Best to let him keep his illusions.

"Are you finished?" he said impatiently, looking at her half-eaten meal. "I want to show you something."

Curious, and with some trepidation, Portia followed him into the great hall and up the stairs to the first landing. Marcus's surprises were not always nice.

It was dark apart from a wavering candle or two—
no gaslights here at Duval Hall. When they reached
the huge glass window, Marcus halted and held up the
lantern he'd brought with him from the hall table, so
they could see.

There were angels and animals cavorting, and a
garden full of flowers and fruit. The colors were not so
bright without the sun coming through from the other
side, but it was still impressive.

"This is the section I had replaced," he said.

Mesmerized, she looked at where he was pointing.

A star in a midnight blue sky and a woman gazing
up at it. She was wearing a scarlet dress and her long
fair hair was loose, tendrils of it twining about her lovingly. It took her a moment to realize who the woman
was meant to be.

"Oh."

Marcus laughed softly, wickedly. "So you do recognize her? I wondered if you would."

She turned to look at him, her eyes wide with amazement. "You put me in your window."

"I did." He set down the lantern and slipped his
arms about her, holding her against him, his lips close
to hers. "I'd rather have you in my bed, though."

She leaned into him with a sigh.

His hand slid up from her waist, cupping her breast
with a familiarity that should have made her cross but
instead made her want to giggle. He kissed her, his mouth
warm and tasting of the wine he'd drunk at dinner.

Her resistance, what there was left of it, crumbled.

"Come on," he murmured, "it's time I showed you my bedchamber. Just so you know the way if you ever get lost," he added, and taking her hand, began to lead her up the stairs.

She went willingly. He might be arrogant and manipulative, but he was a god in bed. Her god.

At the door he kissed her again, and she forgot about the past and the future. He had put her in his window, in his home, and his gift to her touched her almost beyond bearing.

He kissed her cheeks, tasting her tears, but when he was about to speak, she pressed her mouth to his, wildly, passionately. "Make love to me," she whispered. "Make me forget."

And, being the well-mannered gentleman he was—on the surface anyway—he obeyed.

In London there was hysteria. Newspaper sellers shouted out the dreadful news from street corners, politicians demanded action in Parliament, and the queen wrote letter after letter to her police constabulary. The question was the same wherever you turned.

Where is Lady Ellerslie?

Was her disappearance a plot to disrupt the queen and her government? Was there to be a ransom for her return? Already several prominent people had suggested a collection be taken up to cover such a possibility, so that Lady Ellerslie could be saved. But of course there was always the concern that some wretched fellow with designs upon the beautiful widow had decided to kidnap her. Take her away to some secret hideaway and wreak his terrible will upon her.

The public shuddered, some with horror, some titillated, and some with a combination of both. Speculation was rife, and no more so than in the household of Sebastian, the Earl of Worthorne.

"I'd be much happier if I knew exactly where Marcus was," Sebastian said grimly. "I have a feeling he's involved in this."

"Surely not," Francesca soothed, but her expression was apprehensive.

"He's obsessed with the woman. Remember that madness when she fainted in Green Park? Marcus isn't one to display caution when it comes to something he wants. He goes after it."

"What will you do if he has her?"

"Strangle him?"

They were distracted by raised voices outside in the entrance hall, and both turned as the door was flung wide open. Aunt Minnie, in her traveling clothes and wearing an Indian turban, made a dramatic entrance.

"It's all my fault!" she burst out.

"Minnie, what on earth . . . ?" Sebastian stared at her.

Francesca was already moving toward the elderly lady. "Minnie, whatever is it? Sit down, do, before you fall down."

Minnie allowed herself to be assisted to a chair and restored with a glass of cordial.

Sebastian watched her, struggling with his impatience. As she drained the last drop, he said, "What is your fault, Minnie? It must be important if you've come all the way from Little Tunley to tell us."

Minnie looked up at him, her eyes beneath her turban were sorrowful, yet Sebastian could have sworn there was also a gleam of pride in them.

"Marcus has kidnapped Lady Ellerslie."

Sebastian and Francesca exchanged a glance.

"I would insist upon boasting about my Duval ancestors," Minnie went on. "They were robber barons, you see. They used to ride out and take what they wanted. I told Marcus all about it. I paid especial attention to the way they kidnapped their wives—although of course they weren't married to start with. That came later. He pretended to scoff at the story, but he must have been listening more carefully than I imagined. Now that I think back on it, there was a definite glint in the dear boy's eye. He must have been planning it even then."

"You mean to say that my brother really has kidnapped Lady Ellerslie?" Sebastian said in a voice like thunder. "And you encouraged him, Minnie?"

Minnie shrank a little, but her chin was still very much up. "I am afraid so, Sebastian."

"Where are they? At Worthorne Manor? Or have they fled to France?"

"He's at Duval Hall, of course," Minnie said with a

flash of scorn. "Surely you've guessed that? Marcus is wild about the place, just as Roger was. They are very much alike, you know. Now that I think of it, Roger also fell in love with a totally unsuitable girl."

Francesca stood up, as if planning to set off at once for Norfolk. "Oh, this is dreadful! He could be sent to prison, or worse . . . Sebastian, my love, what are we going to do?"

"Yes, Sebastian, as head of the family I think you should take charge of the situation at once," Minnie announced.

Sebastian nodded soberly. "You're right. I'll have to go to Norfolk," he said quietly, "and try and mend this before it gets too far out of hand. If anyone else finds out what he's done and where he's gone and spreads the word . . . he'll be torn to pieces."

Francesca shuddered. "Oh God, imagine the angel in widow's weeds being found in Marcus's clutches? The man who stormed the dais and tried to . . . to molest her, or whatever those dreadful broadsheets were saying at the time. Even if they do not literally tear him to pieces, they will visit their anger upon him. Poor Marcus will be ruined, unable to show his face in polite society—in any society—ever again. His life will be over."

"Exactly." Sebastian sounded as grim as he looked.

"Yes, yes, you must go at once and save him," she said. "Go now, my love, before it is too late!"

He clasped her in his arms, kissing her long and soundly, and then he was gone.

Aunt Minnie took out a painted fan and waved it in front of her face. "Actually . . . " She smiled wickedly at Francesca. " . . . it's quite romantic, isn't it? I always knew Marcus was impetuous, but never quite so dashing. If I were Lady Ellerslie, I think I would be very pleased to be whisked away by Marcus on a secret tryst."

"Lady Ellerslie may not be pleased at all," Francesca said worriedly. "Imagine the scandal? Her reputation will be ruined. Society can be very cruel to women who do not live up to its high moral standards. Do you know, I heard some silly woman saying at a supper last night that it would be better for Lady Ellerslie to die than for her reputation to be smeared?"

Minnie snorted. "What pish."

"Exactly what I thought. But this is what Portia will have to deal with, if the worst comes to the worst. And as for Marcus . . . if he doesn't go to gaol, then he will be ostracized as well, and just when he was beginning to take an interest in Duval Hall."

"A scandal," Minnie said breathlessly, her eyes shining. "How exciting!"

Francesca sat down beside her aunt by marriage and gave her a searching look. "Minnie, you said that your uncle Roger fell in love with a girl who was completely unsuitable."

"That's right. Tavern owner's daughter, of all things. Roger stayed at the tavern on his way to London and by morning he was in love. I think she served him supper and he prevailed upon her to sit and talk with him. But that was enough."

"Did he get over her?"

"Not at all. He married her. It was very shocking and caused a great scandal. There are snobs in all levels of society, you know, and the tavernkeeper was just as appalled as my parents. But neither of them minded a snap. Roger loved her until she died and was never the same afterward. Marcus is like that—steadfast. You'll see."

Francesca put a hand to her eyes. "Dear Lord, I don't know if I want to see. I just hope there will be no scandal, and that Sebastian can smooth things over before it becomes generally known . . . for all our sakes."

Lara Gillingham was horrified to find herself in such a situation. Everything had been going along so well. Portia was behaving herself, invitations were flowing in, life was as it should be. And now this! Everywhere they went they were pestered by well-wishers and scandal mongers, and she had to pretend to be distraught, when in fact she was furious. She wanted to tell them what she actually thought, but couldn't say anything. Arnold had forbidden it.

"She must have planned it all along!" she wailed. "The lying, devious cow. She has ruined herself, and us with her."

Arnold had his own thoughts on who had planned Portia's disappearance. Despite rigorously questioning the servants, he was able to extract very little from them, and nothing about any accomplice. Marcus Worthorne had done this. He was sure of it. The man was a immoral savage. The question now was where he had taken her.

Until he knew that, his own plans had been put on hold. He had chosen Portia to be his instrument, and so she would be. No, he had not given up and he never would. He'd already hired several appropriately qualified persons to hunt Portia and her lover down, and when he found out where they were, he would decide how to deal with them to best advantage. *His* best advantage.

Something still might be salvaged from this mess.

"What will we do?" Lara's voice finally penetrated Arnold's thoughts. He turned to look at her, noting her wild eyes and flushed face. She was probably picturing a flood of refusals for her latest dinner party if Portia wasn't there.

"Deny any knowledge," he instructed her. "Say you are certain it is just a mistake and very soon she will come home again and explain it all to everyone's satisfaction. You are worried, naturally, but confident all will be well."

"I don't know if I can. I am so very angry, Arnold. I find myself wishing she would come to some dreadful harm . . . she and that man. How can I pretend to love her as I should when she is such an unnatural stepmother?"

"Well, you must," he retorted coldly. "This isn't about you, this is about the family. Remember, your father's memory is untarnished, and it will remain so as long as you rise above any gossip to the contrary. Portia may be destroyed—in fact she seems intent on destroying herself—but not him, and not you. We may even be able to use her downfall to better ourselves in the eyes of the queen and the public."

His wife gazed at him admiringly.

Arnold had noticed before that the more of a bastard he was, the better she liked it. Probably reminded her of her father, and the way he used to order her around as if she were one of his subalterns. Of course, if she knew his ultimate plans concerning Portia and the queen, she might not be quite so admiring. Or maybe he wronged her; maybe she would think him a hero for what he was going to do.

It wasn't every man who changed history.

Chapter 26

Portia was limp and replete. She hardly had the strength to lift her hand to stroke one of Marcus's dark curls back from his brow. He opened an eye, looked at her and smiled.

"Masterful enough for you, my lady?"

Portia smiled back. "Very masterful."

His smile turned quizzical. "Do you know I have the strangest feeling sometimes when I look at you. As if we've met before."

She lowered her eyes and pretended to smooth the bedclothes. "I can't think why."

"I'd like to believe it's because we're soul mates, but I suppose I've seen you at some function or other. You on the stage taking all the glory, and me on the outer reaches of the crowd, looking on."

Did he really believe she was so far above him? Not that it seemed to bother him; he was proud of her and who she was. She could see it in his eyes, in his smile. And it certainly didn't effect the way he made love to her, which was far more earthy than reverential, thank God.

He climbed out of bed and went to the window, naked as the day he was born. "The fog's gone," he said with satisfaction. "I want to try and have that sluice gate working tomorrow. We need to start thinking about planting, if we're to make this place pay."

We.

Portia let the word go without a fight.

He looked at her over his shoulder, a smile hovering about his handsome mouth. "Come and see."

A little reluctantly, she climbed out of the warm bed, the floor cold against her bare feet, and joined him at the window. He drew her back against him, folding his arms about her. He was so warm, even naked, and with a smile she remembered what he had said out on the causeway about being hot-blooded.

Then she looked out of the window.

The fog had dispersed and the moon had risen. It was like a huge round ball, hanging low in the sky, shining its pale cool light over the marshes and the water. There was something ethereal about the scene, as if it were a kingdom belonging to a mythical hero.

Marcus's kingdom.

No wonder he loved it here, Portia thought. He probably imagined himself as a king, all powerful. But that wasn't fair. He had ideas for the future, and he was more than willing to put them into practice. This was no vain despot. Marcus was an intelligent and thinking man, and although he might be a little impetuous, and blind when it came to danger, he was admirable in so many ways, she'd struggle to list them.

She had wronged him when she thought him nothing more than a handsome man of the town, a womanizer who only knew how to drink and gamble and enjoy himself in the London fleshpots. Perhaps she'd always known, in her heart, that he was capable of far more than she credited him with. Perhaps it had just been easier for her to pretend otherwise.

"Beautiful, isn't it?" he said against her hair.

"Yes."

"We will live here, you and I." It wasn't a question.

"Marcus . . ."

He tilted up her chin so that he could see her face. "I love you," he said. "I don't think your husband did, not like this. No one will ever love you like this. Why can't you trust me to take care of you?"

"I do trust you," she murmured.

"Do you?" Startled, he searched her eyes in the moonlight, seeking the truth.

"Of course. I went to St. Tristan when you asked. I went to Aphrodite's Club. I have risked being discovered time after time. Marcus, I trust you."

He seemed touchingly pleased with her answer.

"It's other people I don't trust," she added.

"Let me worry about 'other people.'"

She didn't want to say something that might spoil this precious moment, so instead she stretched up and kissed him. Their kisses grew deeper and more passionate, and with a groan he swung her up into his arms and carried her back to bed.

Marcus woke early, as he always did at Duval Hall. He saddled his horse and set off across his land, enjoying the mist swirling around him and the smell of the sea. London seemed far away, and he did not miss it at all.

Last night had been perfect. Portia trusted him; she'd said so. The magic of this place, of being here together, was winding its spell around her. He only needed a little longer and she would agree to stay with him forever. Surely a few more weeks of peace and solitude with the woman he loved was not too much to ask?

Despite what she seemed to believe, he was not being willfully blind or naïve when it came to the future. He knew there could be a scandal, and a bad one, but they would weather it out, just as they would weather out the storms that blew in from the sea. Matters might be difficult for a while, but Portia placed too much importance on what might be happening in London. The people around here weren't interested in that. They would look at him and Portia, see that they were honest and true, and accept them for what they were.

Later on, when the gossip died down or was replaced by some other juicy tidbit, they could begin to resume their lives farther afield. Time was the thing, and he had more than enough of that. He would lock his gate against the outside world, retreat behind his walls and prepare for a siege.

But when he turned his horse for home and came in sight of the hall, he saw that the outside world had already reached inside his kingdom. There was a stranger's mount in the cobbled courtyard, still steaming from its journey, and his heart sank.

"More trouble," he muttered as he dismounted.

The groom came to take his reins.

"Who is it?" Marcus demanded, jerking his head toward the other horse.

"Said he were a friend of yours, master. Mercy took him indoors to give him some breakfast. He said he'd ridden hard all the way from London."

London. Maybe it wasn't as far away as he'd thought. Marcus strode toward the house, determined to send his visitor back as soon as possible. Thank God Portia wasn't up and about, and he'd warned the servants not to gossip.

It wasn't until he was almost upon them that he recognized the voice. Unceremoniously, he thrust the door open on the cozy parlor.

"What the blazes are *you* doing here?"

Portia heard the voices as she reached the turn in the stairs. Marcus and another man. The light shining through the window was glorious this morning, and she couldn't help but look up at the figure in the scarlet dress with a wistful smile.

I love him, she thought. *I thought I loved him when I was a young girl but that was nothing to what I feel now. I will love him until I die. But I cannot let him throw away his life for me. I cannot allow that to happen to this wonderful man who has so much to give. As much as I would like to stay here, in his arms, hidden from the world, I know that eventually it will find me.*

" . . . You have sent a storm through Westminster, all the way up to Buckingham Palace. Not to mention the rabid newspaper headlines. To date, people have claimed to see Lady Ellerslie from Land's End to John o'Groat's. Don't think this is going to go away. They're after blood, and it's only a matter of time before they catch your scent and find you."

"Seb, I know what I'm doing."

"Francesca is worried about you, brother, and I won't have her worried." He sounded as if he meant it.

By now Portia had recognized the second man as Sebastian, the Earl of Worthorne and Marcus's brother. The fact that he was here at all was worrying, she thought, as she stole down the stairs toward them.

"You can't expect to hide away from the world forever, Marcus."

"I don't. Just until the worst of it blows over."

"They won't let you. Can't you see that? Too many important people have a stake in Lady Ellerslie. They will be looking for someone to blame, and it won't be her."

"In the days of the first Duvals, when they were under attack, they took away the causeway."

"What? So you intend to stay here under siege and pour boiling oil over your walls? Marcus, wake up. These aren't the days of knights and dragons; this is the nineteenth century!"

"Your brother is right."

They both looked up as Portia approached them. Marcus was unshaven, his hair tussled from his ride in the dawn light, while his brother was hollow-eyed from the journey. They were suddenly far more alike than she had realized.

"Lady Ellerslie." Sebastian gave her a formal bow.

She saw the way he glanced over her old-fashioned clothing but was too polite to comment. "I'm afraid your brother did not think to provide me with a wardrobe, my lord, so I've had to make use of what was available in the attics."

Sebastian's dark eyes warmed with laughter. "My brother can be a thoughtless wretch, Lady Ellerslie."

"Nonsense, I'm her hero."

She smiled at Marcus, and somehow their gazes got tangled up and she could not seem to look away. It was Sebastian clearing his throat that cut through the moment. She took a breath, stiffening her spine, knowing that any news from London must be bad.

"Do they know?"

"Not yet. I have heard that your stepdaughter's husband is paying for information as to your whereabouts, and some of the people he is paying are by no means scrupulous. They will find you, it is only a matter of time. Then it will be up to him whether he spreads the word or comes here himself to persuade you to return."

"Arnold," she murmured, and knew her face paled. "He is a dangerous man, and he hates me, although I don't understand why. Because I don't admire him as Lara does, I suppose. She is much easier to fathom . . . she hates me because her father married me. She would have hated any woman in those circumstances."

She frowned.

"Are they still living in my house in Grosvenor Square?"

"I believe they have moved back to Curzon Street. Lord Ellerslie's sister, Jane, has put herself in charge of your household."

Portia brightened. "Good."

"So, you do not intend to return to London if Arnold Gillingham sends for you?"

"Certainly not! Even if he comes in person and tries to drag me back, I will refuse to go."

"Let him try," Marcus said in a quiet, deadly voice. "My ancestors used to chain their enemies in the marshes and wait for the tide to come in. Less messy than a dungeon."

"Thank you, Marcus, but as much as I am tempted, I don't think that would be a good idea," Portia answered him with a smile, as if she enjoyed the image he painted for her. "If Arnold—when Arnold comes for me, I want to be gone. I won't stay here, shivering and hiding. I must return and explain before the scandal breaks." She looked to Sebastian. "Will you take me back to London, my lord?"

Marcus interrupted. "Bugger that," he said angrily, "if anyone takes you back, it will be me."

"No!" Both his brother and Portia spoke together.

Portia reached to clasp his arm, speaking urgently. "Marcus, if you come with me, they will arrest you. You must stay here where you're safe until everything has been sorted out."

"Stay here where I'm safe?" he repeated in amazement, his eyebrows raised. "I'm not some schoolboy afraid of the dark. I have been a soldier. I can fight. I demand to come with you and face my enemies."

"But I don't want you to."

He looked as if he wanted to rant and rave, and shout and stamp around the room, but instead he gave her one long infuriated look and strode away.

Sebastian waited until he was gone before he spoke again. "I apologize on my brother's behalf."

Portia moved gracefully toward an alcove where a window seat offered some privacy. "There's no need."

"He's a brilliant man, clever and kind, beneath that devil-may-care attitude, but he doesn't see things the way the rest of us do. I blame our mad Aunt Minnie. She more or less brought him up after our mother died."

"I have met your Aunt Minnie," Portia admitted. "I found her enlightening. She reminded me of . . . of someone else I know who also lives an unconventional life. There is an honesty about them both. They do not say something just to please others, nor do they fear being out of step with the rest of society. They say what they mean. Marcus is like that, too."

Sebastian sat down beside her and glanced through the dusty windowpane. "I haven't been here in years," he admitted. "When Roger Duval left the hall to my brother, I was appalled. I didn't think for a moment he would ever live here, unless it was to sell it and use the money for some scheme or other, or to buy himself out of difficulty. But it seems to have been love at first sight."

"The people here love him, too, so it is a perfect match." She met his eyes, her own full of worry she could not hide. "Is it very bad in London?"

Sebastian grimaced. "Hysteria. The public are beside themselves that their angel in widow's weeds has been stolen from them. Questions have been asked in Parliament. The queen is dashing off letters. No one seems to know where you are or why you left. Your stepdaughter claims to know nothing of your departure."

"She must know. Arnold, too." She shook her head and stared at her hands, twisting nervously. "I told Marcus he would be arrested, and this time he'd go to prison. Or worse."

"Yes, you're right."

"How much time do you think we have?"

"A week at the most. When Arnold Gillingham finds

you, he will act. It would do him no end of credit to be the one to restore you to the world."

Portia laughed bitterly. "Oh yes, that sounds like him. Cold ambition."

"Marcus has told me what you have been made to go through recently, Lady Ellerslie."

"Oh, call me Portia, please."

He bowed his head.

"Yes, Marcus saved me from that. He is my hero. But I fear he has brought much trouble upon himself." She sighed. "I need to go back. I hoped for a little longer, but . . . "

"You love my brother, don't you, Portia?"

She looked up and smiled. "Yes. I tried not to, but I can't help it. I think I've always loved him," she added thoughtfully.

He frowned and tilted his head to one side. "I know you, don't I? I know your face from somewhere else."

That he recognized her shouldn't be a surprise, she thought; Sebastian had been to tea at the vicarage several times when she was young. There seemed no point in denying it. "Yes, you do know me. I was Portia Stroud, my father was the vicar . . . "

"Good Lord, I remember now. Does Marcus . . . ?"

She might have said more, and might have asked him not to tell, but they heard voices approaching. Portia looked up just as Mercy and her mother entered the hall from the back area of the house. Her mother was chattering away and Mercy was nodding.

"There's your daughter, ma'am," the housekeeper said, noticing Portia and Sebastian in the alcove.

"Oh yes. She is a lovely girl, isn't she? Takes after my side of the family, of course."

"My mother is not herself," Portia murmured. "She hasn't been herself for years and she has been getting worse."

"But what is she doing here?" Sebastian asked, puzzled.

Portia looked at him with wide laughing eyes. "Didn't Marcus tell you? Arnold was holding my mother's welfare over my head and I decided I had to send her out of London. It was on the same night that Marcus came for me. He brought my mother with us. And my maid."

"Good God," he said, and laughed.

"Who is this gentleman?" Mrs. Stroud demanded.

"This is the Earl of Worthorne, Mama."

"I've met dozens of earls," she confided to Sebastian. "Dukes, too. They're all the same, if you ask me."

"Mama, that is impolite."

"Is it?" Her mother looked at her as if seeking guidance. "I will take the earl to see the flower garden, then. It is very pretty, you'll see." She took Sebastian by the hand and led him away.

"I hope she isn't a bother," Portia began, when they were out of earshot. "I know she can be difficult."

"She's a dear," Mercy said firmly, "just a little confused about things. I think she likes it here. She keeps asking if she can stay."

"I didn't realize how much she hated London. She wanted me to marry Lord Ellerslie, and when I did, she was ecstatic that she would live a grand life and meet grand people. She was always very ambitious, and being a vicar's wife had not made her happy."

"Well, she's happy now," Mercy assured her. "Maybe she didn't realize how much she enjoyed being a nobody until it was taken away from her."

Portia smiled and walked with her toward the garden. The sun was out but the air was cold. A woman sat nursing a baby in the shelter of the gatehouse, her man—one of the stonemasons working on the house—seated by her side. The picture of them together caught and held her gaze, and she found herself pausing to glance back at the little tableau enviously.

Marcus was her lover, and he had been her obsession for most of her adult life. Could they live a normal life, could they be happy together? She thought so, if only they were left in peace. But that was the problem. The world outside Duval Hall was closing in, and nothing they did could stop it.

Chapter 27

"**P**ortia."
The whisper made her turn.

Marcus was standing by the stables, in the shadows. She opened her mouth to ask him what he thought he was doing lurking there, but he put his finger to his lips.

Portia glanced about her. Mercy had reached the others and they were standing together, admiring the garden. In a moment they would be looking to see what had happened to her.

She walked toward Marcus. "What is it?" she said softly.

"I have something to show you," he said, reaching out to take her hand as soon as she was close enough.

"What about . . . ?" She gestured toward his brother and the two women.

"I want you to myself." His eyes held promises, and when he tugged her hand, she was unable to resist. Once they were out of sight he began to run, pulling her along behind him. Portia kept pace, breathless, feeling like a girl again. They slipped out of the gate and followed a path atop a high bank that rose above the surrounding marsh. The tide was in, and steps led down to a small wooden jetty with a boat tied to it. Marcus clambered down into the craft and lifted her after him, making certain she was settled before he cast off the line.

"Do you want to swim?" he asked her as she sat carefully, hands gripping the gunwales for dear life.

"No." Her eyes were big. "Do you expect to tip over?"

His face was serious, but with the hint of his wicked smile. "I hope not, but like most things in life, one can never be sure. But we will hope for the best, my love."

He pushed them off from the jetty, and sitting down himself, began to row. Here on the water they were below the height of the reeds, and other than the very top of Duval Hall, with its bell tower, there was nothing much to see. Portia watched him rowing, admiring the strength of his shoulders and the way his dark hair hung in his eyes so that she longed to smooth it back.

"Better than the Serpentine?" he asked with a grin.

She giggled.

"I love it when you do that," he said suddenly, stopping to give her one of his penetrating looks. "You can be the sophisticated Lady Ellerslie for everyone else, but I flatter myself that I'm the only one who can make you giggle like a girl."

It wasn't flattery. Portia knew that she was different

while with Marcus, and if what he'd been saying was true, then he was a new man when he was with her.

A fish splashed close by, startling her. "Where are we going?" she asked, looking about.

"Nowhere. That's the joy of this place. You can row for miles and never actually get anywhere, just go around and around in the maze of waterways within the marsh."

"You could lose your enemies."

"Arnold Gillingham, do you mean? Or the entire British nation? They probably both hate me equally."

The awful thing was, she knew it to be true.

"There's only one way out of this, Portia."

He was fixing her with his intense look again.

"Marry me."

He didn't ask, it was more of an order.

"To save you from the gallows?"

He gave an impatient shrug. "Don't do it for that, for God's sake! Marry me because you want to, because you love me. Do you love me?"

"I do love you."

He grinned. "Ah."

"There are practical considerations."

"I'm weary of being practical." He glanced over his shoulder, and then drew into the bank, so that the bow was secure among the reeds, and fitted the oars carefully within the boat.

"I like you in that dress," he said softly, crawling toward her over the seat. "It's so white and pure. It makes you look like a debutante at her first ball. Fresh and untouched."

"Instead of a jaded old woman?" she retorted, not sure whether she entirely trusted the expression in his eyes. She glanced behind her but there was nowhere to go but into the water, and she didn't fancy plunging into the marsh.

"Oh no, never that," he said, and took her into his arms. His mouth was hard and passionate, taking her breath.

It was no use struggling; besides, she didn't want to. And it was no use listing the overwhelming odds against their chances of happiness, either, because he didn't want to hear them.

But he seemed to have read her mind anyway.

"What is it you want from your life, Portia?" He was holding her close, his eyes on hers. "I'm not talking about your responsibilities to other people. I mean, what do *you* want?"

It was a long time since anyone had asked her such a question. Her life revolved around the needs and demands of others, and until she went to Aphrodite's Club and met Marcus, she'd been content to allow it to remain so.

What did she want, truly, in her heart?

Suddenly it was all crystal clear.

She wanted a life of her own. She wanted a husband and children and a place where she was loved for who she was and not what she was. She did not want to stand in the glare of the public eye anymore and pretend. Such things had long ago grown tiresome. *She* was tired of it.

"My love?"

His voice drew her back. She opened her eyes; she had not realized they were closed. He was watching her. His handsomeness did not seem so refined here—there was a wildness about him, an untamed quality. His jaw was not so carefully shaved, his hair was shaggy, and there were shadows under his eyes. His clothes, too, were wrinkled and untidy. He looked less like the debonair Marcus Worthorne of her dreams and more like a real man. The man she loved and wanted to spend the rest of her life with.

"I want you," she murmured. "I want to live here with you."

His fingers trembled as he stroked her cheek. "Portia, my love."

"I know you don't want me to go back," she added quietly, "but I have to make things right. There are people who depend on me, and I must see them settled. There are people who will be hurt by my change of heart, and I must do my best to explain. I do not think I can be happy with you unless I leave my past in as good an order as it is in my ability to do."

"I know that." He brushed her bottom lip with his thumb. "I can help you."

"You can't. I need to do it alone. I need to finish with my past and come to you free." She smiled up at him. "If you still want me, that is."

"I want you," he whispered, bending to press his lips to hers.

They didn't speak again. There was no need. They kissed gently as the water rocked the boat, and then he began to make love to her slowly, carefully, in their secret world. And it was like a promise they made to each other; a vow for the future.

"Duval Hall. In Norfolk." As Arnold said the names, his mouth twisted with scorn.

Lara's face went blank.

"I know, my dear, it isn't a place that immediately springs to mind when one thinks of your stepmama. Evidently, Mr. Worthorne resides there."

"So she has run off with him!"

"Or him with her."

"What will we do?" A glittery light came into her eyes. "Will we tell the queen?"

"I think we might," Arnold said thoughtfully, "but it must be done in the correct way, so that we look like caring relatives. Soon, though. I've wasted enough time."

"Portia has been very bothersome. We should punish her."

"Don't worry, I have every intention of doing so."

Lara smiled up at him, her eyes slanting, and he felt an unexpected bolt of lust. If his friends hadn't been there, he might consider following her up the stairs.

Lara glanced back over her shoulder into the dining

room, where those friends were partaking of their brandy and cigars. "I will leave you, then," she said to Arnold, a little pathetically. Perhaps she had read his expression. "I imagine you will be talking about boring matters for hours . . . ?"

"Quite possibly." Arnold eyed her thoughtfully, then abruptly reached out and stroked her shoulder, feeling the warmth of her flesh beneath his fingertips. His next words surprised even him. "Read a little while, my dear. I will try not to be down here too long."

Startled pleasure flushed her cheeks and she smiled as she turned away.

Arnold waited a beat before he reentered the room and closed the door. They all fell silent, and he knew he had their full attention.

"I will expect my wife to be cared for when the deed is done," he said with quiet intensity. "Although we will triumph, she will face ruin, socially and financially, and she will need your help."

"Of course." The murmur went around the table.

Arnold gave each of them the benefit of his cold hard stare and was satisfied. He did not love Lara, not as he loved the cause he would give his life for, but he'd discovered that he didn't want to see her suffer unnecessarily. Her feelings in regard to him didn't interest him, and he suspected she would hate him when it was done. Although in time her need to preserve her pride would cause her to fictionalize his part in the queen's death, and she would find some way to exonerate him.

It was something he would have found amusing, if he'd been here.

But just now there was the problem of Portia and Marcus Worthorne, who was aptly named, because the man had certainly become a thorn in his side. What he had said to Lara was true, it was immaterial whether Marcus had run off with Portia or she with him. The point was, they were hiding out at Duval Hall in the middle of nowhere, and he had to find some way of getting the queen to them, or them to the queen.

His moment of triumph was fast approaching, and the odd thing was, he wanted Portia there to witness it. He wanted her to know what he was capable of and to share his glory, however unwillingly on her part.

The very thought of it stirred his lust again, the feelings even more powerful than before.

"My friends, I will leave you to make your own way out," he said abruptly, rising to his feet. "Good night."

He closed the door on their startled faces and started up the stairs, as eager as a bridegroom.

By the following morning Arnold was clear-headed again, and had decided on his next move. By nine o'clock he was presenting himself at Buckingham Palace. It was not as difficult as he'd expected to gain admittance to the queen. Once Portia's name was mentioned, doors were opened, and before long he was in the antechamber waiting to be led into the royal presence.

The queen listened to the announcement with disquiet.

"Mr. Gillingham is waiting to see you, ma'am. He says he has some news to impart to you about Lady Ellerslie."

Victoria's plump face grew stern. She did not like Mr. Arnold Gillingham; he had an unpleasant chilliness about his eyes. And there were rumors about his father—she remembered there had been a scandal once, when her uncle was alive. The sins of the father shouldn't taint the son, of course, but in this case she was willing to make an exception.

"Very well, I will see him. Briefly."

When Arnold entered, he bowed low. "Your Majesty."

"Mr. Gillingham. You have some news, I've been told. Quickly, tell me what it is, I have the French ambassador waiting."

"I will, Ma'am, but I fear you will not like it."

"But that is no reason not to tell me," she replied tartly.

Arnold took the hint. "Lady Ellerslie is in Norfolk with Mr. Marcus Worthorne. I fear, Your Majesty, that she is lost to all reason. My wife can hardly bear to think of how this news will affect the memory of her father—"

"Do you mean that she is living there with him? Alone?"

"Well . . . not quite. Her mother, Mrs. Stroud, is also there, and her maid."

Victoria seemed nonplussed. "Then she is adequately chaperoned?"

"Ma'am, I didn't just come here to tell you of Lady Ellerslie's whereabouts. I wanted to ask for your help. My wife and I have tried our best to talk sense into Lady Ellerslie, but to no avail. This man is a rake and a fortune hunter, the worst sort of person to attach himself to a vulnerable lady. You have so much influence over her, and as she admires you greatly, we had hoped . . . But it is too much to ask."

Victoria sighed impatiently. "Ask your favor, sir. You should know by now that I prefer plain speaking."

He bowed. "Very well. Would you go to her, Ma'am? Would you do us the very great honor of meeting Lady Ellerslie and using your influence on her? If we can bring her back to London before her whereabouts are discovered and the scandal breaks, then surely it would be to everyone's advantage. Your Majesty, I ask this not only for myself and Lady Ellerslie, but for the sake of her dear husband, Lord Ellerslie, and his revered memory."

Victoria would have refused him, it was on the tip of her tongue to do so, but the appeal to the memory of Lord Ellerslie had struck her to the heart. And it was true, there would be a terrible scandal. Did the government, the country, need such gossip and distress, when she could prevent it? Despite Portia's recent behavior she was fond of her, and the children adored her. It would be a shame if Portia destroyed herself over a man unworthy to wipe dear Lord Ellerslie's boots.

Victoria might have been a stickler for the rules of

church and society, but she was not a fool, and she was certainly not a prude. She knew that if she could rescue Portia from Marcus Worthorne's clutches, it would be better for everyone concerned.

"What you are asking is very unorthodox, sir," she said coldly.

He was about to reply when she held up her hand to stop him.

"Lady Ellerslie is a dear friend of mine, it is true, and I was extremely fond of her husband. But how do you know she will listen to me? This Worthorne man seems to have her under his spell."

"Your Majesty, this is unfortunately true, but I am sure if she could but speak with you and see what she is risking, she would come instantly to her senses. Only you can save her now."

The words were theatrical, and for him, out of character, but afterward Arnold considered them a stroke of genius. To come here and ask such things of the queen was audacious, but he had nothing to lose by it. And as he watched the expressions flit across her face, he knew that, against all odds, he had convinced her.

She informed him curtly that they were to set off in two days time, and would travel as discreetly as possible, to prevent bringing about the very situation they were attempting to prevent.

When Arnold knew he was going to Duval Hall, it was all he could do not to rub his hands together as he backed away from Victoria's presence.

Chapter 28

❧

The sluice gate had been mended. Portia, watching Marcus, was aware of a sense of pride in him that was growing day by day. It seemed as if new facets of his character were being revealed to her since they'd come here to Duval Hall, or perhaps she had been too caught up in her problems before to look properly.

How could she have ever thought him nothing more than a handsome idler? Oh, he was handsome; her heart still beat faster whenever she saw him. But he was a complicated man, with strength and compassion and determination and intelligence . . . She could go on all day.

When he looked at her with the sparkling warmth in his eyes he saved for her alone, she felt humbled and proud. And afraid. There was so much to be got over before she could think of being his wife. But she did think of it, all the time. It had become the image she clung to.

Sebastian was still at the hall. Portia had asked him

to escort her back to London when the time came, and he'd agreed. They did not mention it, however. Marcus still refused to contemplate such a thing. But it would have to be soon. Would he forgive her when she left him behind? Or would he refuse to remain and come with them?

The thought of what might happen to him made her feel sick, so she didn't say anything. She waited. And time grew short.

"I have asked Portia to marry me," Marcus told his brother, making no secret of it.

Sebastian chuckled. "You do surprise me, brother."

"We haven't set a date," Portia said, giving Marcus a little frown. "Such a thing cannot possibly be decided yet."

"Of course it can," Marcus replied. "You only need to say the word and I'll have you before the altar so fast your head will spin." His smile teased but he meant what he said.

Sebastian had been watching their byplay. "Do you know, Marcus may be right for once. Marriage might be a way of diverting the scandal, and who knows, there could even be some sympathy for you both."

"I can't possibly think of such a thing until I have my affairs in order," Portia said stubbornly.

"See?" Marcus gave his brother an exasperated glance. "This is what I have to contend with. The woman is impossible. And selfish. So used to getting her own way she doesn't consider how she is breaking my heart."

He was teasing, of course, but Portia wasn't amused. "You are deliberately blind to anything that doesn't fit in with your plans."

"Very well. Let Seb take you to Worthorne Manor and we'll be married there. Make it a huge affair, as if we have nothing whatsoever to hide. The Earl of Worthorne can give you away and we will invite everyone who is anyone. Let them come and see that we have nothing to hide."

"If you had nothing to hide, you'd marry her in London, in St. James's," Sebastian said levelly, watching them with amusement.

"And risk a riot?" Marcus asked with mock horror. "The police would outnumber the guests. No, Worthorne is grand enough for the occasion. But I forgot, Portia has never seen it. You're in for a treat, my love. My family home may be in need of a few repairs but it has everything from an ornamental lake to a baronial hall full of rusty weapons and moth-eaten stag heads."

"Portia knows Worthorne Manor, Marcus."

Marcus frowned. "She knows it? Have you visited the New Forest, my love?"

Portia's heart sank. She had known the truth would out, but not like this. She should have told him long ago. Why oh why hadn't she?

"Portia?"

Sebastian, realizing his mistake, said hastily, "I beg your pardon, I did not realize . . . "

"Is there a secret?" Marcus looked from one to the other of them. "Will someone please tell me?"

Portia set down her teacup. "Sebastian, I wonder if you would leave us alone for a few moments?"

Obediently, Sebastian rose quietly to his feet and left the room.

"We have met before," she said, "you just don't remember it." She glanced at him across the table. He was watching her intently, a frown between his brows. "But perhaps you do, in a way. You have mentioned several times that I seem familiar."

"Tell me," he growled.

"My father was the vicar when you were a boy at Worthorne Manor."

He stared at her hard. "You are the vicar's daughter," he said blankly.

"Yes, I am."

He didn't smile. She had grown so used to his smiles that his sternness was unsettling. Almost as if he was a stranger.

"You should have told me."

"It was a long time ago, Marcus, really I didn't think—"

"You did think. You think too much. That was why you didn't tell me, wasn't it? You had some idea that I would think less of you if I knew, or that I would use the knowledge against you."

He was too intuitive. She tried to brush his words away. "Marcus, you don't even remember me from then! What does it matter?"

"I do remember. You used to walk in the lane when I was riding there. I wondered sometimes whether you did it on purpose."

Suddenly Portia could not bear it if he knew how much she'd loved him in her girlish way. That was why she hadn't told him. She was embarrassed; she did not want to dredge up memories of the poor lovelorn parson's daughter. She had put all that behind her.

"You should have told me," he said again, and he didn't sound like himself. This man was grim and serious, and when she looked into his eyes she saw nothing of her lover.

"You are making too much of this!"

"And you are making too little. If it was nothing, you would have told me long ago. But you didn't. You hid it. And I am wondering why."

Portia rose to her feet, the chair scraping on the floor, her teaspoon clattering against the saucer.

"Portia!" he cried out, but she didn't stop. She was already leaving the room, tears blinding her.

She didn't trust him. All along he had felt that, known it in his heart, and now she'd confirmed it. If she trusted him, she would have told him the truth. Instead she kept it to herself as if it were some dark secret, as if she expected him to think less of her, or maybe she just didn't consider him important enough to tell.

Despite her promises and her kisses, she had kept her own counsel. He had opened his heart to her, spilling out his dreams and hopes, and she'd held onto her secrets. What did that say about his hopes for marriage?

Marcus felt anger and hurt twist inside him.

He heard her footsteps as she ran down the stairs and into the hall. Belatedly, he rose from the breakfast table and set off after her. Whatever she'd done, whatever she hadn't told him, he loved her. He would forgive her.

He was on the landing when the sound of a coach reached him from the courtyard below. He strode to the window, peering through the beautiful colored glass. The coach was a large black one, and there were many outriders, as if the persons inside were important.

Frowning, he watched as it drew to a halt just as Portia appeared outside in the yard. She was also staring at the coach, but there was something about the rigid set of her shoulders that made him think she knew who it was. A sense of foreboding filled him.

And then the door swung open and Arnold Gillingham stepped down. With a curse, Marcus ran down the stairs.

Portia had recognized some of the outriders, despite their somber clothes. They were the queen's guard, which meant that the queen was inside the great black coach. Victoria, here at Duval Hall. For a moment, shock held her frozen in place and she forgot what had sent her out here.

Then Arnold stepped down from the coach in front

of her, and despite his carefully controlled expression, she could see the triumph burning coldly in his eyes.

There wasn't time to turn and run. She wouldn't have anyway. Arnold was not someone she would ever show such weakness to; she'd learned by now that he thrived on bullying others. Portia, alone in the courtyard, straightened her back and put on her public mask, and walked toward the carriage as if she was the mistress of the house and not its prisoner.

Victoria, looking tired and irritable, was descending from the coach with the help of one of her men. "Lady Ellerslie," she said, then raised her eyebrows when she saw Portia's bizarre outfit, the old-fashioned dress.

Portia curtsied. "Your Majesty, I am overwhelmed."

"I'd prefer gratitude. I have had to rearrange my schedule to accommodate you, and I am most put out. You have caused me a great deal of bother, my lady."

"Ma'am—"

"No. We will not discuss such matters out here. Invite me inside, Portia, so that we can speak privately." It was an order, not a request.

"Stepmama, how could you worry us so!" Lara, her insincerity plain to hear, was next from the coach.

"Privately, I said," the queen repeated with an irritated glance toward the Gillinghams that told Portia more than words about their journey together.

Portia led the way inside.

Marcus was standing in the doorway. She ignored him, and so did the queen. Mercy, hurrying from the kitchens, stopped dead in amazement. Portia hastily ordered refreshments before leading her royal guest into the drawing room.

Thankfully, there was a fire and the queen quickly stripped off her gloves and sat down on the chair before it, holding out her hands to the warmth.

"Lady Ellerslie, your relatives are abominable. They think I will believe them sincere if they continue to tell me how much they have your welfare at heart and pull somber faces. Am I such a fool?"

"No, Your Majesty," Portia said. "I apologize, but they are my late husband's relatives, not mine, and I did not choose them."

"Well," Victoria huffed, allowing herself to be mollified. She gave Portia a hard look. "I think it is time for plain speaking, don't you?"

"Yes, Ma'am."

"Sit down. That's better. Now, whatever were you thinking to go off like you did, without a word to anyone? I was concerned. The nation was concerned. And now Arnold Gillingham tells me you were here, with this man, all the time."

"I beg your pardon, Your Majesty. It was a spur of the moment decision. I was not thinking straight. And once I had run away, I did not know how to come back."

"This man . . . it was all his fault. He shall be punished. I shall have him taken back to London and arrested. There will still be a scandal, that cannot be helped, but at least the public will have someone to vent their spleen upon."

"No!" Portia bit her lip, forcing herself to be calm. Hysteria was no way to persuade Victoria to her point of view. "Ma'am, please. It was not Mr. Worthorne's fault. He was only trying to help me escape Arnold."

Victoria stared at her with hard bright eyes. "Escape Arnold?"

Portia felt as if she was entering a maze with traps and snares at every turn, and that every step she took could be her last. But if anyone was to blame for the situation she was in, it was Arnold, and she felt no compunction in saying so.

"Since you have been generous enough to make me your companion, Ma'am, I have seen how happy you and your dear prince are together, and seeing has made me long to have such happiness for myself. But Arnold preferred I remain a widow because that way he could use me to further his own ambitions. I think he hoped to ingratiate himself with you, my dear Majesty, through me."

Victoria nodded. "I knew he was a horrid man."

"When I told him I wished to marry Mr. Worthorne, he threatened to place my mother in an asylum if I went ahead. She is old, forgetful, but he made it seem as if she was violent. I could not bear that, and he knew it."

Her mouth thinned. "I should think not. You should have told me, Portia."

"I am sorry, Ma'am. I see now I should have come to

you and laid the whole matter before you, but suddenly I could not bear it any longer, and when Marcus offered me and my mother sanctuary here in Norfolk, I said yes."

It was the truth, more or less. The queen could probably fill in the gaps without her help, Portia thought.

Victoria was staring thoughtfully into the fire. "I cannot pretend it pleases me, Lady Ellerslie, that you wish to remarry. I suppose you know that, and that is the reason you did not come to me. I was particularly fond of Lord Ellerslie."

"Ma'am, so was I. I loved him dearly, but I was only a young girl when I married him, and now I am a woman. I want to love again, Ma'am. I want to find happiness such as you have. Is that so wrong?"

"No, that is not wrong." Victoria seemed to be mulling over the question. "There must be a sensible way out of the mess you have made, if only we can find it. I quite like the idea of blaming Mr. Gillingham for everything, but I suspect he would protest."

"He might, but that doesn't mean we can't try."

Victoria smiled for the first time. "I am fond of you, Portia," she said, a little stiffly. "I would not like to see your life ruined."

Surprised and touched, Portia didn't know what to say.

"I will give it some thought," Victoria went on, as Mercy arrived with the refreshments, curtsying deeply. "I will take something to eat and drink, and then I will rest. We will discuss this later."

"Of course, Ma'am." A glance at Mercy confirmed that a room would be made ready, although the house-keeper looked a little wild-eyed.

When Victoria, accompanied by the maid she had brought with her, was safely upstairs, Portia went to find Marcus. She wanted to tell him what she had said to the queen, so their stories did not clash. It wasn't until she was halfway down the causeway that she re-membered Marcus might no longer want to speak to her, let alone marry her.

She stopped, the wind tossing her cloak and her hair, and stinging her pale cheeks pink. It was a mess, and she wasn't sure how to fix it, or even if she could.

"Mr. Worthorne."

The cold drawl was familiar, but Marcus didn't turn immediately from his perusal of the plans he'd spread out on his desk in the library. They showed the land as it used to be, the myriad channels and gates, and he could see how much still needed to be repaired and reclaimed.

"I hope you're not too disappointed that your little tryst with Portia is at an end," Arnold went on, as if so pleased with himself he was almost ready to ex-plode with it. "But you have been playing out of your league."

"At an end? I don't think so. We're to be married." Finally Marcus turned to look at him, a scornful glance. "Did you come all this way just to tell me that?"

Arnold laughed, as if he didn't believe it, but Marcus saw the way his hand clenched at his side. "Lady Ellerslie is too important to the nation to marry someone like you," he went on. "You have caused me no end of bother, Worthorne. Don't think I won't get my revenge on you. A nice long prison sentence, I think, would do the trick."

Marcus sat down on the edge of the desk and folded his arms. "What is it you want, Gillingham? I can't believe you came here, and managed to get the queen to come with you, just so you could persuade Portia to return to her life in London. The queen loathes you, and will never rise you up to the heights you seem to think you're worthy of. Are you secretly in lust with Portia, is that it? I'm sorry to have to tell you that she would sooner bed a slug than you."

"Of course. She's slept with you."

Marcus laughed.

Suddenly Arnold's eyes were as hard and savage as a wild animal, as if under his well-dressed urbane exterior there lurked something extremely dangerous. "My father taught me to be ambitious," he said, "and to work hard to obtain my goal. I have worked hard, and you have almost ruined it. But don't worry, in the end you've actually done me a good turn. This is the perfect place."

"I don't know what you're talking about," Marcus began.

"No, I know you don't," Arnold said, and left him alone in the library.

Marcus shook his head. "Completely insane," he murmured, but there was something about the other man that was not so easily dismissed. He had a very unpleasant feeling about Arnold Gillingham.

"My lady, I wish to tell you something." Hettie sounded unlike her usual self, and when Portia glanced into the mirror, she saw that her maid was chewing on her lip.

Hettie was helping her to dress for dinner in the lavender ball gown. Mercy had managed to produce a meal truly fit for a queen, and Portia wanted to dress to do it justice. The ball gown would seem a little strange, but it could not be any stranger than some of the outfits she had been wearing recently. Besides, she wanted Marcus to see her at her best. To remind him that whatever she'd been in the past, she was Lady Ellerslie now.

Perhaps they could mend whatever it was her failure to tell him had broken, and all would be well again. The queen appeared to be on her side, and it would be a shame if they were no longer of a mind to marry.

Who am I fooling? My heart will be broken.

Portia sighed, and turned her attention back to Hettie. "What do you wish to tell me?"

"I think you will not forgive me, my lady."

"It cannot be so bad." *And who am I to play at being perfect when it comes to secrets?* Portia watched closely as Hettie put the finishing touches to her hair. "Hettie?"

"Do you remember when Arnold and Lara Gillingham came to the house in Grosvenor Square? And they seemed to know that you were at Aphrodite's Club with Mr. Worthorne?"

"How could I forget? It was the worst night of my life."

Hettie hesitated and then shook her head. Her face looked old. "My lady, it was I who told them."

Portia sat, frozen, struck down by Hettie's perfidy. "You told them?" she whispered. "Oh Hettie, you told them?"

"I'm so sorry, my lady. I thought I was doing it for the best, for you. I didn't realize." Her expression was bitter. "If I knew then what I do now, I would never have done such a thing." Her mouth wobbled. "Forgive me, *lieben*."

Portia could not take it in. "Oh Hettie . . . "

"I'm so sorry," her maid wept. "I can't live with myself any longer. Forgive me or I'll go now. I should go anyway. Far far away. I cannot bear it that you hate me. I have loved you since I came to you when you married Lord Ellerslie. I have always tried to do what was best for you. But I do not ask you to remember that. I am willing to take whatever punishment you feel I deserve."

Portia swallowed down her disappointment. It was

true. Hettie had always loved her and been her trusted companion. Should she be cast off now, because she had acted in good faith? Trusting Arnold had been a mistake, yes, but Hettie had clearly suffered. Portia decided she would do for her faithful maid what she wanted Marcus to do for her.

"No, you must not go away," she said softly. "Who would look after me as well as you, if you were to go? I forgive you, Hettie."

Hettie's sobs grew louder. Portia clasped her maid's hands, squeezing them tightly. "Hush, you will make yourself ill. Go to bed, Hettie. There is no need for you to stay up."

Hettie wiped her face on her sleeve. "My lady, thank you."

"You may not thank me when you have lived here through a winter," Portia teased. "I believe the weather can be very bleak."

"I am willing to suffer the elements for your sake, *lieben*."

When she had taken herself off, Portia rose and examined her reflection in the mirror. It was like looking at a portrait. This beautiful, sophisticated woman was not her, not any longer. She had changed. But tonight she must pretend to be Lady Ellerslie again, for the sake of Victoria, for the sake of Marcus's future.

As Portia made her way to the dining room the bell began to toll a warning from the tower. Like an ill omen, the fog was coming in from the sea.

Chapter 29

Candles glowed throughout the room, valiantly battling the shadows but not quite winning the war. Mercy had shifted heaven and earth to present a meal fit for royalty, and the table was groaning with dishes. Victoria had pride of place at the head, and behind her stood one of her tall guards. Arnold and Lara were together on one side, while Portia sat on the other, with Sebastian. Marcus was facing the queen from the end of the table closest to the door.

He was being the perfect host, scrupulous and brittle in his politeness, despite the fact that Victoria saw him as the man who had betrayed Lord Ellerslie and taken his wife. He knew she'd never like him, and it was a matter of indifference to him.

Portia was something else altogether.

He needed to speak with her alone. She had barely acknowledged him since the queen arrived; it was as if she was afraid of upsetting her patron. And now here she was, dressed up in her lavender gown, her mask firmly in place. He had a hollow feeling that she would be persuaded by Victoria to return to London and he would never see her again.

He could not hope to kidnap her a second time.

It was so damnably frustrating. Ever since he had set his sights on Portia he'd spent his days either wild with happiness or dark with despair—there didn't seem to be any middle ground. But still he wouldn't have it any other way. He loved her now and forever.

Arnold Gillingham was giving him that look that made Marcus long to knock his teeth out, but he didn't suppose it would go down well in the circumstances. And as for the wife, Lara, she was smiling to herself as if she'd won the lottery, except when she remembered to look like the concerned stepdaughter. It was quite comical, really.

Except that he didn't feel like laughing.

The bell tolled mournfully, warning of the fog. He'd noticed on his way to dinner that the white sea fret was already pressing against the windows, as if trying to find a way inside.

Even if any of them had wanted to leave, they could not do so with safety.

"My dear, your hands are icy." Arnold was rubbing Lara's fingers between his. "I'll fetch your shawl."

Lara opened her mouth then shut it again, looking bemused.

Her husband rose and, with a bow, excused himself. When the door closed behind him, the atmosphere seemed to lighten.

"Are the conditions here always so bracing, Mr. Worthorne?" Victoria demanded, helping herself to more mutton.

"There are compensations, Ma'am."

"Indeed? And what would they be?"

"Early to bed, Ma'am."

She looked at him blankly, then smiled. "You are very wicked, Mr. Worthorne."

"So I have been told."

Portia was staring at him as if she'd like to tell him exactly what she thought of such risk-taking, and in return he gave her his most innocent smile.

The door opened and Arnold returned with Lara's shawl. But instead of placing it solicitously about her shoulders, he stepped up to the table with the garment bundled in his arms.

"I've waited so long for this moment," he said, "I hardly know what to say. The occasion demands some sort of speech, but perhaps explanations can wait."

"Arnold?" Lara was watching him uneasily. "Can I have my shawl now?"

But Arnold wasn't listening. He'd unwrapped the shape in his arms, and now the silk shawl slithered to the floor and they could all see what it was. A brace of pistols, primed and cocked.

Victoria's guard didn't hesitate. He lurched forward, but Arnold aimed and fired and the man fell to one side, clutching his chest. Blood bloomed through his waistcoat. Sebastian was on his feet, helping the wounded soldier into a chair, while Lara uttered little cries of distress.

Portia was white, staring at Arnold as he turned and calmly locked the dining room door. The queen had not moved, and the fear in her eyes was belied by the proud lift of her chin.

"My men will have heard the shot and will be coming for you even as we speak," she announced. "Give up your weapon, Mr. Gillingham."

"I'm afraid not, Ma'am," he replied, his smile broadening. "While I was out a moment ago I went down to the kitchen. Your men were in there feasting with the servants, all very jolly they were. I barricaded the door nice and tight and they didn't even hear me. No doubt they will batter their way out in due course, but by then it will be too late and you will be dead. Remember, I still have a loaded pistol."

"Arnold!" Lara wailed.

"Shut up. I've waited all my life for this moment. England for the English, and you, my queen, are no more English than the kaiser."

Marcus had been watching the scene unfold. He felt cold and alert and remarkably alive. He knew he couldn't allow Arnold to assassinate the queen, that he must do something about it, but he would have to choose his moment well.

Sebastian caught his eye in silent warning. He had

taken off his jacket and was pressing it to the wounded man's chest. On his other side, Portia was pale and shaken but just as unbending as the queen.

Arnold was still talking. Ranting on about his father's beliefs and the books he wrote that were never read. He seemed to believe that by shooting the queen he would spread his message to the world. Marcus didn't think it worked like that but he wasn't going to argue. The more Arnold raved, the more time he had to overpower him and take his pistol away.

"Arnold, please, you know you can't escape. You'll be hanged. And what will happen to Lara then?" Portia, the voice of reason.

Arnold glared at her as Lara began to sob. "If you hadn't decided to indulge yourself, Portia, I would have completed my task long ago. As it is, I've had to wait, and I'm not very happy."

"You could have shot me in the coach on the way here," Victoria said. "Why didn't you?"

"I wanted to make an occasion of it," Arnold replied, but his eyes slid to Portia.

Marcus laughed. "No you didn't," he mocked. "You wanted to do it in front of Portia. You wanted to show her what a bad man you really are. You wanted to impress her. Admit it, Gillingham. You're in love with her."

Arnold was white with fury. The pistol was shaking so much that he had to steady it with his other hand. "You have to reduce everything to your level," he whispered. "My aim is pure and true. The feelings you describe would contaminate me."

But the damage was done. Lara was struggling to her feet, knocking over a wineglass, her face ugly with grief. "Arnold, oh Arnold, I thought you were better than that," she sobbed.

"Sit down!" he shouted, but in that moment of distraction Marcus acted.

He was up out of his seat, launching himself at Arnold and reaching for the loaded pistol. He missed—Arnold moved at the last moment—but he bumped it hard and the weapon clattered onto the table, lodging in a dish of chicken pie. But Arnold was quick, too. He was around the table in an instant, snatching up a peeling knife as he ran. When he reached Portia, he fastened his arm about her throat, holding the knife blade to her cheek.

Sebastian tried to stop him but was hampered by his patient, and Arnold kicked out, knocking the chair from under him and sending him sprawling to the floor, the wounded guard on top of him. Portia cried out; a trickle of blood ran down her face where the point had nicked her.

"Get back!" Arnold ordered everyone. "I will cut her throat. I'll do it. You can't say she doesn't deserve it."

He would. Marcus read the truth in the man's wild blue eyes. Portia whimpered, clinging to Arnold's arm, trying to keep her balance as he pulled her back against him, dragging her across the room and edging toward the door. Her skirts tangled around her legs, threatening to trip her up, but she kicked out, freeing herself in time.

The coldness that had held Marcus in its grip until now thawed into a raging torrent. "Let her go."

Arnold smirked. "Oh no, I don't think so. She's coming with me."

He reached behind him, fumbling open the locked door and stepping outside. Portia squeaked, trying to catch hold of the jamb, but he struck violently at her hands, forcing her to let go. He slammed the door and they heard the sound of the key turning outside, and then running steps.

It took Marcus and Sebastian half a minute to smash their way through the door, and by then Arnold and Portia were gone, out into the fog and the marsh.

Portia tried to keep up. If she didn't, Arnold dragged her by her arm or, once, by her hair. She screamed when he did that. She was bruised and shaken and frightened, and she was tired of being brave.

"I always disliked you," she told him, her voice shaking, "but I never thought you capable of murder."

"Well now you know. This way," he added, pulling her along the path beside him.

She could hear the wash of water below them, and knew the tide was coming in. There was a danger of falling into the marshes and drowning in the swirl of the current, and in her heavy skirts, Portia knew she wouldn't be able to save herself.

"The causeway will be closed," she gasped. "You can't escape, Arnold. Please, give yourself up."

"No." He looked around, but the fog was so thick they could see nothing. Sounds were distorted and muffled, and several times he had been startled by his own footsteps, echoing back at him. It was like being in another world. "Is there a boat?" he demanded.

She was too slow to deny it.

"Show me where it is," he said, shaking her. Her hair was falling down all around her, and she pushed it back from her eyes.

"I'm not sure I can. Everything looks different."

"Portia, you will find it or I will throw you into the water. Don't think I won't. To see you die would give me great pleasure."

She looked into his eyes and knew he meant it.

"This way," she murmured, not knowing whether it was that way or not. It didn't matter. Her plan was to stay alive long enough for Marcus to find her. She knew he was looking. She knew he would never let her die out here alone and frightened.

The path was getting narrower, and on either side the rising water slapped against the banks. Portia held her skirts up out of her way, walking in front of Arnold now that there was no room to walk abreast. He kept glancing behind him, although there was nothing to see. Occasionally the fog warning bell rang out.

Portia tried to think. It was all very well to wait for Marcus to find her, but what if he didn't? And if she stayed with Arnold, she would probably die by his hand or in his desperate efforts to get away. She would be better off getting away from him.

That was when she saw it, several yards in front of her and to her right, riding high in the water. Just a glimpse before the fog swirled in again, hiding it completely. The boat. A glance behind her showed that Arnold hadn't noticed; he was too busy searching at his back for any sign of pursuit. She stumbled, pretending to fall, and picked up a heavy stone from the rubble alongside the path. Arnold cursed her, reaching for her, but she pulled away and struggled on. The next time he turned, she threw the stone as hard as she could into the fog behind them.

The rattle it made echoed all around, seeming to come from all directions at once. Arnold spun about, wild-eyed, and Portia took her chance. She flung herself to the side, sliding down the bank and into the boat.

It rocked dangerously.

She fumbled with the rope, managing to cast herself off from the jetty and giving it a shove.

Arnold was shouting. She saw him briefly, a dark shape above her, and then he vanished again and there was nothing.

For a long time she lay in the bottom of the boat, drifting. The air was cold and clammy and she was shivering with cold by the time she heard the voices calling for her. It was several moments before she could convince herself that they were not Arnold, playing tricks, and call out in answer.

Shouts and running steps. The flare of a torch. And then someone was slithering down the bank toward her. The boat rocked as they grabbed hold of it, and then hands were feeling for her, lifting her, holding her.

"My love," Marcus murmured, his voice hoarse with calling. "My dear love. Never leave me again."

Portia clung to him, burying her face in the familiar scent of his jacket. "No, never . . . " she gasped. "I never will."

The next day the fog was gone.

They searched for Arnold for hours until they found his body, floating in the marsh. Marcus was of the opinion that he had slipped and fallen, but Portia wondered if he'd drowned himself after his plot failed. Lara was inconsolable, but Portia thought she detected a hint of relief in her tears. After all, how did one survive the shame of being married to a live traitor? Lara was her father's daughter in that regard, and tougher than she appeared. Victoria was already on her way back to London, but she had sworn them all to secrecy. It would do no good to spread stories of what had happened at Duval Hall. It would all be put down to a tragic accident.

"I will inform the public that Lady Ellerslie is to be married," she said, "and that I knew all about it. That should silence the doubters."

"Thank you, Ma'am."

"I will expect an invitation to your wedding," Victoria went on, "and your first daughter will be named after me."

Marcus bowed, trying to hide his grin.

But Victoria had seen it and chuckled. "I think I could grow quite fond of your Marcus," she said to Portia. "I'll never love him as much as Lord Ellerslie, but he will do."

Later, walking together in the garden, Portia clung to his arm and said, "I don't know how you do it."

"Do what?" he asked, completely at ease.

"Get your own way."

"It's a talent."

She smiled, then sighed.

He tipped up her chin with his finger and gazed into her eyes. "Tell me about the vicar's daughter."

She didn't pretend not to know what he meant. "I was in love with you. I had a—a girlish infatuation."

"Infatuation?" He kept his eyes on hers, refusing to release her. "What was that story you told Minnie, about the bell ringers? Was that you . . . and me? Good Lord, it was, wasn't it?"

"Yes."

He grinned.

"Don't you dare," she said. "If you laugh I will hit you."

"I'm not laughing," he protested. "At least, I don't mean to. I'm happy. It pleases me to think that you were infatuated with me all those years ago."

He meant it. He loved her madly, and to think she had loved him when they were young, even if he'd been too foolish to know it, made him proud.

She gave him a slow sensual smile, and when she had his full attention, said, "Wait until I tell you about my dreams."

Epilogue

Portia shaded her eyes against the sun. The lane was bathed in sunlight this fine morning, perfect for a walk. She shifted her basket on her arm and set off. At first she saw only the dark silhouette, a man on his horse, but as he drew closer she realized it was him.

Marcus Worthorne.

Her heart began to beat wildly. She slowed her steps, wondering whether he would stop today and speak to her, and what she would say. Perhaps her throat would dry up and she would become dumb, as she did sometimes when he glanced at her in church. He was the most handsome man she'd ever seen and she knew she would love him forever.

His horse was slowing. He was going to stop after all.

She could see him now. Dark hair a little wild, his jaw unshaven, his eyes narrowed. He wasn't wearing a neckcloth and she could see the vee of his chest beneath the white linen shirt. Her hands tightened on the basket.

"Miss Stroud, isn't it?" he said in his lazy drawl.

"Yes, sir."

"Off on your good works, are you?"

"Yes, I—I have a family to visit down the lane."

He smiled. "You are to be commended."

"I do my best, sir."

He glanced behind him. "There's a Gypsy camp down there, by the way. You don't want to take chances with those fellows. I think it would be best if I accompanied you. Here, take my hand."

Dazed, she stared up at him.

He wriggled his fingers impatiently. "Come on. Stand on that log there, that's it."

Portia stepped up onto the log and slowly, as if reaching for the holy grail, placed her fingers in his. He heaved her up onto his horse, in front of him. It was a scramble and not at all elegant, but she was actually in his arms. She felt breathless and excited, and jumped when he leaned against her back.

His breath in her ear made her shiver. "I think we should take the long way past the Gypsy camp, Miss Stroud."

"Is it safer that way, sir?"

"I wouldn't say that. No. But you'll find it well worth it, my innocent beauty. I have something to show you that you won't forget."

And he kicked his heels into his mount and set off at a gallop.

Portia picked a leaf out of her hair and sighed. Beside her, Marcus lay half asleep, his big warm body pressed to hers. She glanced at him and he gave her a lazy smile.

"I don't remember you being quite so lecherous," she said.

"Oh, believe me, I was lecherous. You were just too innocent to know it." He stroked her bare thigh. "I enjoyed that, my love. You'll have to tell me another of your dreams."

"I will." She smoothed his hair out of his eyes, gazing at him with all the love in her heart. "As soon as we're back at Duval Hall—when they've finished the redecorations."

"There is always Aphrodite's Club. She has let it be known, through Francesca, that she is very pleased with the way things turned out."

"The courtesan turns matchmaker," Portia said with a smile.

He propped himself up on one elbow. "You don't regret it? Marrying me? Not being the famous Lady Ellerslie anymore, the angel in widow's weeds?"

"Not one bit. I'd much rather be plain Mrs. Worthorne."

He grinned. "Good." His fingers grew bolder. "We

don't have to go back yet, do we? There's plenty of time before Seb and Francesca are up for breakfast."

"Plenty of time," she murmured as he pressed her down into the leaves once more.